P9-BZO-282

Medal of Dishonor

Medal of Dishonor

George P. Miga

Copyright © 2017 by George P. Miga.

ISBN: Softcover 978-1-5434-2366-2
eBook 978-1-5434-2365-5

All rights reserved. No part of this book may be reproduced or transmitted in any form or by any means, electronic or mechanical, including photocopying, recording, or by any information storage and retrieval system, without permission in writing from the copyright owner.

This is a work of fiction. Names, characters, places and incidents either are the product of the author's imagination or are used fictitiously, and any resemblance to any actual persons, living or dead, events, or locales is entirely coincidental.

Any people depicted in stock imagery provided by Thinkstock are models, and such images are being used for illustrative purposes only.
Certain stock imagery © Thinkstock.

Print information available on the last page.

Rev. date: 05/12/2017

To order additional copies of this book, contact:
Xlibris
1-888-795-4274
www.Xlibris.com
Orders@Xlibris.com
761709

PROLOGUE

June 16, 1945
The East Room
The White House
10:40 a.m.

The room was packed. The ceremony was scheduled for the Rose Garden, but a summer rainstorm forced the nearly one hundred people into the East Room. The lights of the news and army film cameras intensified the heat and humidity.

President Harry S. Truman stood in the center of the crowd. Those closest to the President thought it remarkable that he seemed immune to the heat and the press of bodies. Indeed, Harry was the kind of man who didn't sweat.

Three soldiers stood facing the President — Marvin D. Sanders, 19, Pfc, Muncie, Indiana; John J. Feeney, 25, technical sergeant, Binghamton, New York; Oliver Wentworth Crawford, 22, first lieutenant, Fort Bliss, Texas. All three men were about to receive the Medal of Honor for their actions during the Battle of the Bulge in December, 1944, Hitler's last desperate and bloody counteroffensive of World War II.

A husky, middle-aged colonel read the citations, enunciating the words with a stylistic blend of evangelist and drill instructor. The effect was a command: "You *will* honor these men."

The colonel began to read the lieutenant's citation. Lt. Oliver Wentworth Crawford couldn't concentrate on the colonel's words. Once before, as a boy, he visited this room with his father. Even then he was struck by the history seeping from the white-painted wall paneling, the delicate plaster ceiling decorations, the rich parquet floor. His eyes were drawn to the Gilbert Stuart full-length portrait of George Washington, the only object known to have remained in the White House since 1800. He remembered the story his father told him of how Dolly Madison rescued the painting only hours before the British burned the mansion in the War of 1812.

Then, like strobes of light triggered by the colonel's words, Lieutenant Crawford's mind flashed from the steamy room to that frigid road flanked by snow-laden pines in the south of Belgium. *"...despite intense enemy fire that wiped out most of his squad, Lieutenant Crawford directed accurate and deadly fire that inflicted heavy..."* Lieutenant Crawford heard the clanking of the German tank treads and the numbing crack of their high-velocity guns. *"...his inspired leadership rallied the survivors of his unit, despite vastly superior..."* He heard the screams of the wounded and the hammering machinegun fire. *"...by his superb courage and indomitable fighting spirit, Lieutenant Crawford provided an inspiring example for the men of his command..."* Like a lesion burrowing into his gut, he remembered his fear. He remembered how the rattle of gunfire and the screams of savaged men faded as he plunged wildly into the safety of the snow-cloaked forest. *"...above and beyond the call of duty."*

The bird-colonel picked up three presentation cases and stepped smartly to the President's side. President Truman seemed pleased, even awed, by what he was about to do. He had said that bestowing the Medal of Honor was one of the great privileges of his office. Although Crawford was rigidly at attention, he shifted his eyes slightly to watch the President place the medal's blue silk ribbon, spangled with thirteen stars, around the necks of the two men to his left.

When President Truman stood before Lieutenant Oliver Crawford, he repeated what he told the other two men, what he told everyone he had so honored: "I would rather have this medal than be President of the United States." President Truman smiled, the floodlights reflecting from his metal-rimmed glasses and masking his eyes, as he warmly and vigorously shook Crawford's hand.

Then the President stepped around and behind the lieutenant to shake hands with Major General Oliver Wentworth Crawford and Mrs. Crawford.

"Ollie," the President said, "you must be very proud of your boy."

Lieutenant Crawford heard his father mumble a response. The lieutenant looked back to see that his father, Major General Oliver Crawford, called "Iron Ollie" by the troops he had led in two world wars, would not — could not — look into the President's eyes.

June 16, 1945
U.S. Military Hospital
Near London, England
3:40 p.m.

More than three thousand miles away, a U.S. Army surgeon and a nurse stood next to the bed of a heavily bandaged corporal. The previous morning, the corporal had undergone surgery for the eleventh time.

The nurse carefully removed the bandage from the corporal's head. As the surgeon leaned forward to more closely examine his work, the nurse said, "Remarkable job on this one, Doctor Merkley. Truly remarkable."

Major Donald Merkley, absorbed in his examination, carefully tilted the patient's head and nodded agreement. "Yes, despite a nine millimeter bullet hole in his skull, the loss of a leg, and more shrapnel wounds than I can count, I would say that in a month or so this man can be shipped back to the States."

The patient, a 44-year-old army cook, had been wounded during the Bulge fighting. Although conscious, he seemed unaware of the activity around him, his eyes staring at the ceiling.

When the nurse bandaged the wound and moved on to prepare the next patient for examination, Dr. Merkley lingered at the corporal's bed. For the first time he noticed that one of the man's eyes was staring at him through a small gap in the bandages now covering his head and most of his face.

Dr. Merkley didn't know why, but he felt a growing discomfort as he looked into that single eye. What was the eye trying to communicate, the doctor wondered. Was it fear? No, the doctor thought, he has seen fear all too often.

"We're ready for you, Dr. Merkley," the nurse called from the next patient's bed.

"In a moment." Dr. Merkley lingered, intrigued by what message the eye might be communicating. Perhaps the eye was asking the question most patients ask: Why did this happen to me? Why me?

The surgeon again checked the metal clipboard. Oh, yes, he recalled. This is the one. Several weeks earlier another doctor said this corporal was one of the few survivors of intense fighting at an important roadblock during the Bulge fighting. In fact, according to the other doctor, there were rumors that the soldier had been recommended for a high medal.

The surgeon thought that unusual. He couldn't be certain, but he'd never heard of a Negro soldier receiving a medal for heroism, certainly not the nation's highest honor for valor.

Dr. Merkley knew that only about three percent of Negroes in uniform saw combat. Most were used as orderlies, labor troops, and cooks. He wondered why a Negro had been among the men entrusted with such an obviously important combat assignment. Of course, Dr. Merkley remembered, during the Bulge fighting they scraped the bottom of the barrel for whatever they could find. Even Negro cooks.

Well, the doctor thought as he moved to the next bed, there's no reason why these colored boys shouldn't bleed right alongside the white men fighting the war.

CHAPTER 1

February 19, 1967
The Oval Office
The White House
8:45 p.m.

Spenser McCall was aware that Lyndon Baines Johnson was obsessed by a fear of failure. McCall knew Johnson as a freshman senator from Texas. They'd hunted together and drank too much Kentucky bourbon together. McCall knew that Johnson, driven by deep-seated insecurities, needed to test his power, to assert his control, sometimes in small or mean ways.

Perhaps, McCall speculated as he waited in the corridor anteroom of the West Wing for his turn to see the President, that's why Hubert Humphrey -- his face flushed and his doe eyes averted -- was limping noticeably as he left the Oval Office.

The President did it again, McCall thought. Lyndon must have kicked Hubert. McCall had heard the story from several sources. In dispatching Humphrey on some mission with the order to "get going," the President often kicked his vice president in the shins. Hard.

The President's secretary, Yolanda, whom he had hired when he became vice president, gestured toward the door to the right of her desk. "He's on the phone, Mr. McCall, but he wants you to come in."

When McCall entered the Oval Office, the President was concluding the phone call. Even on the phone, McCall noticed, the President emphasized his words by waving one long arm like a windmill.

McCall had received the call summoning him to the White House the day before. The President wanted to see McCall privately, for the second time in two months.

"Spense, how the hell are you?" Johnson's greeting came before he had hung up the phone and without saying goodbye.

"I'm fine, Mr. President."

Johnson waved McCall toward a chair, then he pointed at a white-jacketed steward. "Get us some coffee."

The President sat heavily into a leather library chair across from McCall's, washing his face with his huge hands. McCall thought the President looked very tired, and he wondered how the folds of skin around his eyes didn't obscure his vision.

"Christ, Spense, sometimes I feel like I'm running a goddamned Chinese circus." Then he leaned forward and squeezed McCall's knee, as he often did with people to make a point. Johnson was a toucher. McCall had often seen him reach out to handshake, while his left hand coaxed and stroked and pressed, drawing the person closer.

"Spense, I sure as hell wish you'd gone into politics. I could use a man like you. You saw Humphrey?"

McCall nodded.

Johnson leaned back and grimaced. "The man just doesn't have enough weight; he cries as easily as a woman." He shook his head briskly, as if to fling away a distasteful image.

McCall knew that the vice president had expressed second thoughts about Vietnam. Humphrey had since recanted his dissent and was shamelessly flattering LBJ in hopes of being welcomed back to high councils. It was apparent that the President still didn't completely trust his vice president.

"Spense, when the hell are you going to get out of the oil business?"

"As a matter of fact," McCall said, "I've got a little over five years to retirement, but--"

"Spense," Johnson said, shifting his weight forward in the chair to rest his elbows on his knees, "I called you to talk about a couple of things that are damned important to me, damned important to the country. First of all, you know how much I appreciate that you're going to work for my campaign again. You raised a helluva lot of money for me in sixty-four, and it looks like I'm going to need a lot more of that kind of help next year."

Johnson leaned back and was silent for a long moment, his eyes turned toward the French doors that opened onto the Rose Garden. Then he sighed heavily -- McCall thought theatrically.

"But I've got a bigger job for you. I know you're the right man for it, for two reasons: you're not an ass-kisser, at least you never tried to pucker up to mine, and you know the Mideast, probably as well or better than anyone I know."

"The Mideast?"

"Spense, the boys at Langley tell me the whole damn place is one big Molotov cocktail and the Jews and A-rabs are playing with matches."

McCall shook his head in confusion. "What does that have to do with me?"

Johnson pulled his chair closer to McCall's, close enough that their knees were touching. "Spenser, I want you to go there for me. I want you to find out what it'll take to stop them from fighting. Then report back to me. I don't want you to put anything on paper. Just come back and talk to me."

McCall shook his head in confusion. "Mr. President, I wouldn't have the foggiest idea of where to start. Surely you have qualified people there to advise you."

"Of *course* I've got people there. I've got the military saying we should go in on the side of the Israelis, and I've got State Department people telling me that we shouldn't do a damn thing."

"Then what good could I possibly do? I'm not a diplomat."

"God*dammit*, McCall, I know you're no diplomat. That's why I want you to go. What you know about those people isn't muddled by your politics -- or mine. And I'll tell you exactly where to start -- Hussein of Jordan. You know him and his wife. She's English, I think."

McCall nodded.

Johnson quickly rose and began to pace. "I've arranged for you to be briefed by the CIA, but I'm convinced Jordan is the key. You won't have diplomatic status; you won't even be a special envoy. But the right people will know that you're my man and why you're there."

McCall thought about Hussein, the young king, whom he knew as a gentle, sensitive man whose personal charm was admired by even his bitterest enemies, a man who regarded life as an adventure and who preferred to be thought of as the Brave Young King at the head of his army, rather than the sophisticated statesman.

"I know that Hussein doesn't want war," the Johnson said. "He's got the smallest army in the Mideast. Christ, he's only got a dozen jet fighters, and he knows the A-rabs can't agree on the time a day, let alone how to fight the Jews." Johnson paused, his hands deep in his pockets as he looked out at the rose garden. "You know, those Jews remind me of the boys at the Alamo -- surrounded, without hope. The Texas boys didn't run, and they kicked a lot of ass before it was all over. The Jews aren't going to run either, Spense. In fact, the word I've got is they're going to attack."

"Who...who will they attack?"

The President shrugged. "First, they'll knock out all the A-rab air power. Then they'll move their troops against the Egyptians in the Sinai."

"When will they attack?"

"Even if I knew -- and I'm not saying I don't -- I couldn't tell you, at least not until you commit to coming to work for me. But you're going to have to decide pretty damn quick."

McCall sought for a way to tell the President that he didn't want to go. He couldn't. The New Mexico project was at a critical stage. Going to the Mideast might take weeks away from his work.

"Talk to me, McCall."

"I'm sorry, Mr. President, I really don't see what I can contribute."

The President leaned back in his chair, his head cocked, holding his glasses in one hand resting in his lap. McCall thought the President looked like the school teacher he once was, and that he, McCall, was the errant pupil.

"Spenser, this country can fight only one damn war at a time. The only thing the generals tell me about Vietnam is to bomb and send in more troops and bomb some more." Johnson cupped his hand over his eyes, as if he were staring into the distance. "They keep seeing lights at the end of the tunnel, and they don't even have a tunnel. Hell, they can't even find the damned tunnel."

The President threw up his hands in a gesture of helplessness. "Christ, Spense, that *pissant* country is tearing us apart. The last thing I need is a damn war in the Mideast."

McCall knew that, despite Johnson's bombast and theatrics and duplicity, he truly believed in his Great Society; he wanted to be remembered as the President who helped the "little man." McCall knew that deep within the bogus politician, there was great good and an honest sense of justice.

The President folded his glasses and put them into his shirt pocket. Then he leaned close and squeezed McCall's knee. "Spense, you do this for me and I'll take care of you." He smiled broadly. "Old friend, after the election, how would you like to be the next ambassador to Iran?"

"Me? An ambassador?"

The President laughed. "Hell, yes, and you'd be a damned good one."

McCall had thought tonight's meeting would just involve planning campaign strategy, primarily the recruiting of other business CEOs to support Johnson. McCall was confused and concerned. Did Johnson know of the friction developing between McCall and his board of directors? McCall knew there were links between his board and this man. Was all this a ploy to gracefully move him out of the company?

"Mr. President, I'd have to think about all of this."

McCall could see that the President was disappointed.

"No, dammit, you don't have to think about it. I need you in the Mideast, and I've already had someone talk to the Shah. He likes you, Spense. He says your company has been good for his people. He'd like to see you take the job."

"You can count on me for whatever I can do for the campaign," McCall said. "But the rest of it? I can't give you an answer tonight. Besides, I can't imagine that I can accomplish anything the State Department can't."

"Look," Johnson said as he leaned close again, wiping his mouth with the back of his hand, "you know I never liked that damned striped-pants crowd. The nut of it is I don't trust them in-bred, Ivy-League sumbitches. I need somebody I do trust. I need you, Spense. Your country needs you."

"Mr. President, I'm flattered by the offer. But if you think I'm expecting some special favor because I've supported your campaign or because we go back a lot of years--"

"Hell, I know better than that," Johnson said, dismissing McCall's words with a huge wave of his hand. "You're the only guy around this damned place who hasn't asked me for a favor. And listen, if you're worried about the media vultures making a fuss because you're an old Texas buddy, don't spend a New York minute thinking about that." The President laughed. "Hell, if Jack Kennedy could get Bobby some legal experience by making him attorney general, I sure as hell can make an old hunting buddy an ambassador."

McCall knew that the President would flatter and cajole. He was a master of theater. His voice would rage, then descend to a hoarse, aggrieved whisper. Tracking his moods, his eyes could pierce like lasers or be as moist and sorrowful as a hound's. Eventually, if he really wanted something, he'd start building the pressure, and who could resist the calls to glory and honor, especially with the entire Free World teetering in balance?

"Mr. President, the fact is that I don't want to leave my company -- at least not yet."

The President raised his eyebrows. "Why the hell not? You just turned sixty, you've got enough years as man and boy in that business, and you've got more damned money than one man can spend. Besides, I know that it's mandatory for the chairman of the board of your company to retire at sixty five, so why not get out now when you have an opportunity to do something damned important for me."

"Well, there's a project I'd like to finish up. It'll take a couple of years."

The President tilted his head, his eyes narrow and laser cool. "What the hell's going on, Spense? I thought you'd jump at the chance to come work for me."

If he accepted the job, McCall wondered whether LBJ would kick him in the shins before sending him on some assignment. No, McCall thought, he wouldn't do that. If he did, he knows I'd kick him back. Then McCall considered the ludicrous image of two old men in the Oval Office kicking each other in the shins. He could see it as a cartoon in Eleanor's Chicago *Times.*

"It isn't that at all, Mr. President. I want a little more time to see if I can develop a plan our people have for rejuvenating those old West Texas oil fields. If it works, it'll be like rediscovering the Permian Basin."

"What does your board think about that?"

"Well, frankly, at the moment, the cost of the project scares hell out of them. But if I get enough time to put a small-scale field test together, I'm certain I can convince them to buy the program. It'll mean millions of barrels of oil that otherwise couldn't be recovered."

The President nodded slowly. "Yes, I see the value in that. We are getting too damned dependent on foreign oil."

"As a matter of fact," McCall quickly added, "our marketing research people see a serious tightening of gasoline supplies, perhaps by early nineteen seventies. If for some reason the Arabs cut off our oil, this country could be in serious trouble."

The President slapped his thigh. "Dammit, Spenser, that's why I want you to take this job. The damned A-rabs are going to get their act together, especially if Israel attacks. Mark my words," the President said, jabbing a long finger at the ceiling, "they're going to force the free world to deal with OPEC. Then they're going to cut off *our* peckers because we keep sending roses and candy to the Jews."

The President rose quickly from his chair and began to pace. "God*dammit*, Spense! Can't you see that you're going to be a helluva lot more important to me -- to this country -- working in the Middle East for peace than if you're tinkering around in some played-out oil fields in West Texas?"

McCall knew now that he'd have to be firm. "I'm sorry, but I can't give you a commitment -- at least not until the board makes its decision. I don't know if I can even explain all the reasons why, but I've got to try to get this project going."

Lyndon Johnson was standing on the presidential seal woven into the carpet. Clearly disappointed and angry, he nodded slowly. "Okay, Spense, I suppose I can understand. I'll wait until you do what you feel you've got to do." The President raised a long arm and pointed it like a rifle at McCall. He wasn't smiling. "Then, old friend, your ass is gonna belong to me."

February 19, 1967
Randolph Street
Chicago
5:12 p.m.

The patches of ice always concerned Cordell Jackson. He limped slowly, close to the buildings, wary of both the ice and the streams of hurrying commuters. He glanced at his watch. His bus stop was less than a block away on Wabash. He'd make the 5:18.

Less than fifteen minutes earlier he had stowed his shoe shine cart, as he had every working day for almost twenty years, in a closet on the executive floor of the Horizon Building, the Michigan Avenue headquarters of Horizon International Oil Corporation.

Cordell Jackson shined shoes for a living. Each day he rolled his cart through the office corridors, shining the shoes of executives as they worked at their desks. It was a job he enjoyed because he earned a decent wage, and because he was well treated by the men whose shoes he shined. Besides, he knew there weren't many jobs available to an elderly Negro, at least not one with an artificial leg.

Cordell knew there were several reasons why he was treated so well, even generously, by Horizon employees. Of course, he did good work. And he worked hard. He began at 8:30 and worked straight through until five without a lunch break, because a lot of the executives ate lunch at their desks and it was a good time to catch them. Besides, the money he saved by skipping lunch was how he'd helped his son through college and law school. Cordell also knew that the fact he was treated well had something to do with his personality. He wasn't exactly sure what it was that made him so popular with the forty to fifty executives whose shoes he shined each day, but he knew they liked him. He could tell because of the way they talked to him, the things they told him about their jobs and their families. In fact, the rumor was that Cordell probably knew more than anyone, including the chairman, about what really was happening in the company. Certainly he was privy to the latest gossip that seeped and ebbed through the executive suites. Whatever Cordell heard, he kept to himself.

Cordell understood that the most important reason why the nearly twenty years had been so good was because of *The Man.* That's how Cordell and the few other blacks in the company referred to Spenser McCall, Horizon's chairman of the board. Nearly everyone in the company was aware of the friendship between the man who shined shoes and the man who ran the company.

Spenser McCall didn't pay for his shines, at least not directly. Cordell didn't want to accept the money because of what McCall had done for Cordell's son. Cordell had no choice but to accept the fifty dollars deposited each month in his savings account.

At Randolph and Wabash, Cordell still had a couple of minutes before his bus arrived, so he leaned against a building to shield himself from the cutting northwest wind. As usual, there was a crowd at the intersection, people huddled together waiting for the light to change.

They reminded Cordell of cattle he'd seen one winter in Colorado, all herded together, jostling each other, their breath generating funnels of steam. Cordell pulled his head deeper into his collar as an elevated train thundered overhead, the nerve-stretching squeal of its wheels and brakes reverberating in the canyon of buildings.

The bus was late. Cordell didn't want to be late tonight because he planned to stop to see Robert Robinson, his 81-year-old neighbor. Cordell checked on Robinson at least every other evening. It wasn't a chore, because he enjoyed Robby's stories about the days before the turn of the century when he laid track in Montana, and later when he'd worked on a barge on the Ohio River. Besides, Robby clearly enjoyed telling the stories.

Cordell had known Robby for as long as he could remember. Robby's nine sons and daughters were all gone. They rarely came to visit. Robby didn't have anyone now, except Cordell.

Cordell cupped his hands to his mouth and blew on his chilled fingers. He huddled against the building, away from the wind and the crowd. That's probably why the boy, no more than fifteen or sixteen, didn't see Cordell. The boy, shabbily dressed and his long blond hair hanging almost to his shoulders, did see the two women chatting while they waited at the curb for the light to change. The boy obviously was especially interested in the middle-aged, fashionably dressed woman, whose expensive leather purse hung casually from her shoulder.

When the boy stepped behind the woman, Cordell knew what would happen. Cordell started forward, looking toward the heavily bundled policeman directing traffic in the middle of the intersection, but the policeman was preoccupied with preventing a rush-hour gridlock. Then Cordell heard a scream and looked back to see the boy knock the elderly woman to the pavement as he yanked her purse roughly from her shoulder. The younger woman screamed again as the boy reached for her purse.

Cordell's movements were surprisingly quick. He stepped forward and grabbed the back of the boy's collar, yanking hard enough to pull him off balance. The boy's flaying arms knocked aside other people as he sat down heavily onto the sidewalk, releasing the purse, a stunned expression on his face.

The dozen or so other people standing on the corner stepped back quickly as Cordell looked down at the boy. "Now, son, I'm going to give you a chance to get up without any more trouble. Just get up easy and leave this place."

The policeman, now conscious of the commotion, held his arms up to halt traffic, the whistle clenched between his teeth screeching shrilly in the brittle air. He walked cautiously from the middle of the intersection toward the curb.

The boy jumped to his feet to face Cordell. "You old black bastard," the boy spat with such fury that spittle dribbled over his cold-numbed lips, "what are you messing in this for?" The boy, his fists clenched, took two steps closer to Cordell.

The policeman now was a dozen feet away. "You, there!" he said to the boy. "Don't move!"

Cordell saw the boy's hand flash to his jacket pocket as he whirled toward the intersection. It was a moment before the old man could see the blue-steel automatic pistol swing up and toward the policeman. Cordell saw people standing nearest to the boy begin to back away, at first slowly, their eyes darting from the boy to the policeman. Then there were screams of panic as people ran. Several of the men sprawled onto the pavement.

The boy leveled the weapon at Cordell. "Stand right there, nigger. I'm going to take care of you next." Then he almost casually swung the pistol toward the policeman.

The policeman froze. His mouth opened and the chromed whistle, attached to a lanyard, dropped to his chest. He started to reach for his service revolver, buried under two layers of clothing.

When the pistol fired, a jagged tongue of blue-white flame blossomed from the barrel. The 9mm bullet struck the policeman about an inch below his left eye, the impact of the 123-grain bullet snapping the officer's head back. Cordell saw the policeman stand motionless for a long moment, caught in the glare of headlights, his head tilted far back, as if he were inspecting the tracks over his head, or perhaps noticing for the first time the squeal and thunder of a passing elevated train.

When Traffic Patrolman Richard Morovic's body finally crumpled to the street, he'd been dead for several seconds. The people who had been standing on the corner, moments before bustling and impatient to cross the street, were hiding in doorways. Some had fled into nearby stores. A few were cowering behind parked cars. Even the drivers of the cars near the shooting, their movement blocked by the policeman's corpse, abandoned their vehicles. Over the radio of onc abandoned car, Cordell could hear a helicopter pilot report the traffic jam on the Dan Ryan Expressway. The elderly woman, semiconscious, still lay groaning at the curb, the younger woman shielding her body.

Cordell was amazed at the boy's casual, deliberate actions as he examined the weapon. The badly worn German Luger had jammed, failing to completely eject the fired brass cartridge. As the boy turned to face Cordell, he slid the pistol's bolt back to eject the spent shell, then released it. The bolt sprang forward with a frosty snap as it chambered a bullet.

Cordell winced at the cold, metallic sound of the Luger's bolt snapping closed. That *sound!* Cordell stared at the pistol, shuddering as if he'd touched a bare electric wire.

The boy pointed the gun at Cordell's chest. "You messed me up, old man. Now you're gonna die."

Cordell didn't hear the words clearly, but he could see the anger, the blond hair sticking out from under the stocking cap, the looming muzzle of the Luger.

"*No!*" Cordell shouted, "you're not going to shoot me this time... you're not going to kill any more of my people."

Cordell's lunge surprised the boy. As Cordell tried to push the muzzle away, the pistol fired, and the old man felt as if he had been struck with a hammer in the left side of his chest. Despite the intense burning sensation, he held onto the weapon with both hands. Cordell, a head taller and heavier than the boy, used his height to lever the boy's arm straight up, twisting the weapon out of his hand.

The boy, looking around warily, slowly backed away into the intersection. He paused near the policeman's body, then reached down, roughly pulling up the dead man's coat to unsnap the holster, but the revolver became entangled in the policeman's coat. Crouched over the body, the boy panicked when a siren wailed a few blocks away, and he tried to rip the gun free of the coat.

Cordell slowly shook his head. "No more," Cordell said as he raised the Luger. "I'm not going to let you hurt Bobby no more."

The impact of the first shot slammed the boy to the pavement. Almost immediately he got to his feet, the blood spurting through the fingers that clutched the chest wound, and faced Cordell. "You didn't kill me, you sonofabitch." Tottering, and his movements lacking coordination, the boy once more reached for the policeman's revolver. The second and third bullets spun the boy in a half-circle before he fell.

Cordell dropped the pistol and clutched at the wound in his lower left chest. When he looked down at his hand, the blood appeared purple under the street lights. The old man moaned softly and staggered against a newspaper vending machine chained to a lamppost, then slid to a sitting position. Cordell was conscious of people standing around him, of muffled voices shouting. He thought he could hear the squealing brakes of another elevated train coming, then realized the sound was a woman screaming and screaming.

The old man knew his lung had been pierced because he could hear the air rasping through the hole in his chest, and he could feel the warm, bloody froth bubbling through his lips.

He remembered the cold, metallic ring of the pistol's bolt snapping closed. The anger. The blond hair. He had heard it and seen it a long time before. It was a memory he thought had been safely submerged.

Cordell became very cold. Even the pain and cold were familiar. The old man began trembling so violently he could hear the hollow thump of his artificial leg rapping against the pavement.

CHAPTER 2

February 19, 1967
Wesley Memorial Hospital
Intensive Care Unit
Chicago
9:20 p.m.

"How is he?" McCall asked.

"He was very lucky." Dr. Michael Jacaruso sounded as if he were delivering a lecture, one he wanted to complete quickly so he could get back to work. The young doctor, standing behind and to McCall's right, spoke in a low monotone. "The bullet didn't penetrate his chest. But it did shatter a rib, then traveled around the rib cage under his skin to within three inches of his spine. People presume that a bullet travels in a straight line through a body. In fact, when a bullet hits a bone or heavy muscle it's likely to move in any direction. The rib fragments are what punctured his left lung, which was collapsed when he was rolled into ER.

"The lung is what concerns me," the doctor continued. "When a bullet shatters a bone, the bone fragments can do more damage than the bullet. That's the situation we have here. That lung has been badly damaged."

McCall stepped closer to Cordell Jackson's bed. Cordell's eyes were closed. A lamp on a flexible arm attached to the wall on one side of the bed cast a harsh contrast of light and shadow over Cordell's face that disturbed McCall. It didn't appear as if Cordell were breathing. McCall's eyes were drawn to the electronic instruments that pulsed and hummed on a shelf over the head of the bed, and to the tangle of tubes that carried fluids into and out of the old man.

"You didn't answer my question, doctor. How is he now?"

The doctor hesitated a moment. "Critical, but stable."

McCall turned to look at the doctor. *He's young, and he looks tired, probably because he did the surgery. The kid probably comes from an old-money family, and probably knows his business. But I don't like doctors who talk to people as if they had the IQ of a house plant.*

"What does critical, but stable mean, doctor?"

"Mr. McCall, it's much too early to make definitive judgments about his chances, which I presume is what you're asking me. After all, we've got to consider the trauma he experienced and..." the doctor looked at the metal clipboard he held... "the fact that he's sixty-seven years old."

McCall nodded slowly. Horizon's senior managers learned quickly that McCall demanded they walk a narrow line; he didn't have much patience with bad decisions, but he had zero patience with managers who lacked the courage to make high-risk decisions or judgments.

Well, it's been my experience that the medical profession isn't immune to the cover-your-ass syndrome.

McCall stood for a long moment at Cordell's bed, then motioned for the doctor to step with him into the corridor.

"I want a straight answer, doctor," McCall said as soon as the door was closed. "Is he going to live?"

"Look, Mr. McCall," Jacaruso said, "I can't give you an unqualified yes or no. All I can tell you is that we'll be in a much better position tomorrow morning to make a judgment. The next few hours are very important."

McCall looked closely into the younger man's eyes, then nodded slowly. "Okay," McCall said. He looked to his left down the corridor and motioned slightly with his right hand. Within seconds two men dressed in dark suits were standing in front of him. One of the men was older, perhaps as old as McCall, and his suit was slightly rumpled and ill-fitting. The other man was tall, trim, almost dapper, and looked to be in his mid-forties.

McCall nodded to both men before turning to Dr. Jacaruso. "Did Mr. Jackson say anything, anything at all, about what happened tonight?"

"He was conscious when I saw him in ER, Mr. McCall," the doctor said, "but he was very confused."

"But did he say anything?" McCall repeated.

Dr. Jacaruso shook his head. "If he did, I was too busy to hear it. But I am curious about how he lost his leg. There's also a lot of scar tissue on his back and thighs, and there's that plate in his forehead. The x-rays showed there are still several pieces of what must be shrapnel in his lower back."

"It is shrapnel," McCall said. "Cordell was a soldier during World War II. He still receives periodic treatment at Hines Veterans Hospital. I would imagine they'll make his records available to you if you need them."

The younger of the two men standing behind McCall asked, "Doctor, I presume there was a police officer present. Do you remember his name?"

Dr. Jacaruso hesitated before answering, looking at McCall.

McCall gestured toward the taller man. "This is Fred Guthrie, Horizon's chief of security. And this is Bill Lowry, also an employee." McCall didn't like to introduce Lowry as his driver.

"There were a lot of cops here," Dr. Jacaruso said. "There always is when a cop has been shot or killed. The one handling the investigation is a detective sergeant who works homicide. His name is Feeney, Jim Feeney, who we see all too often. He has the bullet I removed from Mr. Jackson."

"Do you know the caliber of that bullet?" the security man asked. Dr. Jacaruso ran his fingers through his thick, unruly brown hair. "Ah, yes, I think Detective Feeney said it was a nine millimeter. Actually, Mr. Jackson was fortunate that it was a copper-jacketed bullet, which generally remains in one piece. If he'd been hit with a twenty-two -- I hate the damned things -- they tend to break up into pieces that go every which way in the body."

The doctor hesitated when he apparently realized he'd told McCall more than he wanted to hear about ballistics. "The detective also said the gun was recovered at the scene. It was an old Luger."

There was a moment of silence. McCall started to leave, then paused. "Can you tell me whether Cordell Jackson's son has been informed about his father's condition?"

"I wouldn't know about that kind of thing, Mr. McCall. "You can ask at the nurse's station."

McCall's eyes narrowed slightly. "I'll do that. When his son gets here, he'll want to see his father and he'll want to speak with you."

"If I'm available, I'll arrange for it," Dr. Jacaruso said. "But he'll be able to spend only a few minutes each hour with him,"

"Thank you," McCall said. "Cordell and his son are very close. Tony Jackson is an assistant U.S. Attorney in South Bend, Indiana. My people have contacted him and we're certain that he's on his way here."

The doctor looked at his watch. "Gentlemen, I don't want to be rude, but it's been a very busy night."

McCall turned to leave, then paused again. "One thing more, doctor," McCall said. "I don't know if, or what kind of, insurance Cordell has, but I want to assure you that all of his expenses will be paid."

"Mister McCall, I don't concern myself with how -- or whether -- people pay their medical bills. Other people around here worry about that. Check with the admissions people. Besides, I thought as an employee of yours he would receive care under your medical plan."

"He is not *my* employee, doctor," McCall said, his voice low and even. "I will indeed talk to admissions. I just want you to understand that I expect Mr. Jackson to receive whatever treatment is required, whatever the cost. Have I made myself clear?"

Dr. Jacaruso, his face slightly flushed, didn't answer. McCall turned down the corridor, the two men following, toward the nurse's station. The duty nurse was on the phone.

While they waited, the security chief shook his head in disgust as he handed McCall two stapled sheets of paper. "It was a damn kid, Mr. McCall. Only fifteen years old. He must have been high on something, to kill that cop the way he did. Like the doc said, he used a Luger. This is just a preliminary report."

McCall could see that his security chief had obtained a copy of the police report. He wasn't surprised. Fred Guthrie had been an FBI agent for twenty years and joined Horizon Corporation after he had retired.

"Have any charges been filed against Cordell?" McCall asked.

"No, and I don't think charges will be filed," Guthrie said. "Hell, the cops think Cordell's a hero -- and not only because he shot a cop killer. They're pretty sure that kid was responsible for twenty or thirty purse snatchings. Nearly all of them were older women, and he put eight of them in a hospital. No, I can't imagine they're going to file. Although I wouldn't be surprised if the politicians play it safe by sending it to the grand jury. But I'm sure it'll be no-billed."

Relieved, McCall quickly read the report, then folded it and put it into his pocket.

"There is one thing, though," Guthrie said, then hesitated a moment.

"What is it, Fred?"

"Well, witnesses said that Cordell was saying some things...you know, when everything was going down...things that just don't make sense."

"What kinds of things?"

"I know it doesn't make sense, Mr. McCall, but just before Cordell took the Luger away from the kid -- before Cordell was shot, he said, *You're not going to shoot me this time...you're not going to kill any more of my people.* Then, just before he shot the kid, Cordell said -- and a half-dozen people heard this -- he said, *I'm not going to let you hurt Bobby no more.*"

"Bobby? Who's Bobby?" McCall asked. "And what did he mean by *You're not going to shoot me this time*?"

Guthrie sighed. "We don't know. The police think Cordell may have been talking about crime in his neighborhood -- he lives near ninety-second and Michigan Avenue -- and maybe Bobby is a friend or someone he knows, someone who was a victim. They're checking that out, and they're also checking out whether Cordell's been shot before."

McCall was silent a moment, then asked, "What do *you* think Cordell was talking about, Fred?"

"Well, you know him better than I do, but what the cops think doesn't fit."

"Why not?"

"Because I don't believe that Cordell is a violent man. I mean, he wouldn't have settled it that way, no matter who this Bobby is or what might have happened to Cordell in the past. Hell, witnesses said that after he knocked the kid down, he told him to get up and run. Cordell wouldn't have deliberately popped that kid unless, well..."

"Unless what?"

Guthrie scratched his chin, grimaced, then abruptly shook his head. "Well, there's more to it than just street crime. I don't know what it is, but I feel it's a helluva lot more complicated than the way the police report says it went down."

McCall took the police report from his pocket and read it more carefully. After a minute or so he refolded it and put it away.

"Okay, Fred. Follow it. Call me, or come to see me, whenever you've got anything."

McCall noticed that the nurse was finally off the phone. He looked at his watch, then turned to the two men. "Listen, there's no sense both of you hanging around. Bill, take Fred home, then come back here. I'll wait for a while to see if Cordell's son shows up."

"Mr. McCall," Guthrie said, "there are some reporters with television cameras in the lobby. They know you're here."

"Thanks, Fred. I'll see you later." As McCall turned to the nurse's desk, he glanced down the long corridor and saw a man hurrying toward the intensive care area. McCall realized that he hadn't seen Tony Jackson in more than a year.

When Jackson approached the desk, McCall stepped toward him.

Jackson stopped when they were a few feet apart, their eyes locked. For a moment neither man spoke. "How's my father?"

"He's in intensive care. I just talked to the doctor." McCall paused a moment. "Tony, they're not certain -- it seems they never are -- but the doctor seems to think that if he gets through the next few hours the odds are in his favor. I can assure you they're doing everything possible."

"I want to see him."

"The doctor said you could, but only for a few minutes."

"Then let's find the doctor."

McCall asked the nurse to page Dr. Jacaruso. A few minutes later the doctor escorted Jackson into the intensive care unit. McCall remained in the waiting room.

If Cordell is conscious, McCall thought, it will do him good to see his son. McCall recalled that Cordell had always been proud of his son. Cordell often talked about what a good student Tony had been and how well he'd done in law school. McCall remembered Cordell's proudest moment, when his son had been honored in Washington for achieving more convictions of felons on ITAR -- interstate traffic in aid of racketeering -- than any other U.S. attorney's office in the nation. J. Edgar Hoover, director of the Federal Bureau of Investigation, had invited Jackson and his wife to Washington so he could thank him.

Hoover personally had conducted Tony and Valerie Jackson on a tour of FBI headquarters. McCall also recalled the phone call he'd received from Lyndon Johnson, during which the President expressed his appreciation for McCall's recommendation that the Justice Department recruit Tony Jackson.

Jackson returned a few minutes later. The young man slumped into a chair, his right hand covering his eyes. It was silent in the waiting room, then Jackson sat up in the chair, leaning forward to rest his elbows on his knees.

"What the hell happened, Spenser? All I've heard -- after your security guy called -- was a news report that dad had killed a purse snatcher who'd shot a cop."

McCall retrieved the police report from his inside pocket and handed it to Jackson.

Jackson read for a moment, then slowly shook his head. "I don't believe this. Why the hell would dad shoot someone -- a kid, for Christ sakes?" Jackson looked up at McCall. "This makes it sound as if dad executed him. My father wouldn't do that. He *couldn't*."

"There are many witnesses, Tony. The kid was trying to get the dead policeman's gun. It wouldn't take a very good lawyer to prove that your dad fired in self defense."

"I don't give a damn what the witnesses say. I know my father. He wouldn't shoot anyone, not even a cop killer." Jackson slammed his fist down onto the armrest. "There was no damn reason for him to get involved."

"That's a helluva thing for you, of all people, to say," McCall said. "We still don't know enough about what happened on that street corner, but your father had a habit of helping people when they needed it most."

Jackson looked at McCall. "Is that an observation you made while he was sitting at your feet shining your damned shoes?"

McCall slowly shook his head. "Tony, you don't know what the hell you're talking about. You're way off base, so drop it."

"That's a lot of crap, McCall. He's groveled for you people in that marble tower for more than twenty years. What the hell was he to you?"

"Look, we both know why you're angry with me, and it has nothing to do with why we're here tonight. We'll talk about it later."

Then McCall recalled something from the police report. "Has your father ever been shot -- during a robbery attempt or some other street crime?"

"Shot?" Jackson again read the police report. "Somebody must have misunderstood what he was saying," Jackson said, handing the report to McCall. "My father has never been shot..." Then Jackson looked at McCall. "...but I suppose he might have been shot during the war, but you know he never talks about any of that."

McCall folded the report, tapped it against the chair's armrest, then put it into an inside jacket pocket. Then he gestured toward the hospital lobby. "There are some reporters out there who want to talk to you. The police told them your dad's a hero. The reporters know who you are and they want to ask you some questions about your dad."

"Screw the reporters. I saw them when I came in."

"Look, it'll only take a few minutes. Besides, your dad will probably enjoy reading your interview when he's better."

"He wouldn't be interested."

"You're going to have to face the reporters now or later," McCall said more firmly, "so you might as well get it over with."

Jackson leaned his head back against the seat. "Ah, hell, Spense, why did this have to happen to him. He's known nothing but pain for all these years..." Jackson slowly sat up and looked at McCall. He looked down at his hands, then sighed deeply. "Okay. I suppose you're right."

They turned down the corridor toward the emergency room entrance.

"Do you have a place to stay?" McCall asked, their footsteps echoing down the tiled corridor.

"Not yet. I thought of staying at dad's place, but it's too far from the hospital."

"You know I live alone. You're welcome to come home with me. There isn't anything more you can do here tonight."

"No thanks," Jackson said quickly. "I'm sure I can get a room downtown for a couple of nights."

McCall nodded. "Suit yourself. I was only trying to make things a little easier for you."

"Yeah, I know, Spenser," Jackson said. "You have a habit of working too hard at doing that."

There were three camera crews and a couple of print reporters waiting in the lobby. They immediately recognized McCall, and in moments the lights and cameras were on.

"Mr. McCall," one of the reporters called, "we heard you were here. Is Jackson one of your employees?"

"Mr. Jackson works in our building, but he's not a Horizon employee," McCall said, then gestured toward Jackson. "I'm sure you know his son, Tony Jackson."

The reporters immediately circled Jackson. Even though he was the assistant U.S. Attorney for the Northern District of Indiana, Chicago reporters knew Jackson because his convictions involving interstate racketeering cases had been a national story.

"Mr. Jackson, have you learned anything new from the cops about the details of your father's shooting?"

"No, I haven't had an opportunity to talk to the police yet. I'll do that first thing in the morning."

"The police superintendent called your father a hero for helping that woman, and for shooting a cop killer. There's talk about giving him some kind of medal. How do you feel about that, considering you're a U.S. Attorney?"

"I'm an *assistant* U.S. Attorney. Of course I'm proud of my father."

Another reporter pushed his microphone closer to Jackson's face. "One of the nurses said your father had been very seriously injured some years ago. He lost part of a leg. How did it happen?"

"My father was in World War Two, but he's never said much about how he got hurt. All I know is that he was a cook and was wounded in the closing months of the war."

"Did he get any medals for bravery?"

"If he did, I've never seen them." Jackson paused for a couple of seconds, then began to take control of the interview. "The important thing to me, ladies and gentlemen, is that my father saw a crime being committed and did something about it. That took courage, but I've always known my father to be a courageous man. As Americans, we no longer can afford to be complacent about crime. Frankly, I think my father would be embarrassed to receive a medal for doing what he felt was his duty, his responsibility, as a citizen."

McCall saw the reporter for the Chicago ABC affiliate, Channel 7, who had asked the question, look back at her cameraman and nod.

McCall knew they'd just been handed their sound bite -- that lean, concise combination of words demanded by the time-constricted medium of television to tell a story.

As the interview continued, McCall was impressed by how well Jackson handled the questions, how well he handled his emotions. He was articulate, quick on his feet, and did a good job of hiding his personal feelings about what his father had done.

McCall quietly walked away from the circle of lights and reporters. He shrugged into his topcoat and walked through the exit into the parking area. His driver immediately spotted him and pulled the limousine to the entrance.

"The apartment, Mr. McCall?"

"Yes, Bill," McCall said as he got into the back seat. "And plan on picking me up at seven in the morning. I want to stop here before going to the office."

McCall thought back to the doctor's comments about all the scars on Cordell's body. McCall knew that Cordell had been wounded during the war, but he didn't know the wounds had been so extensive. The fact that Cordell had been in combat was unusual, a fact that Cordell didn't like to discuss. Not many Negroes had been involved in combat during the war. Most were assigned to labor battalions or were used as cooks.

Then McCall thought of the police report. How or when was Cordell shot before tonight? Who was Bobby? And why would a gentle, religious Negro kill another man...a boy? Because of this Bobby?

McCall shook his head. *Why the hell am I so curious? Maybe it's just because Cordell is such a decent human being, that I can't imagine that he'd hurt anyone, not even a cop killer.*

McCall suppressed a yawn. His eyes were gritty with fatigue. He could hardly wait to take a shower and crawl into bed. *Hell, I'm too damn tired to think about it tonight.*

CHAPTER 3

February 20, 1967
The Times Tower
Chicago
11:15 a.m.

Eleanor Harrison reached for the day's edition that her secretary had just placed on the corner of her desk. There was something she always found exciting about a freshly printed newspaper. She couldn't describe it. It involved more than just the touch and feel of the newsprint, although certainly that was part of it. Each new edition represented the culmination of an incredibly complex chain of events -- from the disciplined chaos of the newsroom, to the "back shop" where the words were cast into metal, to the giant presses in the basement that rumbled throughout the Times Tower as they accelerated to speed.

Eleanor often speculated that magazine and book publishers must experience the same sense of accomplishment when an issue rolled off the press. The difference, of course, was that her presses rolled out a new edition every day.

Her husband, recognized as one of the nation's premier journalists and news executives, felt the same excitement during the twenty eight years he'd published The Chicago *Times*. For the seven years since his death, Eleanor's name appeared in the paper's masthead under the title of publisher.

She carefully unfolded the paper and reached for her coffee cup, then paused. Above the fold was a headline in forty two-point type that caught her eye. The two-column story was about a black man who shot and killed a teen-aged purse snatcher who killed a policeman. A police spokesman was quoted as crediting Cordell Jackson's actions with helping to clear up as many as thirty such assaults, many of them on elderly woman who were injured in the attacks. According to the article, police said that Jackson, who was shot and seriously wounded during a struggle with the youth over a pistol, risked his life to prevent bystanders from being shot. Although police said they believed that Cordell's shooting of the youth was justified, the case would be considered for submission to a grand jury.

Eleanor had met Cordell Jackson on many occasions when she'd visited Spenser McCall's office. Reaching for the phone, Eleanor dialed her managing editor's extension.

"Russell, do we have an update on the Cordell Jackson shooting?"

"Nothing at the moment, Ellie, but we've got people standing by at the hospital and at the cop house. The mayor's press secretary says *his honor* will have a statement later this morning. If we get it early enough, we'll replate page one. Thought you'd like to know -- Spenser McCall was at the hospital last night and again early this morning. Jackson's son is at the hospital now."

"What's the latest on Jackson's condition?" Eleanor asked.

"He's in intensive care. Still critical. I guess it was touch and go during the night, but now they think he'll make it."

"Keep me advised."

"Sure thing, Ellie."

"By the way, who did the sidebar on the son?"

"Wilkinson talked to him last night and pulled together what we had in the files."

"Tell Wilk it was a nice piece." Eleanor paused. "Russ, do we have anything in the files about Tony Jackson's political ambitions?"

"Nothing I've seen suggests he's interested in politics. But you know that a lot of U.S. attorneys use the job to run for the state house or Congress. But I'll tell you this -- any political ambitions he might have will depend on whether he gets Izzy the Animal into U.S. District Court. And if he does get him into court, everyone will be watching how he handles the case."

Eleanor looked at the profile that Gary Wilkinson, the paper's top investigative reporter, had written. She remembered that Wilkinson had covered the original story on Izzy when it broke three months earlier.

Israel "Izzy The Animal" Arnold was a key suspect in the murder of an undercover ATF -- Alcohol, Tobacco Tax, and Firearms -- agent in Indiana. The agent's body had been found on an abandoned farm near South Bend. The agent, Harold Pinkins, was found sprawled over the hood of his own car with two bullets in his head.

Eleanor recalled that Pinkins had been the first black agent assigned to his division. He was only twenty six, married, and had a young daughter. Pinkins had been assigned to watch Arnold, who federal agents were certain headed a gunrunning and drug operation.

"Russ, ask Wilk to quietly check out Tony Jackson. Only you and I will see copies of his report. I think Hoosiers are long overdue for a talented black candidate for state office -- maybe even Congress -- someone who can go toe-to-toe with the downstate Republican power structure. If Tony is as good as he looks...well, let's just see what we find."

"We'll have something for you this time tomorrow."

"Thanks, Russell."

Eleanor then dialed Spenser McCall's private number.

"Yes?"

"You sound tired. Are you alone?" she asked.

"Good morning. Yes, I'm alone and, yes, I'm a little tired. I was just leaving for the gym."

"Spense, I'm sorry about Cordell. Have you heard anything more about his condition?"

"No, he's still critical. The bullet shattered a rib, and the doctor says that bone fragments sometimes can do more damage than a bullet. They were worried at first, but this morning they seemed to feel he's going to make it."

"Yes, that's the report I got from one of my people." Eleanor hesitated. "Spense, I know you're concerned about Cordell, but something else seems to be troubling you?"

McCall didn't respond immediately. "Yeah, I suppose there is. Bob called a few minutes ago."

"And it sounds as if it didn't go well."

"Ellie, that kid and I can't exchange a complete sentence without one of us getting pissed."

"McCall, I know I can safely presume that you did a good job of controlling your temper," Eleanor said. "Correct?"

McCall didn't respond.

"*Correct*, McCall?"

"Ellie, explain to me what the hell the difference is between a movie and a film?"

"I don't know that there is a difference. Why?"

"I called his damned movie a movie and, as only my son can do, he made it clear that he doesn't make movies. He makes *films*. Now, I'd like someone to explain to me what the hell the difference is. I suspect, Ellie, that if I would have called the damn thing a film he would have--"

"Spenser McCall."

"What?"

"Listen to yourself."

McCall suddenly realized how agitated he sounded. He took immense pride in his reputation for self-control, in his ability to remain calm during crises. But McCall's son was his great weakness.

"What is Bob's film about?" Eleanor asked.

"He said he's doing a documentary on Caesar Chavez, that guy who started the farm workers union. He's probably going to make the guy look like a hero."

"He is a hero," Eleanor said. "I think Chavez is an excellent subject for a documentary, and Bob does very good work."

"Now don't you start spouting that liberal crap, Ellie, and if the kid's work is all that good, then why the hell doesn't he make any real money with his damned *films*.

"He will, Spense. I'm sure he will. He just needs a little more time. But listen, why don't you let a girl take you to lunch? We can talk more about this then."

McCall hesitated. "I've got a better idea. Why don't you come here and I'll have sandwiches brought up to my meeting room. I'll finish up at the gym by noon. Say, twelve thirty?"

"Deal."

Spenser McCall rested his head against his high-back chair. Through his nineteenth floor window he could see that ice had formed along the Lake Michigan shoreline, although the lake appeared to be free of ice. Wave action had piled great slabs of ice into ridges several feet high. Visibility in the cold, clear air was excellent and he could see the Indiana-Michigan shoreline. Far out into the lake, a vessel, perhaps an ore carrier, was eastbound.

McCall couldn't shake the image of the old Negro lying in a hospital bed. Spenser McCall and Cordell Jackson had known each other for almost twenty years. McCall had joined the company's research division before the war, where he'd been selected for the fast track. By the age of twenty-four he was a department supervisor. He was named president when he was only thirty-seven, and chairman when he was forty. Under McCall's guidance, Horizon grew in twenty years from a modest Midwest refiner-marketer to become one of the nation's top ten fully integrated oil companies operating in more than forty countries. In all of those twenty years, Jackson had shined McCall's shoes, as well as those of the other company executives. McCall had ordered that Jackson have unlimited and exclusive rights to shine shoes in the massive headquarters building. And McCall dropped a not-so-subtle hint among his executives that Cordell should be well paid for his services.

Why? McCall didn't think of himself as a champion of Negro rights. In fact, in recent years, there had been criticism from Negro rights groups that Horizon Corporation had made little progress toward achieving equality for minorities.

There were things about Cordell Jackson that McCall admired. It was more than admiration. McCall envied the bond between the man and his son. Despite the fact that Cordell, whose wife had died in 1957, shined shoes for a living, he managed to make enough money to help his son through college and law school. The odds had been against the boy -- the neighborhood he grew up in, the color of his skin, the death of his mother, a crippled father, the lack of money. Yet, McCall knew that Cordell had inspired the boy, and the boy had achieved his goals. That's why McCall had helped Tony get the appointment as assistant U.S. attorney by making certain that young Jackson was noticed by the right people in the Justice Department.

McCall balanced all of that against the splintered relationship with his own son. He felt the pain of it deep in his gut. He looked at his watch. A half-hour had passed since Bob's call. It had been almost three months since he'd heard from him. Their last argument had been over Bob's divorce.

Predictably, Bob needed money -- five thousand dollars -- to finish the Chavez project. McCall intended to give him the money, wanted to give it to him, but he'd made the mistake of asking Bob why he needed it. It was a habit, part of his culture, his training. You didn't spend money on things without knowing what you were buying.

McCall knew that he and the boy had never been really close, and McCall accepted the responsibility for that. It was just that McCall never discovered how to structure a father-son relationship. The hope that one ever could be developed was all but abandoned when McCall's wife died. McCall recalled how on the night after the burial, Bob accused him of sacrificing his family for success in the oil business.

Perhaps, McCall thought, perhaps Bob was right. McCall recalled his relationship with his own father, who had been state superintendent of schools in Ohio. He was a capable and highly respected man who was admired for his accomplishments -- all the more significant because he was blind, having lost his sight in a boyhood accident.

Perhaps that's why McCall's father constantly urged him to excel in his studies. Success in life was everything, his father had said. McCall graduated from high school at sixteen, completed his undergraduate work in petroleum engineering at nineteen, and received his doctorate when he was twenty two.

McCall, however, never really knew his father. Even now, although he hated to admit it, he suspected during those years that his father was trying to see the world through his son's eyes.

McCall wondered if he hadn't intruded into Cordell's life to vicariously share the relationship the man had with his son. Cordell and Tony sure as hell didn't fight over the difference between a *film* and a *movie.*

McCall realized that he and Cordell were nearly as different as two men could be. The only thing they had in common was that they'd both served in World War Two. But McCall had been stationed in England, where he felt the only important contribution he had made was to help develop the plan to ensure the flow of gasoline and oil across the English Channel for the Normandy invasion.

Cordell, seven years older than McCall, had been a cook in a parachute regiment, although he had never trained as a paratrooper. He'd joined the Army in 1936 because he couldn't find work. McCall never saw combat. Jackson was in action during the Battle of the Bulge, where he lost his right leg below the knee and suffered a wound that disfigured his forehead. Although McCall and Cordell often had discussed their experiences in the army, Cordell had never once discussed details of how he was wounded.

McCall shook his head. *I can't overlook the possibility,* he thought, *that I've helped Cordell Jackson simply because he is a very decent human being. Maybe it's as simple as that.*

McCall looked at his watch. The hell with the gym. He reached for the intercom and called his secretary. "Kathy, give Jim Austin a call. See if he can come up before he leaves for lunch."

James R. Austin had for more than a year been Horizon's manager of public and government affairs. A native of Alabama and a recently retired army lieutenant colonel who had served with distinction in Vietnam, Austin's final tour of duty had been as a public information officer at the Pentagon.

Four minutes after receiving the call, Austin was standing in the doorway of McCall's office.

"Come in, Jim." McCall gestured toward a chair.

"Thank you, sir."

McCall liked Austin's efficiency. The man got things done without a lot of fuss. McCall also liked him as a human being. Despite Austin's military background, he seemed a gentle man -- his gentleness accentuated by his soft drawl -- and he was respectful almost to a fault. If there was a flaw in Austin's tenure with Horizon, it was that he apparently found it impossible to stop being a soldier.

"Jim, you know Cordell Jackson.

"Yes, sir." I heard about the shooting."

"Read that." McCall handed Austin the copy of the police report.

Austin looked puzzled when he placed the report on the corner of McCall's desk.

"I know what you're wondering, Jim. What did Cordell mean when he said he wasn't going to be shot again? And who is Bobby?"

"Yes, sir. The police obviously think it's related to something that might have happened in his neighborhood. I guess he lives in a pretty tough area."

"I've got Guthrie in security working with the police to check that out," McCall said.

Austin nodded. "But you're also wondering if it had anything to do with his military service?"

"Yes. Cordell is a World War Two veteran, and I know he was wounded during the Battle of the Bulge fighting. But he's never discussed the details of how he was hurt. He shrugs it off, saying that he hadn't really been a fighter, that he'd been -- in his words -- 'just a cook.'"

"How would you like me to help with this, Mr. McCall?"

"How are your contacts at the Pentagon?"

The question surprised Austin. "Well, I don't know. I guess it depends."

"I'd like this carried out very quietly. I'd like you to find out where and how we can examine any after-action reports that describe the circumstances under which he was wounded."

"Mr. McCall...ah, that may be very difficult. I've had occasion to search for such records involving that period once before. A lot of those reports -- if they were made at all -- were written on scraps of paper, even the backs of envelopes."

"I can imagine. But I'd like very much for you to try, and to do so as soon as possible."

"Do you know what unit he served in and the date he was wounded?"

"One-Hundred Sixth Division, 442nd Regiment. As I said, he was a cook. I don't have the exact date when he was wounded, but it obviously had to be sometime around mid-December of forty-four when the Bulge fighting occurred. Maybe Hines Veterans Hospital has it."

"His rank?

"Corporal."

"Can you tell me what we're looking for?

McCall hesitated. "I don't know. I guess I'd just like to know the details about how he was hurt."

"Especially if he'd been shot?"

McCall nodded.

Austin closed his note pad. "I'll make some calls immediately. How soon do you want to do this?"

"As soon as possible. Call me the minute you've got a lead on the procedures involved."

"Yes, sir. I may have to go to Washington to look for what we need."

"Do it. I'll probably be going with you."

February 20, 1967
The White House
9:22 a.m.

The secretary ushered Oliver Wentworth Crawford into the Oval Office. "The President will be with you in just a few seconds, Mr. Crawford. I'll keep Mrs. Crawford company."

"I appreciate that. Thank you."

Crawford's eyes were drawn to the blue carpet with the interwoven presidential seal, the marble fireplace, and the leather wing chairs in front of the desk. The room's air seemed charged with power and flavored with history -- not at all diminished by the bank of television sets and the small models of oil derricks and the figurines of cattle that marked the Lyndon Johnson style. Crawford desperately wanted a cigarette. He reached for his lighter, shook a cigarette from the pack, then changed his mind.

Crawford looked at the Zippo lighter in his hand. It had been a gift from his father when the younger Crawford had graduated from the U.S. Military Academy at West Point. The lighter showed the wear of years of use. There was an inscription on one side that read:

Duty
Honor
Country

Above the inscription was a single gold star. Crawford retired from the army with twenty three years of service and the rank of brigadier general. The other side of the lighter bore the emblem of the unit Crawford had served with during World War Two. It had been his first combat command. When he retired, he was named an assistant secretary of the army. That was two years ago. And now, he thought, two days ago I was named Secretary of the Army. *Damn,* he surged with pride, *if only dad could be here today.*

The door opened so suddenly that Crawford almost jumped.

"Morning, Ollie." Lyndon Baines Johnson, carrying his suit coat, walked briskly past Crawford to his desk. Crawford was surprised to see that the President held up his trousers with suspenders. Although it wasn't yet noon, Crawford noticed that the President's dark blue suit already was badly rumpled.

Johnson put his jacket over the back of a chair. He put on his half-glasses and quickly scanned a paper, then scowled and crumpled it, tossing the paper toward the wastebasket. He then poked his long finger at the intercom button. "Yolanda, honey, let me see the report that Rusk brought over last night."

A moment later the secretary handed the President a sealed manila envelope and left the room. Johnson held the envelope, scowled again as he seemed to weigh it with one hand, then placed it on the corner of the desk. Then he looked over his glasses at Crawford and smiled.

"Well, Ollie, today's your big day."

"Yes, sir, Mr. President."

"We've got a couple of minutes. Let's sit down and talk."

Johnson gestured toward a chair, then sat heavily onto the couch. He draped his right arm over the back of the couch and stretched one leg onto the cushion.

Crawford was tempted to look at his watch. The announcement in the press briefing room was scheduled for nine-thirty. It was nearly that time now.

"Don't worry about the media vultures," Johnson said. "Most of them like to circle a spell before they feed."

"Yes, sir. Ah...Mr. President, I want to take this opportunity to thank you again for appointing me to this position. I'm going to work very hard to justify your confidence in me."

Johnson, his head tilted slightly and his eyes narrowed, the folds of flesh all but obscuring them, said, "Son, the first thing I want to do with you is clear away all the cow plops. I wanted your predecessor to stay on, but he decided he wanted to teach at that damn hippie college -- at least that was his excuse. So, although you've got the job, you're second-best until you prove to me that you're first-best."

Crawford could feel his face flush.

"Among the reasons I appointed you is because you carry your daddy's name, and your family has friends in high places. You did a good job as an assistant secretary, and you also have the Medal of Honor. Right?"

"Yes, sir."

"Well, I'm counting on you to help me with this Vietnam thing. My domestic programs aren't moving fast enough because the goddamned pepperpots, those liberals, don't understand that the Communists don't respect anything but force."

The President swung his leg to the floor so quickly that he startled Crawford, then the President leaned forward close enough to poke the younger man in the chest with his forefinger to punctuate his words.

"Why the hell should *I* be blamed for this war when Ike committed us in Asia in 1954 and Kennedy got us even deeper?" Crawford could see the anger and frustration etched in the President's face. "I'll bet you didn't know that *I* had to pound on Ike's desk to stop him from sending American paratroopers into Dien Bien Phu when the French were getting their asses wiped. Did you know that? Huh? Did you know *that*?"

Crawford shook his head.

The President leaned back and breathed deeply, rubbing his forehead. "Well," he said, as if Crawford weren't in the room, "if everybody says it's *my* damn war then I'm gonna *win* the sumbitch. I'm gonna show them that I've got the biggest guns and the toughest heart."

LBJ, his face flushed, looked up and pointed his long arm like a rifle at Crawford's face. "What I want *you* to do is to help me destroy those pajama-wearing bastards -- we're gonna eat those goddamned Communists." The President leaned forward and held his open hand, palm up, very near Crawford's face. "I want Ho Chi Minh coming to me begging to put his balls in this hand." Then the President, smiling without humor, snapped his fingers closed into a fist so tightly clinched that it quivered with emotion. "You understand what I'm trying to tell you?"

Crawford quickly nodded. "Yes, sir."

The President nodded briskly. "Okay. Now, when I introduce you to those reporters waiting out there, I know you've been briefed on the right answers."

"I feel I've been thoroughly briefed, sir."

Johnson again tilted his head, looking hard at Crawford. "Understand me good, Ollie. What I'm saying is that they're going to drop horse-size turds at your feet and I don't want you tracking anything smelly into *this* office."

"I understand, sir."

"Make damn sure you do. One of your first problems is in that envelope." Johnson gestured casually with his arm toward the desk. "That new helicopter gunship is so full of maggots it's killing damn near as many of my boys as the Viet Cong. Find out who's screwed up and get it *fixed*. You *hear* me?"

"I understand, Mr. President."

"Good." Johnwon rose and Crawford got to his feet at almost the same instant. The President reached for his jacket and shrugged into it. Then he ran his hands over his massive head to smooth his hair.

Standing almost six-feet four-inches, Johnson was at least a half-head taller than Crawford. The President stood in front of Crawford and smiled, this time with a measure of warmth, and he placed his huge hand on Crawford's shoulder. "Ollie, I'm sorry if it sounded like I was jumping on your ass, but another problem I've got is those politicians in Saigon who are beginning to think *they're* running the war."

Johnson chuckled. "Hell, where I come from, when you buy a politician he stays bought. Now, introduce me to your lovely lady before we go feed the vultures."

At that moment there was a knock at the door. "Come on in." The door opened and Presidential Press Secretary George Christian stood in the doorway. "They're getting a little restless, Mr. President."

"Okay, George, Okay. Tell them we're on our way."

When Christian had gone, Johnson leaned toward Crawford and said in a stage whisper, "He's a damned good man. Pierre Salinger was a damn good man, too, but having a man named *Pierre* around made me afraid my pecker might go limp." The President chuckled.

Julie Crawford was standing in the corridor with the President's secretary. Julie wore a dark blue suit; her long, dark hair complemented her fair complexion.

"Mr. President," Crawford said, "this is my wife, Julie."

The President held Julie's hand in both of his. "Honey," he said, tilting his head to the side and smiling warmly, "I want you to know how proud we are to have Ollie running the army. I know he's going to do a fine job for the country."

Oliver Crawford knew that the President had a special appreciation for attractive women. That's why he wasn't surprised when he saw the President's eyes fixed on his wife's bosom while he talked.

CHAPTER 4

February 21, 1967
Georgetown
Washington, D.C.
6:07 p.m.

Julie Crawford hesitated, trying to decide whether to set the tray of champagne glasses down to answer the phone. The dozen or so guests were clustered around the living room television set eagerly awaiting the evening news.

"Switch it to ABC," someone shouted. "They'll have it." An undersecretary said, "Maybe we'd better watch Uncle Cronkite -- we know LBJ does."

Julie carefully put the tray onto a sideboard and picked up the phone. "The White House! Yes, I'll hold." Julie gestured frantically to the people in the living room, but no one noticed.

"Yes, Mrs. Johnson, this is Julie Crawford. Why, yes, I am very proud of Ollie. That's very nice of you to say that. Friday? Of course I can. Yes, I can be there at that time. And thank you for calling. Ollie and I appreciate it very much."

Julie started for the living room, then remembered the tray. "Ladies and gentlemen; may I have your attention, please." Julie placed the tray on a low table and beamed as the heads turned toward her. "Lady Bird Johnson and I just had a little chat on the phone, and she said some very nice things about the new Secretary of the Army."

The room erupted into cheers and whistles. "Not only that, but I am having lunch on Friday with the First Lady..." Julie curtsied "... at the White House, thank you."

Julie reached for Crawford and hugged him tightly, whispering so that only he could hear, "Your dad would be so proud of you." He looked knowingly into her eyes before turnnig to the crowd.

"Turn up the volume," Crawford said, "and everybody grab a glass."

Thirteen minutes into the news, the screen showed the press briefing room in the White House. Again the room erupted into cheers. President Lyndon Johnson was standing at the lectern, Crawford standing to his left.

Crawford had, of course, seen Johnson on television many times. After this morning's meeting in the Oval Office, Crawford was struck by how different the man's personality was in front of the cameras. He was stiff, uncomfortable, his use of the language almost paternal. Crawford recalled how, in private, the President was earthy, gruff, intimidating yet magnetic. The man overpowered people.

On television, Johnson was attempting to look and sound dignified, trying to be what he apparently thought was presidential. Crawford realized that the television camera was one of the few things that intimidated Johnson.

The President read from the prepared manuscript. He talked about Crawford's military career, emphasizing that he was the recipient of the Medal of Honor. Then he described the positions Crawford had held as a soldier and a civilian. Secretly, Crawford had to admit that his credentials, as they were read by the President of the United States, did sound impressive.

Then Crawford stepped to the microphones. He had been briefed to anticipate questions dealing with problems confronting the Army in Vietnam -- its morale, fighting ability, drugs, and complaints about equipment like the new helicopter gunship. But he wasn't prepared for the question from Judd Michaels, the Washington press corps's senior wire service reporter.

"Mr. Secretary," Michaels asked, "there is an allegation that the military has been awarding an unusually high number of decorations for bravery -- including the Medal of Honor. Historically, it seems that whenever the fighting doesn't go the way the military had planned -- by that I mean when casualties are high -- or if the fighting doesn't have the full support of the people, the military creates heroes by handing out more medals."

Crawford asked, "What is your specific question, Mr. Michaels?"

"My question is whether you agree -- considering that you've won the Medal of Honor -- that decorations, including the Medal of Honor, are being liberally handed out because the Vietnam war is rapidly losing the support of the American people?"

Crawford paused before responding, then smiled. "No, Mr. Michaels, I don't agree with your allegation. The American Army in Vietnam is as good or better than any army this nation has ever fielded." Crawford pointed at Michaels. "Your statement short-changes the American soldier. He's fighting a tough and disciplined enemy in some of the world's most hostile terrain -- and the American soldier will win that fight.

"Finally, Mr. Michaels, I didn't *win* the Medal of Honor; I was the recipient of that honor." Crawford now moved his eyes over the group of reporters. "That distinction isn't an exercise in semantics. Those of us who have received the medal don't think of it as a contest. The approximately thirty-three hundred men -- and one woman -- who received that piece of bronze and silk ribbon understand that it recognizes a very few from among the tens of millions who have served this nation since the Civil War. They understand that it recognizes the courage and sacrifice of those who put their lives on the line for their country.

"That's why, ladies and gentlemen, I am honored to have been named Secretary of the Army. I will do my utmost to help ensure that the U.S. Army will be so strong, so formidable, that our young men and women will never again have to face the conflicts that involved my generation and the generation of young men and women now fighting in Vietnam."

Crawford paused dramatically, his eyes moving deliberately around the room. "My sincere hope is that no one ever again will have cause to be the recipient of the Medal of Honor."

The camera moved from Crawford to President Johnson, who was smiling broadly as he began to applaud, his head bobbing as he looked around the room, obviously urging others to join him. There was sporadic applause, mostly from aides and other governmental officials.

The news spot was no more than ninety seconds. When it concluded, everyone in the Crawford home whistled and applauded. Julie was at Crawford's side. She held his hand, grasping it tightly.

Crawford felt it was one of the most important moments in his life. Yes, it was a shame that Major General Oliver Wentworth Crawford Senior was not alive to share his son's glory.

February 22 1967
Wesley Memorial Hospital
Chicago
5 p.m.

"Dad?"

Tony leaned close to his father's face. The man looked incredibly old and fragile. The loose skin around his neck was gathered in dark folds. A gray stubble covered his face. The tubes running into his father's nose, arm, and chest almost made Tony physically ill. Four containers, one obviously a unit of blood, fed their contents through the tangle of tubes into the old man, who was propped up at a forty-five degree angle. On the wall over the bed was an oscilloscope-like monitor, rhythmically beeping as wave forms undulated across its green screen. Another machine hummed softly next to the bed. The nurse had said it was a vacuum pump that maintained a negative pressure inside Cordell's chest to keep his damaged lung from collapsing again.

"Dad, it's me, Tony."

The old man's eyes opened, eyes that were unfocused and wet and rheumy. Cordell raised his right hand slightly and his son grasped it.

Tony leaned closer and smiled. "You're going to be okay, Pop. It'll be a little while before you get out of here, but you're going to be fine. Then I'm going to take you home with me."

Tony saw his father slowly shake his head. The old man's lips quivered with emotion and his eyes welled with tears.

Tony patted his father's hand. "I told you," he said gently, "the doctors say you're going to be fine. It's just going to take a while."

Cordell shook his head again. "It all came back to me in my dream." His voice was soft and phlegmy.

"What are you saying, dad?"

"I killed that boy." Cordell took a deep breath that rattled.

"Dad, you did what you had to do. You did the right thing. Don't worry about it now. We'll have a long talk about it later."

"I killed all those boys," Cordell said, his voice breaking.

Tony gently squeezed his father's hand. "C'mon, Dad, you're a little confused because of the pain medicine."

Cordell opened his eyes and shook his head. He jerked his hand free and pulled his son closer by the lapel of his suit jacket. "Don't you understand, son? They trusted me." Cordell's voice was almost pleading, his face contorted with emotion. "Especially Bobby...especially Bobby. He wanted to run, but he stayed because of me, because I promised to take care of him. God forgive me. We all should have run away."

"Dad, what are you talking about?"

Cordell's hand fell back to the bed, exhausted by the effort.

Tony remembered that witnesses said Cordell had mentioned the name Bobby during the shooting. Who is he, Tony wondered, and what the hell did he have to do with the shooting?

A hand touched Tony's shoulder. It was the ICU head nurse. "Mr. Jackson, you'll have to leave. You can come back in an hour and spend another five minutes with your father."

Tony hesitated. He looked at his watch, then leaned back and sighed. It was after 5 p.m. He'd spent nearly the entire day in the hospital. "Thanks, but I think I'll clean up and have an early dinner. I'll be back later this evening." He looked at the nurse. "You'll call me at my hotel if there's any change, right?"

"Of course, sir," the nurse said. "Mr. McCall is in the waiting area."

When Tony looked back at his father, he saw that the old man had fallen asleep. Tony took a tissue from a box on the nightstand and gently wiped away his father's tears that had rolled down the side of his face into the gray stubble.

Tony walked the long corridor to the waiting room, reflecting on how he'd always dreaded hospitals. He remembered walking through a similar hospital corridor when his mother died after a lingering illness. He stopped at a pay phone to call his wife. He also talked briefly with his son and daughter, then walked to the waiting room. McCall was seated in one of the lounge chairs.

"He's going to be okay, according to the doctors," Tony said as he sat heavily into a chair.

"Yes. I know the hospital administrator. He'll personally keep us advised."

Tony looked at McCall for a moment, started to say something, then shook his head, smiling ruefully.

"What's the problem?" McCall asked, bracing for what he knew would come.

"You can press buttons all over this city -- hell, all over the country -- can't you?"

"Look, Tony, I--"

"McCall, what I really think is that you get your jollies doing a little missionary work for the poor black folks, don't you? But I think it's a just a power game for you. You want to create the image that you're a big-time, conservative oil guy who has a soft spot in his heart for the little guy. But I hear that you've got trouble with your board of directors and they may take your buttons away. If they do, then you'll be just some poor old guy -- with a measly four or maybe five million bucks to retire on."

"Go ahead, Tony, get it all out of your system, even the cheap shots."

"Yeah, well, maybe I owe you a couple of cheap shots."

"You owe me nothing," McCall said, putting an edge to the words. "Your problem is that you're so damned hung-up with being black that you can't see that to a helluva lot of people it doesn't make any difference."

"McCall, in that marble tower you may be a god. But to me, you're just a meddling old man who's trying to ease his conscience because his time is running short. You're the worst kind of bigot."

McCall got slowly, deliberately to his feet. Tony stood and stepped forward until he and McCall were separated by a couple of feet.

"Why did you do it?" Tony asked through clenched teeth. "Why did you get involved?"

"The why doesn't concern you, Tony. That was strictly between your father and me."

"What the hell do you mean it doesn't concern me?" Tony's voice was rising. "I found out two months after I got there that you'd greased the skids with your cronies in Washington. Don't you understand how that marks me? Don't you understand that I needed to get that appointment on my own?"

McCall's voice was low, measured. "Let me make sure that *you* understand how it was set up. The deal was that you would get a shot at the job -- a fair shot. That's all I got for you -- a chance. No strings. If you couldn't hack it, they would have bounced your ass on the pavement. The people at Justice said they were going to keep your profile low until they could make sure that you weren't just all mouth. They were going to bury you under all the tough cases to see if you could cut it."

McCall nodded. "Yeah, Tony, I know what you're thinking. They wanted a black face so they could show they were doing their share to support Johnson's Great Society. That's true, but they weren't going to be embarrassed by a black face that couldn't cut it. Whether they kept you depended on how you looked, and how badly you smelled, when you crawled out from under all the crap."

McCall saw the anger begin to ebb from Tony's face.

Tony turned and took a few steps to the chair over which he'd thrown his topcoat. He reached into one of the pockets and withdrew a pack of cigarettes. He lit one and inhaled deeply. Then he turned to face McCall.

"Why me?" he asked, edging toward control over his emotions. "Why would you do it for me?"

"Don't flatter yourself, Tony. It wasn't just you."

"My father?"

McCall nodded.

"Why would you bother doing something for an old black man who just shines your shoes?"

McCall walked toward Tony, took the pack of cigarettes from his hand, shook one free, and lit it. "You know, I gave these up almost three months ago." Then he walked back to his chair and sat down. "I suppose it was nearly twenty years ago that I offered your dad a job with the company -- about a year after he started shining shoes in the building. The job wasn't much. After all, as a boy in Georgia, I don't think he finished the fifth grade. I wanted to put him in charge of our mail room."

McCall took a drag from the cigarette, then grimaced and ground it out in the metal ashtray next to his chair. "He took the job for two weeks, then came in one day and said he was quitting. He said he couldn't stand on his feet long enough to do his job right. Besides, he said, there was a young Negro down there with a lot of kids who should be promoted to his job because he could do it better. That was it. He went back to pushing his cart around the building."

"He never told me about that," Tony said softly.

"There was one other thing," McCall said as he reached into his jacket and withdrew his wallet. "When my wife died of cancer ten years ago, my son and I had a tough time dealing with it." McCall found the piece of paper and carefully unfolded it. "In fact," McCall said softly as he looked at the paper, "I guess my son has never learned to deal with it, or to forgive me."

"Forgive you?"

McCall waved the question away with his hand, then extended the paper, no more than four inches square. "One day your father came into my office, handed me this, and walked out without saying a word."

Tony recognized his father's writing. Each letter was written as with a child's careful precision.

But the souls of the righteous are in the hand of God,
and there shall no torment touch them.
In the sight of the unwise they seemed to die;
and their departure is taken for misery,
And their going from us to be utter destruction;
but they are in peace.

Tony carefully refolded the paper and handed it back.

"At the time," McCall said, "those were the most meaningful words said to me. Later he told me that he'd found them in some book shortly after your mother died. He said the words had been a comfort to him."

"My father has always been a deeply religious man."

Tony lit another cigarette, then offered the pack to McCall, who hesitated before waving them away. "How did you meet my dad?" Tony asked.

McCall smiled. "He was recommended to me by a man you probably saw on television news last night."

Tony looked at McCall quizzically.

"The new secretary of the Army, Oliver Crawford."

"You're kidding me. The guy whose father was a great World War Two general?"

"Twenty years ago your dad was shining shoes at the Hilton. Young Crawford was staying there. They met and Crawford remembered your dad, or maybe it was the other way around. He called me and asked if I could find a job for Cordell."

"How did you know the son?"

"I'd known his father when I was stationed in England during the war. In fact, I worked for him during the planning for the Normandy invasion. General Crawford asked me to take his son -- who'd just graduated from the academy -- under my wing to make sure he learned about planning and logistics."

"Why would Crawford take an interest in my dad?"

McCall shrugged. "I suppose because they were in the same outfit, and it was Crawford's first command. He retired a couple of years ago as a one-star general. We've spent a little time together over the years. When he retired, I invited him to join the company, but he said he had plans for staying in government."

"It's obviously paid off for him," Tony said.

"Yes," McCall said. "I sent him a telegram congratulating him on the appointment." McCall paused a moment, then asked, "Well, was your dad awake when you saw him?"

"Yeah, for a few minutes. He seems really upset about shooting that kid. And he's really confused. He mentioned the name 'Bobby' again, saying that he'd promised to take care of him. Then he said something really strange. He said something about all the boys trusting him, and that he'd killed them all."

McCall puzzled over the words for a moment, remembering the police report and what witnesses had been quoted as saying. "Well, after what he's been through, he's bound to be a little confused. I've got one of my people checking into it. I'll let you know if he finds anything."

McCall got to his feet. "Tony, why don't we get out of here and have dinner?"

"Thanks, but I told them I was going back to the hotel, in case they have to call me."

"They'll know where to reach us. They can call us on the car phone or at the restaurant."

Tony smiled, then chuckled as he vigorously rubbed the fatigue from his eyes. "Yeah, I know -- more of your button pressing."

"Like you said, Tony, I may not have buttons very long, so I might as well make the most of it. Humor an old man, okay?"

Tony looked at McCall, then lowered his head and winced. "I'm sorry, Spense. That was a low blow."

McCall smiled. "Apology accepted, but I'm curious about how you heard about it."

"Dad," Tony said. "It's the only time I can remember him telling me about anything he'd heard up there. I'd never seen him so upset. He called your board of directors a board of fools. That's strong talk for dad."

"Too bad I can't get your dad to talk to some of those board members." Then McCall said softly, almost to himself, "But the last word hasn't been said about the matter." Then he looked at Tony. "Let's go have dinner."

"Okay. But, dammit, I've got to buy."

McCall quickly shrugged into his overcoat. "Sorry. You can't. It's a private club. You're money's no good there. C'mon, get your coat."

"Ah, hell, Spense!"

February 25, 1967
The Palmer House
Chicago
11:50 a.m.

"Hello, Frank," McCall said to the maitre'd. "Are you ready for us?"

"Of course, Mr. McCall." Maintaining his practiced smile, the maitre d' motioned discreetly with his left hand for an attendant to take the coats for McCall and Eleanor.

"A Mr. Tony Jackson will be joining us in few minutes, Frank."

The maitre'd penciled the name on a pad. "Yes, sir, Mr. McCall. I'll bring him to your table the moment he arrives."

McCall, as always, was aware of the heads that turned as he and Eleanor were seated at their table. He marveled at how Eleanor appeared to be oblivious to it -- or, rather, she pretended to be oblivious. He suspected that she loved it.

McCall ordered drinks. "Ellie, I'm not sure this is a good idea."

Eleanor lifted her eyebrows in surprise. "Why not? My research shows he talked about running for congress when he was in law school."

"Well, I just don't think I should be here."

"What I'd like to know, McCall, is whether you'll help finance his campaign if he does run?"

"I'll have to think about that. Part of the problem is that he already thinks I'm meddling in his affairs."

Their drinks arrived at that moment. Eleanor smiled mischievously as she touched her glass to McCall's and said with more volume than necessary, "To the hope that oil companies will one day pay their fair share of taxes." She smiled innocently.

McCall, who immediately lowered his glass, couldn't keep his eyes from darting toward the tables to his left and right. He hissed, "Dammit, Ellie, why the hell do you do things like that?"

Eleanor leaned close to McCall and kissed him lightly on the cheek. "I don't want my loyal readers to think I've abandoned the cause just because I'm in love with an oil baron." She sipped her drink, and McCall noted that her large gray-green eyes gazing at him over the rim of her glass were more dazzling than the expensive crystal. When she lowered the drink, she said, "Besides, I've just handed the gossip hacks enough material for a week of columns."

McCall smiled and shook his head slowly. "I'll never understand how such a classy broad can be so nutty at times." He reached for her hand, kissed it, and held it in both of his as he looked into her eyes.

McCall knew that Eleanor was right about the gossip columnists. As a couple, they had for nearly two years provided great copy for writers on major dailies and in national gossip magazines. The columnists were intrigued by the relationship between the flamboyantly liberal publisher and the staunchly conservative oilman, as well as by the power and influence each wielded.

It had been at the fund-raising dinner for the Chicago Youth Clubs, McCall recalled, when he first met Eleanor. They were seated next to each other at the head table. That first meeting had been a complete disaster. At least, McCall felt, it was for him.

McCall remembered that he had been struck by her beauty. She was tall, her red hair was naturally streaked with gray, and she had the kind of figure that flattered expensive and stylish clothes. He also knew that she had earned a national reputation as a tough and highly intelligent journalist -- both print and electronic -- over nearly three decades. Jim Austin, Horizon's public relations manager, had briefed McCall before the dinner, telling him that she'd worked for the Associated Press, the *Detroit Free Press*, and the *Washington Post* before moving to network television. For six years she'd been assigned to ABC's Washington bureau and was on a first-name basis with virtually everyone who counted in Washington.

When Eleanor's husband died, the board of directors of *The Times* thought it natural that she take over as publisher. The decision wasn't based just on her news and business judgment. McCall knew that a key factor was that the board believed Eleanor's politics were even more liberal than her husband's.

Not that the politics of all the board members, or even most of them, were all that liberal. *The Times* had carved a major share of the Chicago market for itself because its liberalism was tough, feisty, and thought-provoking. The paper never hesitated to hurl lightening bolts at city hall, the White House, or even the Vatican.

That's why the paper made money, huge amounts of it, when some major newspapers were struggling. McCall also admired her business judgment. Eleanor Harrison knew how to make money because she recognized good stories, good writers, and good editors. Equally important, she beat the socks off the other Chicago papers with advertising lineage. That's why the paper's directors called Eleanor "The Golden Girl."

On the night of the fund raising dinner, the first course had not yet been served when Eleanor asked her first question.

"Considering the fact that you're a Republican, why did you work for LBJ's campaign in sixty-four?"

Uncertain whether to discuss politics -- especially his politics -- with the publisher of a major liberal daily, McCall tried to avoid a direct answer. "I've known him for a long time, I respect his ability, and I support many of his views."

"I see," Eleanor said, turning her chair slightly to face McCall. "What you're saying is that whatever political convictions you have are based on what benefits you can derive from personal relationships with politicians?"

McCall cleared his throat. "No, Mrs. Harrison. That's not what I'm saying. What I mean is--"

"What you mean is that you were as afraid as the rest of us that Goldwater would go nuclear at the slightest provocation -- real or imagined -- by the Red Hoards. Or perhaps you just recognized what Ike proved: generals -- especially Republican generals -- make lousy presidents?"

"Nonsense," McCall said too loudly. People on either side of the couple couldn't help but hear the exchange. "Goldwater is a reserve Air Force general, and the people of Arizona felt he had served them well in the military and in the Senate. He was -- I mean is -- a very good man."

"Then why didn't you work for him?"

"As I started to say--"

"Yes, as you said, you and LBJ go back a long way, and real buddies -- especially Texas buddies -- don't hesitate to compromise their politics to take care of each other. And I don't suppose that you ever considered that LBJ's home state is where Horizon Corporation produces more than thirty-eight percent of its worldwide oil revenues."

Eleanor smiled. "But, Mr. McCall, I wouldn't presume that oil had anything to do with your decision. As you said, you respect his ability and you support his views." Eleanor turned her chair back to the dinner plate that had just been served.

McCall remembered that he had been angry and frustrated. It had been years since anyone -- especially a woman -- had talked to him that way. He somehow managed to spend the rest of dinner without once looking at Eleanor. What made him furious is that she spent the rest of dinner charming virtually everyone else at their table.

McCall was surprised by her phone call the next morning at his office.

"McCall, the only thing I dislike more than someone afflicted with terminal political views is someone who's a sore loser."

McCall could feel his blood pressure begin to soar. "Look, Mrs. Harrison, I've had enough of--"

"It's Ellie. I'll give you another chance. Meet me at noon today at the Hilton restaurant. I'll even spring for lunch."

McCall hesitated. Yes, he did want to meet this attractive, dynamo of a woman again. In fact, he wanted very much to see her. But...

"It's a deal," he said, finally. "Two conditions: no politics, and no oil-bashing."

"Agreed, although I'm counting on your repartee being more stimulating and articulate than it was last night. By the way, I don't believe in being fashionably late. See you at noon -- sharp."

That's how it started. In recent days, they had clashed -- privately and publicly -- over a rumor that McCall, because of his considerable experience in the Middle East -- was being considered for appointment as the next ambassador to Iran.

It was no secret that Eleanor, and therefore *The Times*, had succumbed to the Kennedy mystique, and that the paper would no doubt support Robert Kennedy in the 1968 election. Commenting on the McCall rumor, a recent *Times* editorial -- although acknowledging that he had in less than two decades skillfully created a major international corporation -- said the White House would make a serious error in naming an oil man to the post because of what it described as LBJ's long history of being "too close" to Texas oil money. Although the President was a Democrat, the editorial contended that -- LBJ's Great Society effort aside -- Texas Democrats were more conservative politically than, for instance, New England Republicans. What the Middle East needed, the editorial said, "...is a U.S. ambassador to Iran who is motivated and experienced to produce solutions for the serious problems afflicting the people of the Middle East, rather than an ambassador with the skills to play world oil politics."

Eleanor Harrison wrote the editorial.

"I don't suppose," Eleanor said coyly, "that you'd be willing to confirm the rumor that your old Texas buddy wants you to be the next ambassador to Iran?"

McCall chuckled. "You muckrakers never give up, do you? For the record, I will neither confirm nor deny such a rumor."

"Hmmm. That's strange. Those are precisely the words the White House used. I *suppose* it could be a coincidence."

Eleanor's smile faded. The game was over. "McCall, I hope you're not seriously considering the job -- and, by the way, I know for a fact it's been offered. You also should know that the way we got the tip makes we think it was deliberately leaked by the White House."

McCall suspected that Eleanor was right. LBJ would have done it for two reasons: he wanted to gauge the reaction of the media, and he wanted to enhance McCall's credentials for the special mission to Jordan.

McCall and Eleanor had learned that their personal relationship could survive only if each respected the other's professional rights and obligations. For them, there always would be information one couldn't share with the other. However, McCall felt he had to discuss Johnson's request with someone.

"Ellie, Johnson wants me to take on a special assignment, a kind of ambassador or special envoy without portfolio, is how I guess they describe it."

"Whatever it is, I recommend that you refuse."

"How the hell can you say that when you don't know what it is?"

"Whatever it is, it can't be good. Does he want you to go to Vietnam for some reason?"

"No, he--"

"Well, you're just about the only one he knows who he hasn't sent over there on some kind of fact-finding mission."

"It's the Middle East. Jordan. He knows I know Hussein, and he wants to see what it'll take to prevent the fighting that he believes is about to break out -- by the way, you understand that all of this is off the record."

"Dammit, McCall, you'll never learn," she said, her cheeks flushing. "Those are the kinds of agreements you reach with a reporter *before* you run off at the mouth." She sighed heavily. "Okay. *This* time. Now, what does he expect you to accomplish."

"I haven't agreed to go, so I haven't been briefed by the CIA. But I gather he wants me to convince Hussein to stay out of the fighting, if it breaks out."

"Do you really think you're going to accomplish that just by asking Hussein?" Eleanor asked. "Spense, the people and the issues are incredibly complex. The Romans, the Crusaders, and the Turks -- and never mind the British and French -- all have tried and failed to bring order to that part of the world. The Arabs themselves can't agree on how or whether to make war or peace -- either with Israel or among themselves."

"Christ, Ellie, don't lecture me. It's not like I don't know the area. Just give me a little of the political situation so I don't seem a complete idiot if I decide to talk to the CIA."

"Okay. Hussein is between two hard places. We and the Brits consider him to be strongly anticommunist, which is why he's receiving so much aid from the U.S. and England. Egypt's Nasser is the one who's rattling sabers, he's the one with troops in the Sinai, and he's the one who will drag Jordan into any fighting that develops. Nasser's objective is leadership of the Arab world. The problem is that the Arab world doesn't recognize his leadership, at least not yet."

McCall admired Eleanor's grasp of politics, especially power politics. In fact, in his private moments, he admitted that it was possible that he could be intimidated by what he described as her aggressive intellect.

"So, what could I offer him as an incentive to stay out of the war, assuming I take the assignment?"

"Only your Texas buddy can tell you that. Ask him what he thinks he can promise Hussein that won't alienate the other Arab nations, the Israelis, those Americans who support the Israelis, or that won't alienate Hussein from his own people. I would be very interested in hearing how your buddy answers those questions."

The conversation ended when Tony Jackson joined them. McCall stood to shake Tony's hand.

"Hello, Spense," Tony said, "I can only stay a few minutes. I've got to get back to South Bend early this afternoon."

McCall nodded understanding. "Ellie asked to meet you. She's very interested in your career."

"Very nice to meet you, Mrs. Harrison."

"Yes, I know you, Tony," Eleanor said. She noted that he was tall, well-dressed, and looked to be in his early forties. Yes, she thought, this could be the man for the job. "I'm sorry about your father. I understand he's doing much better."

"Thank you. Yes, he was sitting up today and fussing about things, so I know he's better." Tony hesitated, quizzically looking at Eleanor. "But I don't think we've ever met."

"Please call me Ellie. We haven't, but I would have recognized you because you look very much as your dad must have looked at your age. I've also been watching your career with interest. I saw where you were honored by the Justice Department -- by J. Edgar himself -- for your interstate racketeering convictions."

"Well, thank you. But those convictions represented a lot of solid work by the FBI."

"I should warn you that I've asked our staff to contact you. We'd like to do a Sunday magazine piece. I'm especially interested in your plans for the future."

Tony laughed uncomfortably. "I'll have to check with the department about the interview, but I can tell you now that my only interest is my future with the Justice Department."

"How about congress?"

McCall chuckled when he saw the surprise register on Tony's face. "I think you're discovering, Tony, that Ellie has never been accused of being vague."

Tony looked hard at McCall, then his expression softened. "Is this something you cooked up, Spense?"

McCall smiled. "I think it's a good idea -- as long as you run as a Republican. But relax; this is strictly Ellie's idea."

Tony shook his head. "I'm sorry, Mrs. Harrison, but I won't discuss politics with your reporter. I am interested in running for congress some day. But at the moment, I'm only interested in continuing my present work."

"Well," Eleanor said lightly, "you and I should have this discussion again. I'm certain you have an opportunity to establish yourself as a viable Democratic candidate next year, and you probably could win in seventy."

"What makes you so confident that I'm a Democrat -- and a liberal one at that?"

"Because, before your appointment to Justice, you were active in state politics. In law school you were vice president of the Young Democrats Association, where you were quoted as saying that you could do a lot more for black people as a congressman. You were also a volunteer for the Southern Leadership Conference and..." Eleanor smiled. "Shall I continue?"

"Damn," Tony said smiling. "I wish I had someone with your skills on my staff, but I am serious: I do not intend to become involved in politics in my present assignment."

Eleanor leaned back in her chair, tilting her head as she locked eyes with Tony. "Okay. I believe you, Tony -- at least I believe that you want to stay with Justice for the time being. Besides, I couldn't find any evidence that you used your association with any black leaders, either to help you get your present job or to start building your campaign for congress."

Tony, nodding slowly, said, "Ellie, you should be aware that Spenser used his White House connections to get me my job. It's been a sore point for us – at least for me -- for a long time. Recently, however, I've acquired a better understanding of what his motives were"

Eleanor reached across to put her hand on McCall's. "Why Spenser McCall, there's hope yet for some of you radical conservatives."

"That's a matter of opinion, Mr. Harrison," Tony said smiling as he folded his napkin. "When the time is right for me to seriously consider running for congress, I would prefer to do that on my own." Tony got to his feet. "I'm sorry, Ellie and Spense, but I've got to catch a plane."

March 1, 1967
The Horizon Building
Chicago
8:35 a.m.

"How did you get this document?" McCall asked.

"The chief of psychiatry at Hines Veterans Hospital," Jim Austin said. "He received a phone call from the Pentagon urging him to cooperate with us."

McCall looked at Austin, seated in front of his desk. Then he looked down at the bound document in his hands, thumbing through the yellowed, typewritten pages. "Isn't it...well, irregular for them to have released this document to you?"

"I'm not sure, Mr. McCall." Austin pointed to the document McCall was holding. "We can make copies, but I promised to return the original as soon as you've read it."

"Have you read it?"

"No, sir. I just returned from the hospital and came directly to your office."

"Well, I'll read it immediately. Then I'd like you to read it so we can discuss it before you make a copy and return it. Thank you, Jim."

As Austin rose to leave, McCall opened the document. It was a transcript made in December, 1946. McCall noted that it was a compilation of notes made by an army psychiatrist following a long series of interviews with Cordell Jackson.

In the document's preface, the examining psychiatrist explained that he compiled the report, in Cordell's own words, as part of the treatment of "latent anxieties related to combat experience." The doctor carefully recorded Cordell's narrative as part of a study to determine if "Negro soldiers were more susceptible than Caucasians to combat-induced psychoneuroses," according to the introduction. There was no indication whether the study had been completed or how, or if, it had been used in Cordell's treatment.

The examiner was a Dr. Edward Moyer, who served the hospital on a consulting basis. He was assigned the case, according to the document, when a staff physician treating Cordell's wounds surmised that Cordell was for some reason suffering from feelings of guilt that apparently were related to his combat experience.

It appeared to McCall that the narrative was recorded with court-reporter efficiency. At times, Cordell responded to specific questions posed by Dr. Moyer; at other times Cordell's comments were recorded as free-flowing narrative.

Dr. Moyer: *Mr. Jackson, the records show that you were wounded on December eighteenth, nineteen forty four. Is that correct?*

Patient: No response.

Dr. Moyer: *Okay, Cordell, let's start with what we know. On December sixteenth, two days before you were wounded, the Germans broke through our lines in the Ardennes Forest in southern Belgium. Your unit, the 106th Infantry Division, was in Reims, France. You were a cook in George Company. When the breakthrough occurred, you all were trucked into Belgium and went into combat near the town of Hotton. Now, Cordell, I want you to tell me everything you can remember from that point until you were wounded.*

Patient: Extended hesitation before response. The following narrative is a compilation of four sessions.

I remember that it was so cold in the trucks. It was night. The roads were real slick because of all the snow. Everybody was scared and confused. A lot of us were cooks and clerks and they gave us guns because they said they needed everybody. They taught me how to shoot a gun when I joined the army, but I was no fighting man. I was just a cook.

When we got to this small town -- you say it was Hotton, but I don't know that I ever knew the name -- a young second lieutenant took fifteen of us. I was the only colored man. We went about a half-mile down the road and set up two machine guns and a bazooka. He told us that no matter who or what came down that road, we had to stop them or die trying. We had to stay until relieved.

That kind of talk really scared me. It scared all of us. We cut down some trees and pulled them onto the road so we could hide behind them and maybe stop the tanks.

It seemed like we waited in that snow and cold for a long time. We could hear sounds of fighting, and we could hear tank engines, but couldn't see anything. My job was to carry ammo for the bazooka, and I was supposed to help load it. I was scared I wouldn't do it right, and I was scared that my hands and feet were going to freeze -- sweet Jesus, I was scared of everything.

(Patient pulls his arms around himself, as if he once more is experiencing the cold and fear.)

Then we heard the sound of tanks and everybody got real jumpy. Me and the bazooka man -- I don't remember his name -- were laying behind a tree a few feet off the road, off to the right. He was a four-striper and older than us. He had a lot of anger in him because he had to have a colored cook for a loader. "All they give me are goddamn cooks and clerks and nigger for a loader," he said. "You screw up," he says to me, "and I'll kick your ass all up and down this road." But I knew he was just scared like the rest of us.

Then the first tank came around a little bend and stopped. We could see lots of German troops walking behind it. The tank fired its big gun twice, real quick, and it seemed like about half of us were hit by those two shells.

One of our machine guns was wrecked, but the other one started up. Then the bazooka man fired, but the rocket bounced off the road in front of the tank and went flying off into the trees. Then the tank started moving toward us again and I looked over at our boys who were left and it seemed like they were getting ready to run. Lord knows I surely was.

The Germans were shooting everything at us and I could hear some of our boys screaming. Then the sergeant slumped over. He was laying face down in the snow and I could see the big hole in the back of his helmet. Brains and blood was all over me and the bazooka.

(Patient is perspiring heavily and respiration is elevated.)

I picked up the tube, loaded it, and fired at the front tank. I guess I was lucky. But at first I didn't think it was hit because it kept coming. Then it jerked to a stop and when they opened the hatch and started to get out I could see black smoke and fire coming from inside. One of the German boys had his clothes on fire. Our boys on the machine gun killed them all. Then the second tank and the German troops backed up around the bend. Our boys started to cheer, saying that we'd whupped them. But I had the feeling them German boys wouldn't give up so easy, that they'd be back.

There were seven or eight of us left. The others were either dead or hurt bad. We couldn't do nothing much for them because our medic was dead.

(Patient's eyes are welling with tears; he is struggling for control.)

Oh, my...some of those boys were hurt so bad, and they were afraid they would die, alone on that road in the cold and snow. I crawled around among them to do what I could...the snow was turning red with their blood. I couldn't do much, except to hold each man's hand for a second or two and to tell them that the Lord was watching over us all and that He would help us.

Dr. Moyer: Cordell, what happened to the lieutenant?

Patient: *I don't know. I saw him over by the other machine gun before it was hit. He was yelling at everybody to keep shooting, and he was throwing grenades like a crazy man. One of the tank shells hit right where he was and some of those boys just got blown away -- nothing left but bits and pieces. I suppose the lieutenant was one of them that got blown to bits.*

I was afraid the Germans would come around through the woods and get us from the side, so I asked three men to take the other machine gun into the woods a little ways on the other side of the road. That way they could shoot into the woods and still help cover the road.

Dr. Moyer: Cordell, are you saying that you took command of the unit?

(Long pause while patient considers question.)

No, I wouldn't say that I took command. I guess I was just doing what had to be done.

(Patient refuses to continue beyond this point. It took three sessions for him to overcome his reluctance.)

I stayed on the road with Bobby...oh, Lord, I've forgotten his last name...but he told me he was seventeen and lived in Waycross, Georgia, not too far from my home. He kept calling me 'Corporal Jackson,' like I was somebody. In all the time I was in the Army I never had a white boy talk to me the way he did. There was just me and Bobby hiding behind those logs. He was my loader. He kept asking me if we were going to make it, and he kept looking behind us to see of our boys were coming up the road to help us. I told Bobby I'd take care of him.

But nobody came up that road to help us. We were alone.

Pretty soon we heard the tanks again. They came around the bend and they were shooting everything at us and we're hiding behind the logs and bullets are eating up them logs and I could hear our gun in the woods and Bobby and me were shooting and screaming...Lord...it seemed like the whole world was shooting at us.

When the tank moved around the one we'd already hit, it fired its big gun and blew up most of our logs. Me and Bobby were both hit by shrapnel. But we shot that tank...Bobby and me...we killed it. When the tank started to burn, the German boys hiding behind it came running out to charge us. Me and Bobby fired our rifles and our boys on the machine gun were helping.

(Long pause. Patient is staring at the floor, appears to be shaking his head in wonder.)

Hard to believe, but some of them German boys got to within a couple feet of the logs before they fell. Bobby stayed cool when we started shooting; he was real cool. He was good with that rifle, a lot better than me. He shot most of them that came at us.

When the shooting stopped and we looked out over all those dead boys, Bobby started shaking real hard again...and he kept looking down that road behind us.

Lord, lord...there were so many dead boys lying on that awful road. Bobby was bleeding from the mouth and chest, but he said he wasn't hit bad. He just said he was awful cold. I pulled him close to me, behind what was left of the logs so we could warm each other. His body was trembling.

I could tell he was thinking of something. Then he said, "Maybe, Corporal Jackson, maybe we ought to pull back and get help." I told him, "Bobby, that's what I want to do more than anything. But the lieutenant said we got to stay here until we get relief."

Bobby laughed, nervous-like, and he said he'd heard the order too. "I was just wondering, Corporal Jackson, since you're in charge now, whether you wanted to change the orders."

(Patient is bathed in perspiration and sobbing softly.)

I know that when I was holding him...to keep him warm...when he was trembling so bad his teeth were clicking... the Lord must've told Bobby that he was going to die on that road. Bobby could have gotten up and walked back to town and I wouldn't have done anything about it. But he stayed...he stayed because he trusted me...he stayed because it was what we both had to do.

Dr. Moyer: Cordell, you obviously couldn't stop those tanks and troops with so few men. Why didn't you retreat?

Patient: *Because we didn't have that choice. We were told to stay.*

Dr. Moyer: You mean because the lieutenant ordered you to stay?

Yes. It must have been important. Why else would he have ordered us to stay, to die if we had to?

Dr. Moyer: Okay, Cordell. Then what happened?

Patient: *We'd been on that road most of the day and I knew it would get dark soon. That worried me, because I didn't know how we could hold that road in the dark. Then I could hear a tank engine again. Pretty soon I could see one come around the bend. It began pushing against the second wrecked one and finally pushed it sideways into the ditch. There were more soldiers behind the tank. Then the tank began firing its big gun at us and the boys in the woods. The third shell hit the logs in front of me and Bobby.*

I guess I flew a dozen feet or more and was knocked silly for a while. When I came to I saw part of my leg was gone and I had blood all over me. I looked for my leg but I couldn't see it. I crawled back to the logs, but Bobby was gone. I looked, but I couldn't see him no where. I don't know why I wanted to find my leg, but I knew Bobby needed me to find him. I'd promised him...I promised that I'd take care of him.

Then I found him in the ditch. One of his legs was blown off, high up, so I tied a belt around the stump to stop the blood. The other leg was sideways and I could see the bone sticking through his pants. I couldn't see his face for all the blood.

Dr. Moyer: Are you certain it was Bobby?

Patient: *Yes. It was Bobby. He couldn't talk. It sounded like he was choking because his neck was laid open. But his eyes -- they were blue and clear like a young boy's eyes are -- and they were looking at me while I was trying to take care of him. I still see those eyes.*

Dr. Moyer: What did you do next, Cordell?

Patient: *One of our wounded started yelling that the Germans were coming again. Lord knows I didn't want to leave Bobby, but I had to get back up on the road. My bazooka was gone, so I crawled into the woods to get the machine gun. The boys there were all dead. It looked like most of them were killed by the trees the tank gun tore up.*

The tripod for the gun was wrecked, so I pulled the gun off of it and dragged it back to the road. The Germans were just walking to us, like they figured we were all dead. My leg was really burning and paining me, so I packed snow around the stump to cool it.

I cradled the gun with my left arm and started to fire when they were maybe thirty yards away. I just kept shooting and shooting and the German boys were screaming and trying to run away. I remember my coat sleeve started to smoke where it was touching the barrel and then the belt ran out and I didn't have any more ammo. My rifle was somewhere back in the woods, so I guess I just rolled over on my back. I was spent. I just didn't care anymore.

Then I could hear the tank engine get louder and I looked sideways and could see that it was coming. It just kept coming, rolling over some of their own dead boys. I closed my eyes because I knew it was going to roll over me too.

Then it stopped just a few feet away. I heard the hatch open and I saw this German officer get out. He was an SS man. He walked up and stood right over me, his feet either side of me. He had blond hair and I could see all the anger in him. I couldn't hear all of his words because of the roaring in my ears, but I could tell he was angry. I knew he was cursing me. Then he pulled his Luger pistol out of his holster. He looked down at me, then a mean smile came on his face when he pulled back the bolt on the pistol to load it. I didn't have any trouble hearing that bolt snapping closed. It was a sound that seemed to ring through the woods like death itself. Then he pointed the barrel of that Luger at my head. I still can see the muzzle flash.

(Note: Patient has no recollection of events beyond the point where he suffered the gunshot wound to the head, until his recovery in a London hospital.)

McCall placed his hands lightly over the closed document, as if to test whether he could feel the pain and misery it contained. After a long moment, he reached for the intercom. "Kathy, call Jim Austin, please, and tell him I'd like to see him. Then call Tony Jackson in South Bend." McCall checked the time. "You can probably reach him in the federal building. Tell him I'd like him to come here as soon as possible. Tell him it's important. Tell them both it's important."

CHAPTER 5

March 7, 1967
Horizon Corporation
Management Committee Conference Room
4:10 p.m.

Spenser drew boxes on his note pad. They were elaborate, three-dimensional boxes of various sizes drawn around the names of Cordell Jackson and Oliver Crawford. He hadn't slept well the night before, his mind consumed by passages from the psychiatrist's report. He had felt the despair and fear of Cordell and the other men abandoned on that road.

McCall struggled to concentrate on the young chemical engineer making the presentation -- the final speaker in the four-hour meeting. The room was semi-dark for the twin-projector slide show of the various new polystyrene products proposed by the foam products subsidiary. Hopefully, McCall thought, the other twelve members of the corporate management committee around the table also thought the boss was taking notes.

Even though the lectern was in the far corner of the room, to the right of the screen, McCall could tell the young engineer was nervous, as were most presenters when the chairman was in the room. The reading light on the lectern reflected up from the young engineer's prepared remarks onto his face. McCall could see the beads of perspiration on the speaker's upper lip and forehead. McCall knew the young man desperately wanted to wipe away the sweat, but to do so would openly acknowledge his nervousness to everyone in the room. So the young engineer would read on. And he would continue to sweat.

The room was too warm, which didn't help the young engineer. How cold it must have been for Cordell on that winter road in Belgium. When does nervousness become fear? McCall wondered. The young engineer standing at the lectern probably knows some fear at this moment. He knows his career may be at stake. But his life isn't threatened -- at least he's not looking down a gun barrel. McCall darkened the box around Cordell's name. *Why wasn't he awarded some medal?* McCall wondered. *How could his contribution have been ignored, forgotten? Did his being a Negro have anything to do with it? Probably. What happened to the lieutenant? Was he killed?*

McCall, with a conscious effort, brought his attention back to the conference room. He remembered his nervousness when, as a young engineer in the exploration and production subsidiary, he had to make presentations to senior management. That's why he didn't have much sympathy for the young man. It was part of the job. He either would learn to overcome his fear or his career would suffer. Those were the unwritten rules everybody understood.

When the speaker concluded his remarks, he called for questions, what many young employees regarded as the most stressful part of a presentation. The good presenters knew their audience; they knew the idiosyncrasies of key committee members.

McCall knew, for instance, that the vice chairman, Larry Thompkins, sitting to his left, preferred presenters who paused a few beats before answering a question, even if the presenter was able to answer immediately. The pause, Thompkins believed, showed that the speaker was thoughtful and precise in structuring his response. It didn't make sense to McCall, but a presenter who ignored it got low marks from the vice chairman.

Thompkins also had a habit of asking questions peripherally related to the subject. Thompkins said he knew the presenters almost always did their homework, had gone through several rehearsals with their immediate management, and had been briefed on how to handle the tougher questions. Off-the-wall questions, Thompkins believed, were a good test of the depth of a presenter's knowledge and character. McCall felt Thompkins was unnecessarily adding to the pressure on the younger people, that he was playing games.

In some ways, McCall conceded, it was a game, one that tested intelligence and spirit and courage. In some ways -- except for the highly polished mahogany and the leather and the blue pin-striped corporate three-piece "uniforms" -- the process could be as brutal and unforgiving as an alley fight.

Finally, the questions were exhausted. The young engineer, obviously relieved, gathered his papers with shaky hands and left the room. McCall knew that the moment the young man left the conference room and was out of sight of the executive secretary just outside the door, he would reach for his handkerchief and wipe his face. Then he would find the nearest washroom and check his appearance in the mirror. He didn't want to look disheveled when he got back to his work area. When his colleagues would ask, "How'd it go?" the young man would say, "Piece of cake."

Yes, the players changed, but the game would always be the same.

"Well, gentlemen," McCall said as he looked around the wishbone-shaped table, "unless there is further business, we'll do this again in two weeks."

There was no response as the others rolled back their padded leather chairs from the table and left the room. In a few moments, McCall was alone in the room. At first, that confused him. What the hell's going on? he asked himself, as he looked around the empty conference room. Then he realized what was different. Always, at previous committee meetings, various members or speakers would be waiting to talk to him, seeking a few moments of the chairman's time.

The committee members not only left without saying anything, it appeared to McCall they'd left hurriedly. McCall looked down at the boxes he'd drawn around the names. He closed the suede-bound notebook and stepped into the corridor between the conference room and his office. To his left, he noticed a half-dozen committee members standing in a circle around Larry Thompkins, whose office was adjacent to McCall's. Thompkins was saying something that McCall couldn't hear. McCall noticed that several of the men who looked his way quickly averted their eyes.

McCall hesitated a moment, then walked into his office. He pulled back the drapes of one of the windows and looked out over the city. There was no horizon. The gray, overcast skies seemed to melt into the slate-gray water of Lake Michigan.

Some weeks earlier he had recognized that his subsidiary presidents and corporate executive vice presidents seemed to avoid coming to him for some important decisions, especially those involving major long-term projects. Although he had to admit that it bothered him -- bothered him a lot -- he recognized that Larry Thompkins probably was just exercising another of his periodic rounds of corporate intrigue.

McCall certainly didn't attribute any of it to his current problems with the board of directors. He had to admit, though, that his prestige would suffer considerable damage if the board scuttled the New Mexico project, a project Thompkins opposed.

But dammit, he thought, the least they could do is wait until the board decides whether to approve the New Mexico project.

McCall felt it first in the pit of his stomach. Then it spread through his body with such force that it momentarily blurred his vision. *What if*...McCall said aloud...*what if they made the decision? What if they even decided they want me out? What if everyone knows? Except me.*

That the board would turn him down was a possibility he'd never seriously considered. All he needed was a minimum of two years to prove the project. That the board would want him out was a possibility he'd never considered.

McCall was committed to the corporate organization. For him it was everything. Without it, there would be chaos. Despite its faults and weaknesses, he believed that the corporate structure was more efficient and effective than government or military structures. Corporations did a better job of ensuring that its brightest and strongest rise to the top, something McCall believed long before his rise to the top. Although corporate politics was a force to be reckoned with -- he had seen the occasional consummate corporate politician move into a key position, people like Thompkins -- McCall believed that the corporate politicians by their nature lacked the courage to make the tough decisions, to take risks. In the end, the arbitrator between success and failure always was the Bottom Line. He believed that the board would soon see that Thompkins lacked the qualities essential for a CEO.

McCall remembered the men standing in the corridor around Thompkins, his future replacement. For the first time in his more than twenty years as chairman, McCall wondered whether his power and influence were indeed slipping away. It was a strange, alien feeling. He always knew it wouldn't last forever. Yet, he'd never honestly visualized the day it would end. McCall could feel his jaw muscles working. He could feel the anger now.

Hell, I've earned the right to be chairman of this company. I'm personally responsible for the plans and policies that helped make it the world's eighth largest oil company, and I can't remember how many times I've hung my ass on the line to get that done. Christ, they can't just throw me out because the damned calendar has turned a certain number of pages.

McCall suddenly realized that his hands, clenched into fists, were damp. He felt the light sheen of sweat on his forehead. Then he smiled ruefully as he thought of the perspiring young engineer. *Yes, the game's the same. Only the players change.*

He moved to his desk. *Well, the last damn thing I can afford is to feel sorry for myself.* He gazed for a long moment at Lake Michigan.

But I wonder how the hell I can avoid doing that?

The private phone attached to the side of his L-shaped desk buzzed three times before he decided to reach for it.

"Yes," McCall answered.

"Hello, Spenser. Catch you at a bad time?" It was Eleanor.

"Hell, no. Not at all. I just spent forty-five minutes listening to a presentation about some new work we're doing in polystyrene -- plastic foam. They're going to make cups and other food containers out of it. It was show-and-tell time, cleverly designed to keep the old man from meddling."

"Now, Spense." Her voice was soft with understanding. "I don't like what I'm hearing."

McCall sighed. "Okay, but I don't think I'm going to make it through another...let me see, forty-eight months. Maybe I ought to leave sooner." McCall was surprised to hear the words he'd just said. Not once had he ever considered *quitting.*

"Nonsense, Spenser McCall. You keep your buns in that chair. We'll use the months ahead to decide what you're going to do after that."

"I'm pretty sure I've got a job offer. The White House called again."

Eleanor hesitated a long moment.

"Ellie?"

"I'm here. That's wonderful, *dearest*. Yes, I think you'd fit in very well with Lyndon Johnson's ring of eunuchs. Most of them hung their balls on the wall when they took those jobs. So pick your favorite wall, my friend, because I'll be the one to decorate it with your privates if you take that job."

"Eunuchs?"

"The decision is yours, of course. And it sounds like you're going to do it. That means this relationship has thirteen months to go, and I want to make the most of it. So, I have a suggestion."

McCall smiled. "I can hardly wait to hear your *suggestion*."

"I'd like us to dress very casually tonight. Then you can take me to the greasiest pizza joint we can find. After we pig-out on beer and pizza, I want to take a long walk down Michigan Avenue. Maybe we'll find a movie."

"Which one?"

"I don't give a damn which one. What difference does it make? Just some place where we can be alone and hold hands. Then I want to spend the night at your place. I'm in the mood for debauchery, and I want to debauch with you."

"I can't, Ellie."

"*Excuse* me? You *can't?*" Her voice was shrill with feigned indignation.

"I mean about the apartment, dammit. Tony might be staying there tonight. I'm expecting him to come in from South Bend, and he needs a place to stay. I asked him the other night, but he refused. I think he'll stay tonight."

"Well, my friend, that's your loss. You know what you guys say about women -- we get crazy when we can't get enough of it. So maybe I'll take a copy boy home with me."

McCall laughed, and he realized how badly he needed to laugh. "Ellie, I've seen those pimply-faced kids. Besides, there are only a couple of them left since you people started to put in those computers." McCall suddenly realized how much he needed to be with Eleanor. "But I'll tell you what we can do."

"This should be interesting."

"Be ready by..." McCall looked at his watch "... by, say, six-thirty. We'll take the company plane to New York, which has the kind of degenerate food and life style that turn you on. We'll spend the night in the company apartment. We'll have maybe twenty-four hours alone. And don't worry, the stockholders won't be paying for it. It'll all be charged to my personal account."

"Why Spenser McCall." Her voice was almost lyrical. "What a *wonderful* idea. Yes, I want to be with you. But I insist on paying for the plane."

"Ellie, it'll cost several thousand dollars."

"That's wonderfully extravagant," she said. "I can hardly wait to tell my friends -- who'll tell the gossip columnists -- that I hired a jet to take a man to New York to seduce him. Wonderful. It's beautiful! You have no idea what stories like that can do for a woman's ego, especially for a woman my age. I'll be looking for you at six-thirty. Precisely. Bye."

McCall leaned back in his chair, smiling. He'd never known a woman like Eleanor. She was bright and street-tough, aggressive as hell, and she had a mouth like a dockworker. Yet, she could be incredibly vulnerable. McCall knew that Eleanor, despite her mock sarcasm, was indeed angry when she had hung up the phone. She didn't want him to continue as chairman of Horizon and she especially didn't want him to work for LBJ. She wasn't explicit about what she did want, other than the hint that she might be ready to give up the paper if he gave up the company. They'd never openly discussed marriage because, McCall suspected, neither of them could overcome their pride to admit how much each needed the other. He was certain she loved him, and he knew he loved her, and he knew she wouldn't marry him unless he retired. But there was important work to be done before he could think of leaving Horizon.

McCall pressed the intercom to his secretary. "Kathy, please call the hangar and tell them there'll be two of us going to New York. I'd like to leave in about two hours, and we won't be having dinner on the plane. I can be reached in the New York apartment tonight, but only if it's absolutely necessary."

"Yes, Mr. McCall," his secretary said. "Mr. Austin and Mr. Jackson have just walked into the outer office."

"Good. Send them in."

McCall glanced at the issue of The Chicago *Times* on his desk. The page-one story he had read earlier reported the deaths of the federal agent and the undercover investigator. He looked again at the quote by a spokesperson for the Northern Indiana Crime Commission who blamed the deaths on poor planning by federal agents and the U.S. attorney's office. Tony was named specifically. *Israel Arnold not only killed our investigator and an FBI agent,* the spokesman said, *he also escaped using a sixteen-year-old girl as a hostage.*

"Spense, I'm sorry it took me so long to get here," Tony said as he and Austin entered the office. He gestured toward the newspaper. "But I see you know why I had trouble getting away."

McCall nodded. "Any word about the hostage?"

"Nothing," Tony said, shaking his head in disgust. "They've disappeared." Tony's tie was pulled down and his shirt collar was rumpled. His eyes were rimmed with fatigue.

"Well, this won't take long, Tony. Have you had a chance to read it?"

Tony reached into his brief case, retrieved the copy of the psychologist's interview with his dad, and placed it on the corner of McCall's desk. "Yeah, I read it while Jim was driving me in from the airport." Tony grimaced, shaking his head slowly. "Not once did he ever talk about any of what's in there. Oh, I asked him, lots of times...when I was a kid, but he always said that it had all happened a long time ago and wasn't worth talking about. Can you imagine that?"

"Tony," McCall said tentatively, uncertain that now was the time to discuss what he had in mind, "there may be something very important in that document, something we should look into."

"I know what you're going to say, Spense." Tony gestured toward the document. "It's clear to me that the shooting the other night brought it all back. For him, that Chicago street corner became a road in Belgium."

"I think it tells us a lot more than that," McCall said. "For instance, I wonder what happened to the second lieutenant who led Cordell's unit?"

Tony, puzzled, looked at McCall. "Why? What the hell difference does he make?"

"He had responsibility for the squad."

"So? He was probably killed."

"Maybe," McCall said. "But I think we should find out."

Tony leaned back in his chair and rubbed his eyes. "How are we going to do that?" There was irritation in Tony's voice. "How the hell can we go back nearly twenty five years? I haven't got time for that. Besides, what difference would it make?"

"Don't you see, Tony?" McCall moved from behind his desk and began to pace. "Think of what your father is quoted as saying. They were fighting at that roadblock from early morning until almost dark...

against what sounds like an elite SS Panzer unit." McCall paused and looked at Tony. "Don't you see? He and the others blocked that road for maybe ten or twelve hours. That had to give our people behind them the time to prepare defenses."

Tony didn't respond. Austin sat quietly, watching both men.

"Tony," McCall said, "I heard your father say several times that he wasn't a *real* soldier, a fighter. He said he was just a cook, but he took command -- despite his fear and despite how he'd been treated because he was a Negro -- and he held that damned road. We've got to find out why the Army never recognized what he did."

Tony placed his hands on McCall's desk, spreading his fingers wide. "You want to get my father some kind of medal. Well, I can tell you right now, without having to go through any investigation, that he wasn't recognized because he didn't count to the Army." Tony suddenly slapped the desk with his open hand. "To the Army," Tony's voice was a rasp, "Cordell Jackson was just a dumb nigger cook. He was left to die on that damned road."

"Yes, that's very possible," McCall said, his voice even and low. "But it's possible that *all* of those men were left to die because that road had to be held."

Tony started to say something just as McCall's intercom buzzed.

"Yes, Kathy?" McCall answered.

"Mr. Austin has a phone call. It's a Warrant Officer Parker from Washington. He says it's important enough to interrupt your meeting."

Austin rose quickly from his chair. "I'm sorry, Mr. McCall, but I've been expecting this call. I'll take it in the outer office."

McCall waved his hand to dismiss Austin. The room was quiet for a long moment. Tony lit a cigarette. He drew deeply, releasing the smoke slowly. "Spense," he said, "all these years and I've never known what my dad went through. I've always been so wrapped up in myself that I never took the time to consider how much he really was hurting."

Tony leaned forward, his head bent. Then his hands went to his face. "Oh, man..." his voice was muffled. McCall could hear the soft sobs, the emotional pain. McCall had realized that Tony's anger often was a buffer for his emotions.

"It's just that he...that poor old black man has been jacked around all his life. To me, he's always been an old man -- hell, I was born when he was thirty six."

Tony reached for his handkerchief and wiped his eyes. "Ever since I was a kid I remember the sick feeling in my gut when I'd see him hobbling around. He can't sit or straighten up without pain." Tony leaned his head against the high-back chair, looking up at the ceiling, struggling to control his emotions.

"You know, Spense, when I was a little kid I asked him to show me the stump." Tony raised his head to look at McCall. "Can you believe that? He never took his artificial leg off in front of me. Not once."

Tony leaned back and again looked at the ceiling, blinking away the tears. "He wouldn't show it to me. I could tell I'd hurt his feelings." Tony shook his head, as if to fling away the memory. "Damn...how I wish I'd never asked such a dumb-ass thing."

Austin returned to the room.

McCall looked at him quizzically.

"My contact in Washington is ready for us."

McCall nodded, then picked up the report. "Tony, don't be upset with either yourself or your dad because he hasn't told you what's in this document. It appears that he buried it all so deeply that he probably couldn't tell you much about it even if he wanted to."

"Mr. Jackson." Both men turned to Jim Austin. "My guess is that your father would never have talked about it, at least not to you or other people who are important to him. He was afraid you wouldn't understand or, worse, that you would misunderstand."

"What do you mean, *misunderstand*?" Tony asked.

"He didn't want you to think he was a hero," Austin said. "More importantly, he didn't want you to think he was a killer."

"A killer?" Tony said. "Hell, man, he was fighting to save his ass."

"*Now* you understand that," Austin said softly. "But would you have understood it when you were a lot younger, when you were a boy? Nearly all men," Austin said, "take pride in being called a hero if they save lives. Most men, at least most thinking men, are uncomfortable when they're honored for taking lives."

Austin paused for a moment. "Remember how Cordell answered Doctor Moyer's question about whether he had taken command of the squad?" Austin asked. "Your father said, *No, I guess I was just doing what had to be done.* To me, the implication of what he said is a lot more complicated than the words suggest. It probably means..."

Austin suddenly glanced at McCall. “I’m sorry, Mr. McCall, I didn’t mean to run on like that.”

McCall realized that he’d never had much in the way of conversation with Austin, certainly nothing beyond business. “No,” McCall said, “please continue.”

Austin looked at Tony. “Well, he certainly wanted to save his own life. But he also wanted to save Bobby – after all, he’d made a commitment to save him -- and the other Americans. The easy thing would have been for them to just get up and run.”

Tony asked softly, “Then why didn’t he run? My father’s a good man, but I guess I’ve never thought of him as especially brave.”

Austin hesitated as he rubbed his forehead with the tips of his fingers. “There’s been some work that has tried to define what happens to a man in combat that makes him a hero. I don’t think your dad could have held that road if he hadn’t focused more on the safety of Bobby and the others, rather than on his own safety. It’s what the psychiatrists call denial or reaction formation. They say it’s the way we drive fear from our conscious minds.”

“Jim, maybe that’s how the shrinks explain how a white man becomes a hero,” Tony said, “but it’s got to be a lot more involved than that for a black man.”

Austin nodded. “Probably. Perhaps because of his race, your dad may have decided that he would rather die on that road than risk coming home and being thought of as a coward. But there are some pretty fundamental reasons why men become heroes -- whatever their race. I can tell you that your dad wasn’t fighting on that road for his country. In combat, your world narrows down to the men around you. They become your family -- hell, they’re more important than family.”

“I’d hate to think that my dad stayed on that road just because some southern boy treated him decently -- like he was a white man.”

Austin shrugged. “I don’t know about that. What I can tell you, Mr. Jackson, is what I saw in Nam. When men are under fire, they don’t notice the color of the man sharing the foxhole with them. Whether he’s black or white, all they want to know is if they can count on him. On that road in Belgium, Cordell Jackson demonstrated to his troopers that he could be counted on.”

McCall asked, “But why did Bobby stay?”

"I think Cordell made that decision for both of them," Austin said. "Cordell said he wouldn't have stopped Bobby from leaving, and Bobby probably would have left had it not been for Cordell."

"So my father's been carrying around that guilt because Bobby stayed?"

"I don't think Bobby ever got a handle on his fear, but he stayed because he felt it was the right thing to do, and he obviously respected your father. Maybe he didn't control the action the way Cordell did, but in my book Bobby is very much a hero because he stayed despite his fear."

Austin hesitated a moment, then said, "To answer your question, I'd say your father is indeed carrying a lot guilt. And he'll probably carry it with him always, but he assumed the obligation for that guilt when he assumed command."

Austin looked at McCall and Tony. "I've lost people -- too damned many of them -- and I'll always wonder if I did everything possible to prevent their loss. When your dad said he was *doing what had to be done,* that meant -- to me -- that he knew that in order to hold the road, some of his own people certainly would die." Austin pointed to the document in McCall's hand. "From what I read in that report, Cordell probably realized that *all* of the Americans might die."

Austin reached for the report. "I would say that for a lot of years, Cordell had bad dreams nearly every single night."

"Do you suppose my mother knew?" Tony asked, his voice soft.

"About the dreams?" Austin asked. "No doubt she knew he had them, and that they had something to do with the war, but I'd be willing to bet he didn't tell her specifics. He would have been afraid to, because he knew she just wouldn't understand, she couldn't understand."

Austin continued. "It's likely that even during his waking hours the memory of that road can be triggered by some ordinary event. When that happens, he probably experiences a great deal of unfocused anxiety. He probably doesn't always link it to the war." Austin sighed audibly. "There were times, probably, when he must have felt that he was losing his mind."

Austin looked at Tony. "He needed to talk to someone, all right, but you least of all, because you are too important to him. He needed to talk to other people who'd been in combat, and my guess is that some of those other people should have been other black combat soldiers."

Austin was silent for a moment, then said, "Based on what we're learning about Vietnam veterans, when Cordell was shot the other night, he experienced what they're now call post traumatic stress disorder -- a kind of flashback."

Tony stood and walked to the window. After a moment, he returned to his seat. "Christ. I never knew. I had no idea that he's still carrying around all that baggage from that damned war, even after all these years." Tony looked at McCall, then at Austin. "Okay. Maybe he couldn't talk to me about it, but why didn't he ask for some help?"

Austin smiled. "I certainly don't claim to have much expertise in these matters, Mr. Jackson." Austin glanced at McCall before he continued. "But for the last three months I have been a member of a pilot study in which eight other Vietnam veterans meet as a group. Under the guidance of a counselor, we discuss our experiences. I think it may be helping some of us."

No one spoke for a long moment.

Tony took a deep drag on his cigarette, then ground it out, looking at Austin as he exhaled the smoke. "Thanks, Jim. Thanks very much. When my dad is recovered, I'd like to talk to you about who we need to see to get that kind of help for him."

Tony turned to McCall and smiled. "So what do we do now, boss?"

"You've obviously got your hands full, Tony. Jim and I are going to Washington tomorrow night. He has a contact who may help find the records that'll tell us more about what happened on that Belgian road."

"Okay," Tony said, "I'll stay in town tonight and head back home in the morning."

"Now, Tony, I don't want any static over this, but I've made arrangements for you to stay at my place."

Tony, too tired and emotionally drained to argue, merely nodded. Then McCall remembered his date with Ellie. "However, I have to leave for New York in..." McCall looked at his watch... "damn, in less than an hour, so I'm sorry, but you'll have to fend for yourself. There's a good restaurant right around the corner from the apartment."

Austin rose from his chair. "What arrangements should I make for Washington, Mr. McCall?"

"I'll meet you there tomorrow night. Let's plan on staying at the company's Washington apartment. What'll this take, Jim, maybe two days?"

"It's hard to say. We may find it in twenty minutes, or it might take us a week. That phone call was from an old friend in the records center. He's trying to speed things up for us."

"Okay, let's plan on no more than two days. If we don't find it, we'll have to go back another time. Just get a one-way ticket to Washington for yourself. You'll be coming back on the company plane with me."

Austin turned to Tony. "Mr. Jackson, I know the restaurant Mr. McCall is referring to. I would be happy to be your host for dinner tonight."

"On one condition," Tony said, smiling. "Please remember that *Mister* Jackson is my father's name. I'd really prefer for you to call me Tony."

"Yes, sir," Austin said, his ears a light shade of pink.

McCall laughed. "I've been trying to get him to drop that *Mister* and *sir* business for a year. Thanks, Jim. I'll see you tomorrow night."

After Austin had left, McCall moved to one of the chairs facing his desk, next to Tony. "You're worried about that young girl who's being held as a hostage, aren't you?"

"Yeah, and I'm worried that the families of those dead agents probably think I screwed up the bust." Tony tried to rub the fatigue from his eyes with his fists. "Spense, it seems like all the cars are coming off the track. My dad getting shot...reading what's in that report about him... the bust that went sour last night. I'm getting a lot of pressure to get Arnold behind bars."

"Seems to me that someone's got to find him first."

"Before last night, my case wasn't good enough to get a murder conviction, to prove that he killed that ATF agent. I didn't want to lose him, so we tried to get him on the illegal firearms charge."

"Well, you clearly can get a murder conviction now."

"Yeah, but I wanted him for killing that young agent."

"Why, Tony, because the agent was black?"

Tony's head snapped toward McCall, his jaw muscles working. Then the expression softened.

"Maybe," he shrugged. "Yeah, maybe that's part of it. Mostly, it was because of the way that agent died. He was assassinated. The damned newspapers ran front-page pictures of him lying across the hood of that car, blood running all over the grill and bumper. Don't those bastards realize that his parents, his wife, maybe even his young daughter would see that picture? Would they have done that if the agent had been white?"

McCall had always been mystified by the criminal justice system. He felt that the gathering and weighing of evidence was far too subjective, too often affected by emotions. He was much more comfortable with business decision making, which rarely involved passions, and which often could be measured by a financial statement. In business, the lines of responsibility and accountability were clear.

"I'm a little confused, Tony, about who's running the case. I've read about the ATF, the FBI, and the Northern Indiana Crime Commission."

Tony nodded as he lit another cigarette. "That's part of the problem. I'm caught up in an inter-agency rivalry between the ATF and the FBI."

"Which one has jurisdiction?"

"They both do, at least technically. The ATF guys obviously want Arnold because we're certain he killed their agent, and because he's running guns. The Bureau's involved because of the gambling and drugs, which is how Arnold finances the gun-running."

"It seems to me that they ought to be working together," McCall said.

"Well, hell yes, they should be, but the ATF has kept busy for a lot of years tracking down moonshiners. But there aren't that many stills around anymore, so they want to expand their scope of operations."

"What are you doing about it?"

"I've tried to cut through the bureaucratic crap by forming my own strike force staffed with ATF and Bureau people. We went with the crime commission investigator so we could show local involvement, and because he was a damned good man."

"And because it's good politics?" McCall asked, with more sarcasm than he intended.

"Yes, that's one of the realities," Tony said. "That's one of the realities I've learned is a part of this business. Last night was our first team action. Obviously, our leaders and the media weren't impressed." Tony stubbed out his cigarette with more energy than the task required. "And I suppose I can't blame them."

"What are you doing about Arnold now?"

"We've got the net out. But I've got to get the media off my ass because of the pressure they're putting on the brass."

"Don't worry about the media, Tony. I learned a long time ago that it just doesn't pay to get excited about what they say."

"Hell, it's my boss who's getting excited." Then Tony smiled. "One of the older hands told me that if the media think you have a problem, then you have a problem. If I don't nail Arnold, and soon, the best I can hope for is to inherit my father's shine cart."

"C'mon, Tony, it can't be that bad. After all, just a few weeks ago J. Edgar was patting you on the back."

Tony chuckled. "My father said a long time ago that I've got to be better than anyone else just to be considered equal. That pat on the back was yesterday. Their only concern is what I'm doing today."

"Well, you know that you don't have to ask for whatever help I can give you."

Tony nodded.

McCall looked at his watch. "We've got to leave for the apartment right now or *I've* got big trouble."

"You know, Spense, you were pretty damned confident that I'd agree to stay at your place."

"Think of it this way, counselor," McCall said as he took his topcoat from the closet. "You've got the responsibility to set the world straight for a deserving old man, and you've got to find some way to cage an animal called Izzy. That's a lot to worry about it, and you might as well worry about it in comfort."

March 9, 1967
55 Park Avenue
New York City
1:40 a.m.

They held each other closely. Spenser's breathing was slow and deep, but Eleanor knew he wasn't sleeping. She reached around him and felt that the muscles in his neck and shoulders, still slick with perspiration, were relaxed. These were the moments when she knew that she possessed him completely. She knew that even a strong and confident man needed to be vulnerable to someone, someone he could love and trust.

Eleanor was concerned about Spenser's uncertainty about his future. No man could be forced to walk away from that kind of power and responsibility without worrying about how to fill the void. She did not want him to accept either the assignment to Jordan or the post in Iran. She knew that Johnson wanted Iran's oil, and that the Shah had openly expressed admiration for Spenser. No, she didn't want him to take the job because he could do so much better, something much more meaningful. She knew that if Spenser did accept the offer, she would support him, but the paper wouldn't and her editorial policy would continue to criticize the administration's Middle East policies. Eleanor would support Spenser, because she loved him deeply, but she couldn't marry him if he went to work for LBJ. She also thought the mission to Jordan was doomed. There would be war, and McCall couldn't do a thing about it.

Eleanor leaned closer to Spenser and kissed the lobe of his ear, then whispered, "The copy boy I mentioned earlier today wouldn't be lying there half asleep next to this incredible body." Spenser sighed deeply, feigning irritation. "You know, when I was in the army they used to mix something with the potatoes to control urges like yours."

"I know all about that," she said. "It was called saltpecker."

"Salt*peter*."

"Whatever. Same thing." She pushed her pillow up against the headboard and pulled herself into a sitting position. Did you ever eat any of those potatoes?"

"I don't know -- I don't even know if they really used the stuff."

"Well, just to be safe, neither of us is going to eat another potato. Not ever."

McCall chuckled. "Where were you when I was nineteen?"

Eleanor twisted slightly toward McCall. "You know, Spense, I read something that said elderly people -- which we are rapidly becoming -- can make love well into old age, but only if they keep doing it. In fact, they say it gets better the older you get."

McCall sat up against the headboard, then leaned over and lightly kissed her neck and cheek. "Eleanor, I don't have any intention of retiring from *that*."

Eleanor leaned closer. "Oh, hell, Spense, I know that." She ran her fingers lightly through the mat of hair on his chest. "It's just that, well, I'm concerned about how you feel about leaving your company.

I realize that it's probably the most important move in your life, and I want to help."

"I should have considered that screwing my brains out would be your solution to the dilemma."

"Damn you, Spenser McCall," she said softly, "you know what I mean."

He took her into his arms and hugged her. "Yes, I know what you mean, and I love you for it." He leaned back. "It's just that there is so much more that needs to be done. And it would be so much better if I did it. I hope that isn't just my ego talking, but it'd be a helluva lot safer if I did it than if my replacement does. It'll take him at least a year, maybe longer, to get a handle on things and--"

"Spenser," Eleanor said softly, but firmly. "Be thankful that there is unfinished business. That's something about which you should be proud. Look at it this way. Your leadership helped create a major corporation that is constantly growing and expanding. If it ever reaches the point where all the important decisions have been made and all the challenges have been met, then that -- by definition -- is stagnation."

McCall was quiet for a long moment. Then he pulled Eleanor close, her head resting on his chest. "Ellie, you're not only smart as hell, but you've got more balls than most men I know."

Eleanor grabbed a handful of hair on Spenser's chest and tugged lightly. "Smart is wonderful, but a beautiful woman doesn't need to be told she has *balls.*"

McCall laughed. "Ellie?"

"Uhmm-m?"

"There is something I'd like you to do, if you can."

"What?"

"You know that Tony has a lot of trouble over that arrest that went sour. He's catching hell from every direction -- especially from you media types. Do you think your people can help find that young girl?"

Eleanor thought about the request for a moment. "Yes, as a matter of fact. We have a man who I think could handle it. Yes, I'll put him on it first thing in the morning."

"Good. We need to help Tony wrap that thing up so he can concentrate on helping his father. Besides, you'll never make him a congressman unless he puts Arnold in prison."

Eleanor reached up and kissed McCall. "You know, if you're not careful, people are liable to discover that you oil barons can be very nice people." She drew his head closer and kissed him again.

He loved the smell of her hair and the incredible smoothness of her skin.

Eleanor's hand moved under the sheet and grasped him firmly. "Spense?"

"Y-yes-s?"

"If the army ever gave you any of that saltpecker, I'll bet it didn't take."

"Ellie, it was salt*peter.*"

"Uhmm-m," she whispered, her lips brushing his ear. "Whatever."

Eleanor was sitting up in bed, wrapped in her burgundy robe. She could smell the coffee that McCall had brewed. She looked at the clock on the nightstand. They had a little less than two hours before they had to leave.

McCall entered the room, carrying two coffee cups. He placed the cups on the stand and smiled when he looked at Eleanor.

"What are you grinning at?"

"That robe. As I recall, my grandmother wore something like that."

Eleanor held her arms out to her side, as if she were a model.

"My friend, your sense of female practicality is distorted by the hang-up men have with sheer black lace. Most women are more practical than that."

"Well, it sure as hell doesn't fit your image," he said as he handed her a cup.

She held the cup in both hands until McCall slid into bed beside her. "McCall, there's one thing I want to say before we leave, and I want you to listen carefully so you don't misunderstand. I know a management consultant, a good one, who did a study recently about the circumstances under which CEOs leave their companies. He--"

McCall turned and looked at Eleanor closely. "Do you know something I don't? And why a management *consultant*?"

"I asked you to listen carefully. He said something that may be relevant here. You said on the phone that you might not wait until retirement. Most CEOs, he said, are reluctant to step down if they feel they're facing serious issues or if their company's earnings aren't what they should be."

"Well, hell, my company certainly isn't in financial trouble," McCall said. "We've never made the kind of money most people think we do, and of course I'd like to see an increase in earnings."

"But you are worried about our growing dependence on Middle East oil."

"Hell, yes. Ellie, if I were just a few years younger, I know I could at least take the edge off that problem. Americans don't understand -- or appreciate -- that the price for gasoline has been artificially low. The prices have to be much higher if we're going to pay for the kind of exploration we need to assure a secure source of oil. I've said--"

"McCall, I didn't ask for a speech. I've heard it all before. Hell, I may *even* believe some of it. The point is that, as far as Horizon Corporation is concerned, you have to understand that it's going to be someone else's problem. You've got to let go."

"You mean just walk away?"

"Yes," Eleanor said, "that's precisely what I mean. There are damned few men who have accomplished what you have, McCall. You've created an international giant. All I'm saying is don't stay too long. You're on top; there'll never be a better time to leave."

"I may be on top, but there are some people working very hard to make sure that changes."

"McCall, that sounds like paranoia."

"Maybe so, but I know what I see. They're plotting behind my back to move me out of the way, without regard for the contributions I've made." McCall regretted the words. He knew he sounded petulant. "Christ, Ellie, you don't really expect me to just roll over, do you?"

"No, I don't, but make damned certain that you want to stay for the right reasons and not because you want to engage in some macho pushing and shoving to see whose is bigger."

"Oh, come on, Ellie. It's just that a lifetime in business has taught me that the measure of your worth to an organization is what you stand for when standing for something is most difficult."

"McCall, I'm sorry, but that sounds like something from a textbook. I also want you to ask yourself this: why are you so interested in helping Cordell?"

"What the hell are you getting at?"

"You obviously believe Cordell should have received some recognition for what he did during the war."

"Hell, yes."

"But why are you pushing it so hard?"

"Well, it's...it's the right thing to do. He's a decent human being, and Tony's a good man."

"Are you sure you're not getting that mixed up with what you believe is a lack of recognition for what you've accomplished?"

McCall put their coffee cups on the nightstand. "Christ, Ellie, I always suspected that newspaper publishers reached pretty far to make connections, but that's sillier than hell."

Eleanor reached and turned McCall's head so she could look into his eyes. "And what about us? How far do I have to reach to make things connect for us?"

McCall didn't respond.

"Of course, LBJ has given you an out if the board wants Thompkins to take over -- or if you decide to quit." Eleanor's voice was tinged with sarcasm. "What are you afraid of, Spenser, that unless you're a CEO or an ambassador that you'll just be one of the common folk?"

"That's a cheap shot, Ellie. What the hell's gotten into you?"

Her eyes welled with tears, and she pulled him close, resting her head on his chest. For long moments they held each other.

"Ellie, you know I love you."

"Never doubted it."

"Then why can't we wait until this is all settled -- the New Mexico thing?"

Eleanor raised her eyes to his. "Spenser, if I'm as important to you as you say I am, *nothing* else would have to be settled first."

"Ellie, there's a lot at stake for a lot of people."

"I'm aware of that, but no where is it written that only Spenser McCall can handle the tough ones. If you really believe in the system -- and you've told me that you do -- then the right people will rise to the top to take over and deal with the problems. And despite how you feel about him, Larry Thompkins just may be the right man."

Eleanor put her head back on McCall's chest. Very softly, she said, "Until you understand that, McCall, there isn't much hope for us."

CHAPTER 6

March 14, 1967
The Torpedo Factory
Alexandria, Va.
9:10 a.m.

"I don't know what a Torpedo Factory is supposed to look like," McCall said as he looked through the windshield at the three-story concrete building that covered nearly a block along the bank of the Potomac, "but if someone were to ask me, I'd say this sure as hell is it."

"Officially, it's the Washington National Records Center," Jim Austin said, as he turned the rental car into the parking area. "This is where the military keeps most of its records. During the First World War they made torpedoes here -- or maybe they just assembled them. They loaded them onto barges over there on the river bank and shipped them out."

McCall and Austin were greeted at the entrance by a burly, middle-aged warrant officer who stood well over six feet.

"Good morning, Colonel Austin, sir," the warrant officer's voice boomed as he stepped to within three paces of Austin, braced, and delivered a rigid parade-ground salute. "I can not imagine how the colonel has managed to keep his lily-white ass out of a sling without the skill and courage of his sergeant major." The warrant officer smiled broadly, his even, white teeth contrasting sharply with his black skin.

Austin didn't return the salute. He stepped forward and warmly embraced his friend, each man slapping the other on the back.

"Congratulations again on making warrant, you old bandit," Austin said as he stepped back, his hands resting on Parker's shoulders. "Who did you have con to get it?"

"It's the system, sir. It works -- the same system that made a red-necked, 'bama cracker -- a born klutz who couldn't find his ass in the dark with both hands -- a light colonel. *Sir.*"

Austin laughed, then turned abruptly as if he'd forgotten that McCall was standing behind him. McCall noticed that Austin's ears were flushed pink. "Ah...excuse me, Mr. McCall. This is Warrant Officer John Parker. We served together for two years."

Parker extended his hand. "Pleasure to meet you, Mr. McCall." McCall could sense Parker's effort to focus his attention on the purpose of the meeting. "Colonel Austin has briefed me on what you need from us. He also said you wouldn't have much time, so I've pulled records based on the information the colonel gave me. You can examine the files in a private room I've reserved for you. If you follow me, gentlemen, I'll take you there now."

In the small conference room, there was a large Mylar box on the table. Stacked next to the box were several manila folders.

Parker turned to Austin. "Colonel, to save time, I've short-circuited the process for you to examine any documents you'll need. Normally, you have to submit a research application and have it approved. That can take a day, sometimes more. I've personally signed out for these documents, and I'll be standing by to get others you may need. None of these documents is classified, but if you need any that are...well, we'll handle that if it arises. If you need me, there's a civilian archivist at a desk outside the door. Just tell her. Her name is Miss Morena. Finally, tell me how you gentlemen like your coffee."

Austin nodded. "Thanks, Johnny. Coffee black for both of us."

As Parker was leaving, Austin said, "Johnny, I owe you."

Parker smiled, pausing in the doorway. "Colonel, if we've been keeping score all these years, I'm in very deep trouble. Call if you need me, sir."

When Parker was gone, McCall said, "Your Mr. Parker seems to be a very capable man."

"Yes, sir," Austin said, still looking at the closed door. "I owe him a lot."

"Vietnam?"

Austin nodded. "We got into trouble one night and I became separated from the unit. I stumbled into a ravine and broke my leg. Somehow Johnny found me. He set the leg, then carried me on his back for hours, dodging VC patrols all night. I can't remember being so scared, but I guess I was more afraid of being captured than of dying -- a lot of us felt that way. A helicopter picked us up late the next morning."

"As I said, he's a very capable man." McCall could see that Austin had been moved by meeting Parker. McCall didn't know what else to say, so he turned his attention to the documents stacked on the table. "Well, how do you propose we get started here?"

Austin pulled the stack of folders from the center of the table and opened the top one. "I'm sure that Johnny has culled the files for after-action reports involving the Five-Seventeenth Parachute Regiment for December seventeenth and eighteenth, nineteen forty four. That's probably what's in these folders."

"Does Parker know what we're looking for?"

"I sent him a copy of the interviews that the doctor had with Cordell," Austin said. "I hope that was all right."

"Good," McCall said as he opened one of the folders. "He can be more effective if he knows what we need."

McCall had noticed that Austin's personality changed when he had entered the building. He seemed more confident, more relaxed. Perhaps Austin hadn't found a way to adapt to the corporate environment. Certainly, a U.S. Army colonel wouldn't be as deferential to his senior officers as Austin was to his civilian supervisors. Perhaps, McCall thought, he and I should talk about that.

They had been reading reports for more than an hour when there was a knock at the door.

"Come," Austin called.

Parker came into the room. He had a copy of *Time* magazine in his hand. McCall could tell that something was bothering him.

"What is it, Johnny?"

Parker opened the magazine to a one-column story circled in red ink. "I read this several days ago, but it didn't click. Hell, I don't know if it does now, but I thought you ought to read it."

The article was about the appointment of Oliver Wentworth Crawford to Secretary of the Army. A photo showed Crawford at the lectern in the White House press briefing room. The President was at his side, smiling.

"What about this, Johnny?"

"Well, sir, it says that Oliver Crawford received the Medal of Honor during the big war," Parker said hesitantly. "It says he got it for holding a road in Belgium against a Panzer unit. He was a butter bar..." Parker looked at McCall. "...a second lieutenant and his squad was nearly wiped out. The article says only three other men survived the fighting, and one of them died a few weeks later. It was one of those hold-until-relieved assignments, which translates into 'don't come back alive.' Only Crawford was on his feet when the relief column came up. All of that happened on December eighteenth, nineteen forty four, during the Battle of the Bulge."

Austin held the magazine so McCall could read the article with him. McCall took the magazine and looked for a long moment at the picture, then placed the magazine on the table.

"It might just be a coincidence, Jim," Parker said, "but I wonder if one of those men who survived could be your Cordell Jackson."

McCall and Austin exchanged glances, then looked again at the article. "How do you suggest we determine whether Cordell was one of those men who survived, Mr. Parker?" McCall asked.

When Parker didn't respond immediately, McCall said, "Before you answer that question, maybe I'd better say out loud what I suspect the three of us are thinking."

McCall spread his hands on the table, then slowly rose from his chair, his eyes still on the magazine article. "Based on this article, and what we read in those twenty-year-old interviews the psychiatrist had with Cordell, there is a possibility -- and I stress the word *possibility* -- that Cordell Jackson and Oliver Crawford fought at the same roadblock.

"If it is the same roadblock that Cordell described," McCall continued, "then if Crawford received the medal, why didn't Cordell Jackson receive one?" McCall looked at Austin and Parker. "I guess the bigger question is whether Crawford received the medal that should have gone to Cordell Jackson?"

Parker grimaced. "There is the possibility, Mr. McCall, that during the big war it might have been...shall we say, convenient, for the military to overlook something that a black soldier did that deserved a very high honor, especially the MOH."

Parker was thoughtful a moment. "On the other hand, it's also possible that Crawford deserved his medal. I read those old interviews of Jackson's, and maybe he didn't see where Crawford was fighting. After all, Crawford was there when the relief column came up. Maybe Jackson was confused. Maybe he was hurt too bad to be aware of what was going on around him."

"Maybe." McCall pushed the chair back under the table and walked to the huge window that overlooked the Potomac. He remembered Cordell's description of the German SS officer standing over him, smiling as the Luger's bolt slammed home. How could the German have had the time to do that if Crawford had been present? McCall recalled the phone conversation with Crawford twenty years earlier. Crawford specifically asked McCall to find a job for Cordell. Crawford said he'd felt sorry for him, a wounded GI -- "one of the boys from my old outfit" -- who now was shining shoes in a Chicago hotel bathroom.

"Before we proceed further," McCall said, his back to the two men, "I'm certain that we all appreciate the sensitivities involved here."

McCall turned to look at Parker. "Now, Mr. Parker: you've been a great help. However, for your own protection, I suggest that you forget about this discussion and terminate your involvement."

"Mr. McCall," Parker said softly. "If there is the slightest possibility that Secretary of the Army Oliver Crawford received the Medal of Honor and didn't deserve it, or that Cordell Jackson should have received the medal and didn't -- for whatever reason -- then I want to help uncover the truth."

"You realize the consequences for your career?" McCall asked. "Washington doesn't look kindly on whistle-blowers."

"Sir, if Colonel Austin is involved in this, and he needs my help, that's good enough for me."

McCall walked from the window back to the desk. He locked eyes with both men. He envied the loyalty and respect and friendship these two men shared. McCall thought of the grinding, almost debilitating corporate politics in his company. Of the more than fifty-thousand Horizon employees, McCall could describe only one man as a close friend.

"All right," McCall nodded, motioning the two men to be seated. "Tell us how we can get to the bottom of this."

"First, I'll check the citation for Crawford's medal," Parker said. "That'll tell us more about which roadblock he was fighting at. Then I'll go through these reports to dig out anything on Cordell Jackson that hopefully will tell us if they were at the same roadblock. I haven't had a chance to check whether Cordell Jackson received any honors. Maybe we can even find out whether Jackson was recommended for a medal that he never received. It's happened before."

"You mean that these kinds of recommendations are sometimes lost?" McCall asked.

"It's happened," Austin said, "and it may not have anything to do with his being black -- just sloppy paperwork."

"One other thing, Johnny," Austin said, "see what you can find on a guy named Bobby who was with Cordell at the roadblock. That's all we've got on him, except that he was seventeen at the time, probably had the rank of private, and lived in Waycross, Georgia."

"Right," Parker said. "I remember that name from Jackson's interviews with the doctor. That's not much to work with, but I'll do what I can." Parker gestured toward the files. "These reports may tell us something, but I can also check with the Army Personnel Agency."

Parker smiled as he looked at Austin. "Frankly, sir, I can work faster if you and Mr. McCall weren't here. I can put a couple of the archivists to work on it. Leave everything to me and I'll call when I find something."

McCall closed the folder he'd been reading and placed it in the file box. "Mr. Parker, how many black men have received the Medal of Honor?"

"I can't tell you how many have received it, Mr. McCall, at least not yet. But I can assure you that in the big war and Korea a lot of black men who earned it never received it."

McCall nodded slowly. "Do you suppose that's the case with Cordell Jackson?"

"I can't answer that question either, since at this point we only have Mr. Jackson's version of what happened."

"Well, based on Cordell's version, how would you vote?"

Parker smiled. "My vote doesn't count, Mr. McCall. But you know, during the Civil War, Confederate troops actually did vote to decide who would receive their equivalent of the Medal of Honor."

"I didn't know the Confederates had an equivalent," Austin said.

"Confederate soldiers of course weren't eligible for the Medal of Honor," Parker said. "Only Union troops qualified. So the South decided its soldiers would be listed on what they called the Roll of Honor. For some reason they never got around to striking a medal, nor have any designs for a medal survived. But the law signed by Jefferson Davis a couple of years into the war stipulated that enlisted men from each company would vote to select the one man they believed was especially brave during a particular battle. That name was listed on the Roll of Honor. The Roll of Honor was read to each regiment after a battle and it was published in at least one newspaper in every Confederate state. Some of those names have survived, but unfortunately no citations were written to describe the action that earned the honor."

"How objective could such a vote be?" McCall asked.

"I suspect you're thinking it would end up being a popularity vote, and maybe it was. If I had to be judged by anyone, though, I'd just as soon it be the men I served with."

"Yes, I think I can understand that," McCall said. "I know that many black men fought on the Union side during the Civil War, but did any of them ever receive the medal?"

"Quite a few did, actually. My work here makes it possible for me to pursue a personal interest -- black soldiers who have received the medal and other high honors for bravery." Parker smiled. "I hope that some day I'll write a book about it."

"When you feel the time is right, Mr. Parker, call me. I can put you in touch with a lady who has excellent contacts in the publishing business."

"Thanks. I'll take you up on that offer. But back to your question about Civil War black soldiers. The first black man whose actions would merit the medal was William Carney, a former slave who had planned to join the ministry.

"In eighteen sixty-three, Sergeant Carney and six hundred men of the Fifty-fourth Massachusetts Colored Infantry charged the Confederates at Fort Wagner in South Carolina. When the color bearer was hit, Carney dropped his rifle and seized the Union flag before it fell. He made it to the shadow of the fort and planted the colors. But the Union losses were heavy, and when the Confederates charged the position, Carney wrapped the flag around the staff and ran back toward the Union lines in a hail of fire.

"He was hit in his right arm, right leg, and chest. A New York soldier offered to carry the flag after a bullet grazed Carney's head, but Carney refused. He was most proud of the fact that the flag never touched the ground. But it wasn't until nineteen hundred -- thirty seven years later -- that Carney received his medal."

"Has your research given you any insight into what kind of man typically has received the medal?" McCall asked.

Parker smiled. "You're wondering whether a gentle old black man who shines shoes for a living could be a fire-breathing dragon in combat?"

"Well, I--"

"Your question is a common one, Mr. McCall. Virtually every race, creed, color, and national origin is represented by the roster of medal recipients. Among them are a lot of Cordell Jacksons -- both black and white and shades in between. Some of those men have been singled out for public adulation, like Mr. Crawford. Most of them live very ordinary lives, men whose neighbors and friends are probably unaware of the honor. And there are those who find the spotlight of the medal difficult to handle. The Medal of honor, one recipient said, can be a lot harder to wear than to earn."

"Mr. Parker, I'm looking forward to reading your book." Then McCall reached across the table to shake Parker's hand. "I suppose we'd better let you get back to work. Thank you for your help."

Austin walked with Parker to the door. "Johnny, there's no need for you to walk point on this. Call me if you need help."

"Thanks, Jim. I'll be in touch."

Austin opened the door for Parker. "And give my best to Angie," Austin said. "Tell her I still think you married better than she did."

"She tells me that all the time, colonel. She'll be mad as hell if we don't get together on your next trip up."

"We'll do it. Promise. Thanks again."

Later, as Jim Austin turned onto the George Washington Parkway toward National Airport, McCall once again read the magazine article. McCall recalled that during the war, even General Patton had described the elder Crawford as a hard-ass.

General Crawford had one of the highest casualty rates in the Italian campaign -- so high, in fact, that there was talk after the war about a congressional investigation. But even Crawford's critics couldn't deny that he got results. His troops always moved forward and nearly always took their objectives. Crawford retired in the late forties and died in 1960.

Could Oliver Wentworth Crawford Jr. have been the young second lieutenant on that road in Belgium? McCall wondered. Was Cordell one of the other survivors? On the other hand, there probably were small units like Cordell's fighting desperately all over southern Belgium.

McCall recalled that he attended Crawford's wedding. They'd met several times socially after that. Crawford, always deferential, would introduce McCall to his friends as one of the most demanding teachers he'd ever had, "the man who taught me planning and logistics."

God Almighty, McCall thought. What if it is the same lieutenant?

March 18, 1967
Horizon Corporation
Office of the Chairman
9:25 a.m.

"Gentlemen, I understand that we're looking at nearly two billion dollars, and that it's the largest single expenditure this corporation has ever made for this kind of project." McCall locked eyes momentarily with each of the three men sitting in front of his desk. "Are you telling me now that you don't think we're capable of doing it? Or are you saying that we shouldn't do it?"

Patrick Fitzsimmons, president of Horizon's oil production and exploration subsidiary, shook his head quickly. "No, Spense, we're not telling you that we can't or shouldn't do it. But if you want us to push ahead, I'm going to have to assign more people and resources to the project, and that doesn't make sense until the board approves the money. Hell, I've already got nearly a hundred engineers working on it -- people I had to pull from other projects."

"What are you telling me, Fitz?"

"All I'm asking, Spense, is that we wait until we get final project approval and get a budget. If we move ahead on the schedule you've set for us, every other project is going to suffer."

Mike Burson, Fitzsimmons's exploration vice president, nodded agreement. "Besides, we're having a tough time getting the ranchers in

New Mexico to sign leases. Even if we had the money right now, Spense, we couldn't start up more than a half-dozen rigs."

"What the hell kind of job are your land men doing down there?" McCall asked, unable now to mask his impatience and frustration.

Burson shifted uncomfortably. "Well, Spense, you have to understand that there's never been much drilling in northeast New Mexico -- at least nothing that ever amounted to much. It's an isolated area and there are a lot of big ranches there. Burson glanced at Fitzsimmons beside him, as if seeking assurance, then said. "Frankly, Spense, they want more money than our leases offer."

"What you're telling me is that they want oil or natural gas prices for the CO2?"

"No doubt about it," Fitzsimmons said. "Some of them don't know much about how or why we want to drill for carbon dioxide to use in the oil patch. When we explain that we're going to pump it into old oil fields to recover more oil, they figure they ought to get CO2 royalties based on price of the oil we recover. And some of them get a tad touchy over the idea that we're going to pipe the carbon dioxide to Texas."

"What do you mean *touchy?*"

"A couple of days ago a rancher not only refused to sign a lease, he stuck a gun in a land man's face and ran him off the property," Fitzsimmons said. "Another rancher tried to run down one of our boys with a pickup, at least it sure as hell looked that way. There's always been some bad blood that close to the Texas-New Mexico border. It goes back a long ways."

Fitzsimmons said, more to himself than the other men in the room, "I hate to think what we're going to run into when we start trying to negotiate pipeline right-of-way."

"Have any of you personally been down there?" McCall asked. The third man, who was the regional vice president in Houston, said, "We all have, Spense. I've met with the ranchers several times. They're a special breed of people who have special feelings about the land."

"Hell," McCall said, "all ranchers have special feelings for the land. Talk to me about *their* special feelings."

"Well," the vice president said, "their lives revolve around those ranches, some of which go back to Spanish land grants. Some of the ranchers even arrange the marriages of their kids, especially if they can combine a couple of ranches. Quite a few of those spreads go over a hundred thousand acres. It's a different culture. The big ranchers have a lot of influence in the state. When I was talking to one of them -- he's got a hundred-twenty thousand acres near Clayton -- the phone rang. It was the governor."

"One more thing, Spense," Fitzsimmons said. "The cattle graze on what the ranchers call Buffalo grass, which is fragile as hell. You drive a truck over it one time and it dies. When you consider what's going to happen to that grass when we cut roads and rig pads, we may have to pay those ranchers more in damages than we thought."

McCall leaned back in his chair, the fingers of his right hand lightly drumming the armrest. Then he realized how tightly wound he was, and he made a conscious effort to control his emotions. "What's the local economy like?"

"The ranch owners do pretty damn well, most of the time," Fitzsimmons said. "But the rest of the people, especially the Mexican-Americans, could use our money."

McCall was silent for a moment while he assessed what he'd heard. "Fitz, find someone who understands the people down there. Tell those local people that we'll hire as many of them as we can. Hell, tell them that we'll even train them if we have to."

McCall leaned forward to emphasize his words. "But I want you to move ahead on this project. I'll talk to the board as soon as possible, but devote everything you can spare to this thing. Spud some wells as soon as you can. I want a demonstration project as soon as possible to prove carbon dioxide production."

Fitzsimmons sighed, "Okay, Spense."

McCall looked at the three men. "Gentlemen, the best chance we have to get full board approval is to get the thing started, to show them that it can work. Let's talk again at eight next Wednesday morning."

Fitzsimmons hung back when the other two left.

McCall smiled at his old friend, leaned back in his chair, and sighed. "Okay, partner, tell me how it really is."

"Hell, Spense," Fitzsimmons said as he rested his hand on the corner of McCall's desk, "Larry acts like he's already sitting in your chair. He's pushing hard."

"So what's new about that? He's been romancing the board for the last five or six years."

Fitzsimmons grimaced. “Well, according to him, he’s scoring big points -- at your expense.”

“Obviously you mean because of the New Mexico project?”

“Yeah, that’s the root of it.” Fitzsimmons hesitated a moment, looking closely at McCall. “But he told me -- he didn’t say who told him -- that the board is probably going to turn down your budget request for this project. Larry says that he’s pushing the board members to deep-six the project. Apparently that’s a tune the board wants to hear, at least most of them.”

McCall nodded, hoping his facial expression wasn’t revealing his emotions.

“Spense, I’ve got it from a good source that if we lighten up on this project -- if we scale it back to pilot status -- the board probably will support you. You know that you’ve got some support on the board, but you’ve got to cut them some slack.”

McCall looked closely at his old friend. A generation before, they’d worked in the West Texas oil fields. In fact, when McCall had been assigned to the oil and gas production subsidiary, Fitzsimmons had been his boss.

“What you’re saying is that if I want to keep this job I’ve got to walk away from a project that in a few years will be damned important for Horizon...that’ll be damned important for this country.”

“*Dammit*, Spense.” Fitzsimmons shook his head in frustration. “There’s never been any shades of gray for you. You’ve always got to back everybody up against a wall.” Fitzsimmons sighed in frustration. He was searching for words, his right hand scribing a small circle. “Think of it this way -- if that political asshole gets your job now, nothing’s going to happen in New Mexico until the ragheads find a way to cut off our oil. If you back off, if you scale everything down, then the odds are the board will at least let us get a start.”

“What you’re asking me to do, Fitz,” McCall said, his voice rising, “is to tell them I was wrong to push so hard and that I’ll be a good boy and cut it back if they let me stay.” McCall could feel his face flush. “That son-of-*bitch* can have this job right now before I’ll do that.”

Fitzsimmons didn’t respond. After a moment, he slowly gathered his papers from his side of McCall’s desk. He looked at McCall for a moment, then rose from his chair and started to leave the room.

Just before Fitzsimmons reached the door, McCall said, "Damn it, Fitz, hang on a minute." McCall came around his desk and walked up to Fitzsimmons. McCall smiled. "Fitz, do you remember back in the late thirties, in Lubbock, when we were young engineers? We were working for McKenna. I suppose even then we knew he was one of the real legends in the oil patch."

Fitzsimmons nodded. "It's eight years since you and me helped carry his casket."

"Well, he said something that I've always remembered. He said there is no formula for success. But he said there sure as hell is one for failure, and that's when you try to please everybody instead of doing what you know in your heart is right."

McCall put his hand on his friend's shoulder. "Fitz, I *know* this is right."

Fitzsimmons lowered his head. After a moment he looked into McCall's eyes. "Spenser McCall, you've always been the most righteous, bull-headed, single-laned bastard I've ever known. You've got elephant balls -- I'll give you that, Spense -- but you've never learned that you can't change the world in a New York minute." Then Fitzsimmons smiled. "But, if you really want me to punch some damn holes in the damn New Mexico countryside, then I suppose I might as well get on with it."

McCall chuckled, then his smile faded. "You understand, Fitz, that bucking Larry will cost you."

"Hell, Spense, I never intended to work for that peckerwood. Connie and me just finished building our place on Lake Palestine, up by Tyler. When you fold your hand, I'm gonna throw mine in too." Fitzsimmons smiled. "Hell, man, I've been waiting fifteen years to get the hell out of Chicago and get back home to Texas."

Fitzsimmons turned to leave, then paused. He smiled again as he slowly shook his head.

"What is it, Fitz?"

"You got me to thinking about that damn ornery McKenna. What a bear-of-a-man...and smart like a fox. But he had the damnedest, most contrary sense of humor of any human being I've ever known."

Fitzsimmons looked up at the ceiling, rubbing his forehead with his fingertips. "What the hell was that little guy's name, the guy from accounting? He damn near wet his pants whenever he had to talk to McKenna."

Over the years, the McKenna stories had become a ritual. Perhaps neither Fitzsimmons nor McCall had ever known the accountant's name. But the story always began with the same question.

"Remember? It was before the war," Fitzsimmons said.

"No, Fitz, I've never been able to remember his name."

"Well, McKenna calls me into his office. He tells me to just sit and watch. Then he phones the accountant and tells him that he wants to see him. You remember how he could put a real edge on that gruff voice of his. Then, while we're waiting, he reaches into his desk and takes out some waxed paper that was folded around something."

Fitzsimmons was warming to his story. "And there, in that wax paper, was a damn, slimy, raw oyster. And he pops the damn thing right into his mouth. Looked like he kept it in the side of his cheek.

"Well, the accountant comes in and stands there in front of McKenna's desk. You could almost see his pants wiggling around his knees, his legs were shaking so bad. And the way his hands were shaking I remember thinking that he could probably thread a sewing machine while it was running. Then McKenna shuffles some papers on his desk like he's looking for one in particular. He mumbles something about needing the numbers for the rigs working in the Levelland field, and that's when he starts to coughing.

"Then McKenna *really* starts to coughing. That big chest of his starts to heaving. He's growling like a grizzly trying to cough up a hocker. Then, all of a sudden, he spits out that damned slimy oyster. It shoots out of his mouth, slithers across his desk, and bounces up and hits the accountant just above the belt."

Fitzsimmons shook his head. "Hell, man, I reckon that poor little bastard's been running for all these thirty years."

Both men chuckled.

After a moment, Fitzsimmons said, "Spense, I got to tell you that I feel in my gut that they're not going to let you prove a damn thing. But if it falls on its ass, it won't be because I wasn't busting mine trying to make it work for you."

McCall thought of how he had envied the mutual respect and camaraderie shared by Jim Austin and Warrant Officer Parker. He reached out and patted his friend's huge shoulder. "Fitz, old friend, your support is the only damn thing I know I can count on around here."

Later, McCall sat at his desk and wrote himself a reminder to call employee relations. He wanted to make certain that when he applied for it, Fitzsimmons would receive the most generous retirement that company policy would permit.

McCall leaned back in his chair. He seldom had doubts about a decision once it had been made. The only doubt he had about the CO2 project was whether he'd be around to make sure it worked. He recalled what Eleanor had said about his concerns with whether his board would support the project.

"Well, then get with it, McCall," she had said. "Do a marketing job on your board and get the damn project sold. But I want you to answer these two questions honestly, Spense: Are you really interested in making this project work? Or are you just trying to find an excuse not to leave this job?"

McCall's secretary came into his office and put a folder containing his mail on his desk and quietly left the office. He opened the folder and stared at the top letter, but the words weren't registering.

Damn you, Ellie, McCall thought. Damn you for asking the two questions I'm not sure I can answer.

It was clear to McCall that some of the board members wanted to wait until the price of oil increased. One director had said, "I don't see how we can justify to our stockholders -- or to analysts -- the incredibly high cost of the CO2 project."

Two of the directors openly supported McCall. They, like McCall, felt it was prudent to sacrifice near-term profits in order to assure a future supply of oil.

But the undecided votes were the key to McCall's success. If he could persuade them, he had a chance.

McCall rose from his desk and walked to a window, his hands clasped behind his back. Perhaps...perhaps he was pressing too hard, he thought. Perhaps, if he'd back off, the board might be willing to approve funding for a demonstration project. But all of that might take years. McCall knew he didn't have years.

Then McCall became angry for doubting himself. He knew he was right. What he wanted not only made economic sense for the company, McCall viewed the project as Horizon's responsibility to the future of the country. How would Americans react, he wondered, if -- *when* -- the Middle East oil spigot was suddenly turned off? Who would they blame?

March 20, 1967
Horizon Building
Chicago
11:30 a.m.

When the phone buzzed, Patrick Fitzsimmons saw from the blinking light that it was the direct line from the vice chairman, Larry Thompkins.

"Yes, Larry?" Fitzsimmons answered.

"Hello, Fitz. Have you got anything scheduled for lunch today?"

Fitzsimmons did plan to have lunch with two of his consulting geophysicists. "No, Larry, I'm free."

"Good. Let's make it around twelve-thirty." Thompkins paused. "Fitz, I'd like you to be prepared to talk about the New Mexico project."

"What specifically? I can bring Morris along. He's on top of things."

"No, no," Thompkins said. "I'd like this to be just between us. I'll come by your office and pick you up at about a quarter-after

Later, as they rode the elevator down to the lobby, Thompkins suggested they have lunch in the hotel restaurant next door, rather than in the executive dining room. When they were seated, Thompkins began. "Fitz, you know I have the highest regard for Spenser McCall, and I know you and he go back a long way."

Thompkins hesitated. "But I'm having a little difficulty swallowing those big numbers associated with the New Mexico project. Now, don't misunderstand, I believe, essentially, in what he wants to do. I'm just concerned that we may be pushing this technology too hard too fast."

Fitzsimmons grimaced. "Larry, you know that Spense wants me to push ahead within the limits of my authority until the board makes a final decision. Why don't you and he discuss it before we do any more talking about it."

"Yes, I know that McCall wants to push ahead." Thompkins smiled. "In fact, if I'm not mistaken, that was the subject of your meeting with him this morning."

Christ, Fitzsimmons thought. One of those two people in my group is running straight to Thompkins with whatever happens on this project. And Thompkins is telling me that he's feels strong enough that he doesn't care that I know.

"Fitz, you're a good man, a very good man, the kind of man I'm going to need in a few months." Thompkins smiled. "And in case there is any doubt in your mind about it, you will be working for me, sooner than you might think."

Well, Fitzsimmons thought, unless he's playing head games, it sounds like the board's given him the nod.

"Fitz, I admire your loyalty to McCall. What worries me about you is your very parochial view about what's important to this corporation. The price of oil won't support the investment in CO2."

"It would if the Arabs cut us off," Fitzsimmons said.

Thompkins smiled. "I know that McCall is concerned -- no, I should say preoccupied -- with that scenario. But I believe the Arabs won't cut the flow of oil to us simply because they don't want to cut the flow of greenbacks going to them. The economics are pretty straightforward, really."

"What you're overlooking, Larry, is that your *straightforward* economics can be bent out of shape by Middle East politics. Once the dogs of war are unleashed by either Israel or the Arabs, everything's up for grabs."

Thompkins locked eyes with Fitzsimmons. "What I hear you saying, Fitz, is that McCall has your full support."

"Right down the line."

"And you're going to start drilling those CO2 wells?"

"I've already put in the call to start hiring contract drillers. We'll be spudding wells in a few weeks."

"You're going ahead, despite what I've just told you."

Fitzsimmons, his voice low and even, said, "No, Larry, I'm going ahead *because* of what you told me. Maybe McCall is pushing too hard, but I believe that what he wants to do is right for the company and right for the country."

Thompkins straightened in his chair, his eyes hard. "*My* plans will be good for the company and the country, Fitz. And most of the board supports those plans. How you conduct yourself over the next few months will determine what role you'll play in those plans." Thompkins neatly folded his napkin and pushed back from the table. "I'd like you to consider that fact as you enjoy your steak."

Alone at the table, Fitzsimmons slowly sipped his glass of beer. *McCall, your problem is that your talent got you to the top chair. Even after all these years, you've never understood how boardroom politics makes the wheels turn. You've never been good at playing the game, and in your heart you know it's too damn late to start now. You're in a cage with pythons whose only interest is filling their bellies. You're naive, and you're stumbling around in the dark, and they're going to swallow you head first.*

Fitzsimmons looked down at the untouched meal. The image blurred slightly as his anger surged and boiled. It wasn't a conscious action, and he was surprised when it happened. It was as if the back of someone else's hand had flung the plate from the table with such force that the plate sailed twenty feet to crash and shatter against a wall.

Fitzsimmons ignored the suddenly hushed restaurant, as well as the waiters hovering nervously near his table. He almost casually finished his beer, smiling ruefully. He said in a low whisper, "Spenser McCall, if you believe they're going to approve your project, you believe that lightening curdles milk. Old friend, the bastards will bury you before you're cold."

CHAPTER 7

March 22, 1967
Georgetown, Washington, D.C.
2:05 a.m.

Oliver Crawford was alone at the desk in his study. Julie had gone up to bed several hours earlier.

He held the squat crystal tumbler toward the desk lamp, seemingly mesmerized by the flash and hue of the amber liquid it contained. He'd lost track of how many times he'd refilled the glass during the long night.

Crawford placed the tumbler on a coaster, then fumbled for the key to the lower desk drawer. He opened it. There, on top, was a well-worn Army Colt Model 1911A1 .45-caliber pistol. The customized pistol had been his father's. The gold-filled etchings still gleamed. "U.S. Army" was etched in gold on one side of the slide; "O.W. Crawford" on the other side. The weapon had been a gift from his father. He hefted it for a moment, then put it on the desk near the lamp.

He reached into the drawer and withdrew a leather-bound presentation case. Carefully, he placed the case on the desk under the lamp. Long minutes passed before Crawford, with the exaggerated care and deliberateness of someone who's had too much to drink, slowly lifted the case's hinged cover.

The cool brightness of the fluorescent light washed over the five-pointed star with a profile of Minerva at the center, surrounded by a green enabled laurel wreath. The army eagle rested on a horizontal bar reading "Valor." Attached to the medal was a blue silk ribbon, spangled with thirteen stars. The ribbon was folded neatly under the medal. God, he thought, it is magnificent. July 16, 1945. It seemed like only yesterday when he was standing at attention in the East Room, and President Harry Truman smiled and shook his hand, the flood lights reflecting from his metal-framed glasses, at times masking his eyes. Crawford clearly remembered the colonel, who read the citation, saying the words *...above and beyond the call of duty.* Then the President stepped forward to place the ribbon around Crawford's neck. Crawford's mother was standing behind him. At her side was the major general.

...above and beyond the call of duty... He squeezed his eyes closed as the words echoed and pulsed in his fogged mind.

Crawford carefully placed the battered Zippo lighter next to the case. There, under the single gold star of his general's rank: *Duty Honor Country*

Slowly, as if he were reluctant to read what was inscribed on the obverse side, Crawford turned the lighter over. Under the medallion of the regimental insignia were the words: *517th Parachute Infantry Regiment George Company*

He rested his head against the high-back chair and closed his eyes. Of all the sounds of war, there was one he knew he would take to his grave. It wasn't just the crack of the big guns or even the screams of men. The sound was almost benign, similar to the sharp rap of a knuckle against a ripe melon. Crawford's mind began to slide toward the memory, and he struggled against it as fiercely as a man resisting a shove from the roof of a skyscraper.

"You hear that, lieutenant?" The man lay prone in the snow behind the air-cooled thirty caliber machine gun, the barrel poking between logs blocking the road. Crawford was squatting behind the two-man gun crew, looking out toward the bend in the narrow road flanked by snow-laden pines. Crawford clearly heard the guttural sound of a Tiger tank's diesel engine.

"Get set everyone," he called to the rest of the squad, his voice clear and strong in the cold, crisp air, "they're coming." Crawford could hear the rattle of rifle and machine gun bolts as they were cocked and released, stripping rounds from magazines and belts and chambering them home. There was a low muttering as the men hunkered down behind the logs, the snow crunching as they squirmed into position to set up their fields of fire.

Finally, there was only the sound of the growling tank engine, gradually growing louder. Crawford took six grenades from a canvas pouch and laid them on the snow near the log. He looked once more to see how his men were positioned. A few feet into the woods on the right he could just see the two-man bazooka team. The men behind the logs would have to deal with the infantry, but the bazooka was his only hope to stop the tanks.

The man whose job it was to feed ammunition belts into the machine gun rose slightly in front of Crawford, only a few inches above the top log, apparently to get a better view of the road. Crawford heard the thump and saw the man's head snap back. Curiously, he had already crumpled into the snow when Crawford heard the crack of the killing shot. Crawford looked down at the man. There was very little blood from the neat, purple-ringed hole in his forehead.

"Snipers!" Crawford called to his men. "Keep your heads down!"

The Tiger tank came quickly around the bend, then skidded to a halt when the crew saw the roadblock. Crawford could see the long eighty-eight millimeter tube as it traversed in small increments left and right, up and down, like a predator sniffing out its prey.

"*Now*, dammit!" Crawford shouted at the bazooka team in the woods. "Fire *now!*"

Crawford saw the rocket emerge from the trees, pulling a tail of fire and smoke. The missile bounced off the road at least 10 feet in front of the tank and flew into the woods beyond. Crawford heard the dull explosion when the rocket struck a tree.

"Oh, shit!" Crawford grabbed a grenade in each hand and he rose to a crouch. "Open up!" Crawford screamed as he heaved the grenades. "Goddammit, open up on 'em!"

Crawford just had time to throw two more grenades when he saw flame and white smoke blossom from the tank's big gun.

When Oliver Crawford's eyes opened the next morning, he realized that he'd fallen asleep in the study, still at his desk, his head resting on his folded arms. He raised his head, rubbing his eyes with his knuckles. When his vision cleared, he saw the open padded case that held his father's Colt. Crawford picked up the weapon. He pressed the button on the left side of the grip that released the magazine, looked at the gleaming copper-jacketed bullets, then locked the magazine back into the grip. He remembered the day his father had given him the pistol, the day he had graduated from West Point. "The Crawford name is engraved on this weapon," the general said. "Your duty, your obligation, is to carry this weapon, and the Crawford name, with dignity and honor."

Then Crawford looked at the presentation case. He traced the medal with his forefinger, lightly, as if it were too fragile to touch. Dignity and honor, the general had said. Crawford could feel the fear and frustration surge up from his gut until it throbbed like a jackhammer in his ears. He snapped the lid closed and shoved the case into the desk drawer.

March 23, 1967
640 North Michigan Avenue
Chicago
8:20 p.m.

McCall was shaving when he heard the phone ring. Tony was in the living room watching the televised highlights of the weekend game between the Bears and Vikings. McCall and Tony had just returned from the hospital and were dressing for dinner.

A moment later, Tony called, "It's Jim Austin, Spense. He's calling from Washington; says it's important."

McCall quickly toweled his face and came into the living room and took the phone.

"What are you doing in Washington, Jim?"

"I had a call from Johnny Parker, and he asked me to come down here. He's found something." "About Cordell?"

"It's about the lieutenant that Cordell referred to in that report. Johnny seems convinced that Oliver Crawford was the lieutenant in charge of the roadblock."

"The same roadblock that Cordell Jackson was on?" McCall realized how stupid the question sounded after he'd asked it. He saw Tony get up from the couch and walk toward him.

"Well, sir," Austin said, "that's what strange. There is absolutely no mention of Cordell Jackson, at least not in anything he's read so far. It's like the man didn't exist."

"Well, then, why the hell does Parker think it's the same roadblock and the same lieutenant?"

"Because, sir, there was another survivor. A witness."

"Who, dammit?"

"Bobby. We found Bobby. His full name is Bobby Jerome Geary. It all fits, sir. His name really is Bobby, not Robert -- that's what threw Johnny for a while. Everything checks. He was seventeen at the time. He's from Waycross, Georgia. And he was wounded at the roadblock. The clincher is that Bobby was interviewed as part of the review when Crawford was recommended for the MOH...the Medal of Honor. Johnny found the interview."

"What did Geary say?"

"Geary must have been in bad shape. It's hard to believe, but the only way he could respond to questions was by blinking his eyes -- one blink for no and two blinks for yes. He apparently was able to confirm that Crawford was in charge of the unit. He also confirmed for the review committee what Cordell said in those interviews -- that the lieutenant told them they had to hold the road or die trying."

McCall was hesitant, uncertain of what to do next. "Hang on a minute, Jim." He covered the mouthpiece of the phone with his hand and stared at the television set. "Son-of-a-*bitch!*"

"What's wrong, Spenser? What is it?"

McCall started to say something to Tony, then shook his head.

"Jim, what do you think the odds are that Geary's still alive and that we can find him?"

"Oh, the odds are excellent, sir. I've already found him."

"*What!*"

"Yes, sir. He's still in Waycross. He's receiving full disability payments for his wounds. He's in a nursing home. I've got the address."

"Jim, how can you be so certain it's the same man?"

"I called the nursing home to confirm, sir." Austin hesitated a moment. "Thing is, Mr. McCall, they said he's in a very bad way. Darned near a vegetable, I guess. He's gotten worse in the last few years. He's never been able to talk since the war. I guess he was hit pretty bad. Both legs are gone. He's still got some steel in his throat they can't get. Too close to the spine, I guess."

"Jim, did Johnny find any other survivors?"

"Yes, sir. There is testimony from one other man, a Herbert Wilcox, a corporal, who died a few weeks after the fighting. He was a machine gunner and said Crawford was directing the fire of his gun crew and was throwing hand grenades. He testified that he didn't remember anything after his gun position was hit by an eighty-eight."

"You said Wilcox is dead?"

"Affirmative, sir. Johnny checked it out. Wilcox died of his wounds in England during early January of forty-five. One other thing, Mr. McCall: Johnny found Cordell's personnel file. There are the usual I-was-there honors, but none for bravery. Johnny is still looking for any recommendations for honors that might have been written but never processed."

McCall was silent a long moment. "Okay, Jim, give me a number where I can reach you within the next half-hour." McCall wrote the number on a note pad. "I'll get back to you."

McCall hung up, but stood for a moment with his hand on the receiver. He saw that Tony was losing his patience. McCall took a deep breath, then slowly exhaled. "We have, my friend, uncovered what may be an incredibly complicated problem. Sit down. I'll be right back."

McCall went into the bedroom and retrieved the news magazine from his brief case. He opened the magazine to the article about Crawford and handed it to Tony.

"That man, Oliver Crawford, the new Secretary of the Army," McCall said. "He was awarded the Medal of Honor as a second lieutenant. And there is a strong possibility that he got the medal for the fighting at the same roadblock your father described during those interviews with that hospital psychiatrist."

Tony cocked his head, an expression of doubt on his face. "How can it be the same roadblock?"

"Austin and his friend are reasonably certain it is. Remember your dad talking about that young soldier, Bobby? Well, he survived. Austin found him. He's in a nursing home in Waycross, Georgia. Austin is certain it's the same man."

Tony looked confused. "But how does finding Bobby prove that this Crawford was at the same roadblock?"

"Because Bobby was interviewed as part of the revue process that resulted in Crawford getting his medal."

Tony shook his head in confusion. "What are you saying, Spense, that this Crawford got the medal for what my father did?"

McCall didn't answer immediately. Then he said softly, "Perhaps. But we have to consider at least two other possibilities. Your father also may have been recommended for a medal but the paperwork was lost. Or, he may not be remembering the facts exactly as they occurred. Maybe he didn't see everything that was happening. I've never been in combat, but I know that under that kind of stress, a man's mind--"

"Listen, damn it, we both read what my father said about that fighting. I know my father. He wouldn't have made that up. It sounds to me like Crawford stole my father's medal."

"Cool down." McCall tried to keep his voice low and measured. "We don't know that for certain, yet. We've got to move very carefully here, until we are certain."

"Bullshit, Spense. It'd be a helluva embarrassment to Lyndon Johnson if Crawford -- *his* Secretary of the Army -- lied to get the Medal of Honor."

"Take that damn chip off your shoulder for just one minute and listen to me, Tony." McCall's voice was hard. "I'm not trying to cover for anybody. I would hope to hell you know me better than that."

"What I know," Tony said, "is that you were willing to help my father when it was convenient for you. But now you've got to go up against *The Man* who's going to make you an ambassador, or some damn thing. I've read the stories."

"Tony, I believe your father believes what he said--"

"What the hell does *that* mean?"

McCall sat down in a chair opposite Tony's, then shook his head in frustration. "I don't understand, Tony, how someone with your training and skill, someone who must carefully weigh every facet of the evidence, someone who is bound by the tradition of the law, can be so convinced of Crawford's guilt before all of the facts are available to us."

More subdued, Tony said, "The evidence sure as hell seems clear enough to me."

"All I ask is that you consider this possibility. What if Crawford earned the medal legitimately? What if it's really his? It'd be a terrible mistake to make these accusations without any evidence." McCall took a deep breath and exhaled slowly. "That's what bothers me. What if we're wrong about all this?"

"Ah, Spense, dammit. What bothers me is thinking how the medal might have changed my father's life," Tony said, his anger now replaced by a deepening bitterness. "Maybe he wouldn't have had to push that damn shine cart around all these years. Maybe he and my mother would have had an easier life. If my dad went through all that pain... and someone screwed him out of the medal he deserved...I just..."

He leaned his head against the back of the couch, looking up at the ceiling, struggling to control his emotions.

McCall rose from his chair and walked slowly to the large window that looked out over North Michigan Avenue. The weather had turned mild and the streets were jammed with vehicles and pedestrians. Another consideration crossed McCall's mind. What if this business with the Secretary of the Army, and Cordell, and the medal all got very messy. There was bound to be a lot of publicity. Eventually, he'd have to face LBJ. How would his board of directors react, even if he did back off on the New Mexico project? *Well,* he sighed, *I guess I'll have to worry about that if and when it becomes a problem.*

McCall looked at his watch, then stepped to the phone and dialed the number on the pad.

"Jim Austin? This is McCall. Be at National Airport at midnight your time. I'll pick you up at the general aviation terminal. We're going to Waycross. Tony will be with me, so find a place for us to stay at least one night in Waycross. And arrange for a car. Two other points, Jim: find out what you can about the review procedures required to recommend someone for the Medal of Honor -- involving an incident that occurred more than twenty years ago."

"Got it, Mr. McCall. Warrant Officer Parker can help with that."

When he ended the call, McCall dialed the number for the Horizon Corporation hanger at Midway Airport. "This is McCall. I'll be there in an hour. We're going to Waycross, Georgia, via Washington's National Airport. I'll have one guest and we'll pick up another in Washington. We'll have dinner on the Washington-to-Waycross leg."

The last call McCall made was to his chauffeur. Then he went into the kitchen, poured two cups of coffee, and brought them into the living room. He handed one cup to Tony.

After he sipped his coffee, McCall placed the cup and saucer on the low table and looked at Tony. "We've got a half-hour to pack," he said.

Tony feigned interest in the football game, reluctant to look at McCall. Finally, Tony placed his cup on the table.

"Spense," he said softly, "thanks, man."

McCall smiled. "No big deal, Tony. I sometimes even make coffee for my chauffeur -- and, hell, he's white."

CHAPTER 8

March 27, 1967
Waycross, Georgia
9:45 a.m.

"Jeezus," Austin said as he pulled into the driveway. The nursing home was a squat, flat-roofed, cinder-block building, which perhaps forty years earlier had been covered with stucco painted a dark brown. Most of the stucco was gone; the remaining patches looked like scabs on the cinder block. The grounds around the building were overgrown. The home was five miles outside the city limits of Waycross, on a single-lane road in a grove of scraggly pines.

"It looks abandoned," Austin said.

"If it isn't, it sure as hell should be," Tony said.

Austin turned off the ignition. "Maybe you'd better wait here, Mr. McCall. I'll make sure this is the place."

Austin was gone several minutes. Then he appeared in the doorway and nodded. McCall and Tony walked slowly from the car to the building, examining the building and grounds.

A man who appeared to be in his seventies greeted them at the door. He was at least a head shorter than the three men with whom he shook hands. He wore sneakers, rumpled and baggy slacks, and a bright green sweater riddled with holes that were stretched wider by his huge pot belly. It was also evident he didn't have many teeth. He looked at McCall's suit. "You a state doctor?"

"No, my name is Spenser McCall. This is Mr. Jackson and Mr. Austin. We're here to visit Bobby Geary. May I ask your name, sir?"

"I'm John Mobley. I'm in charge here. You said Geary?"

"Yes, Bobby Jerome Geary. Does he live here?"

The old man cackled. "I suppose you could call it that. Why do you want to see him?"

"Is it really necessary for you to know that?" McCall asked.

"I'm in charge here. Nobody ever comes to visit him, not for a long time. If he's got any kin, they forgot about him a long time ago."

"Mr. Mobley, we'd just like to talk to him," McCall said.

The old man hesitated, closely examining each of the three men standing before him. "You boys ain't from the state, are you?"

"No, Mr. Mobley, we're not," McCall said, struggling to control his patience. "May we please see Geary's room now."

"All right; all right. No sense gettin' riled. You can talk to him if you want, but he ain't gonna do no talking back. Follow me, gents." The old man led the three men down a dingy hallway, cackling again as he repeated, "Nope, he ain't' gonna do no talkin' back."

The sour stench of urine and excrement was almost overwhelming. The smells seemed to roll into the hall from the rooms on either side. McCall made a conscious effort not to look into any of the rooms he passed.

The caretaker paused at a corner room at the end of the hall. It appeared that the door to the room had long since been removed. McCall could see a man lying in an ancient hospital bed. He was covered by a thin, gray-white sheet that from the short stubs of his thighs, was flat against the mattress. The room measured no more than ten by fifteen feet. Except for the bed and a small night stand, the room was barren. McCall guessed the walls had originally been painted pink, but over the years had faded to a grimy gray. The dark green floor tile was cracked and pealing.

"Well, here's Geary," the caretaker smiled, showing his gray gums. "Go ahead and start to talkin'."

McCall turned to Mobley. "Would you please ask your staff doctor to come to this room?"

"Why sure; be happy to. You can take your pick because we got us a staff of specialists who can fix any ailment known to man." Mobley wasn't smiling. "Look, Mister-Important-Man, all I got is two part-time nurses and three Nigra boys to help handle seventeen patients. The doctors from Waycross take turns coming here once a week, and the one who drawed the short straw was already here this week." The old man turned and said over his shoulder, "If you want something I'll be in my office up front."

McCall looked at Tony and Austin, then stepped uncertainly to the bed. Geary's eyes were closed. McCall looked closely at the man. His skin was so pale it was almost transparent. His full head of hair was long and tangled and as white as his skin. His left ear was gone and that side of his face was very badly scarred.

When McCall looked at Geary's throat, he could not imagine how the man had survived for so many years. Nearly all of the neck muscles and tendons were gone. The neck, as thin as a child's, wouldn't support his head. The knotted mass of scar tissue at his throat pulled the skin of Geary's face tightly against his skull. A padded brace supported Geary's head.

The silver metal of the tracheostomy tube, stained with secretions, protruded from the center of the purple scar tissue. McCall could hear a slight gurgling through the tube as Geary breathed. A lunch tray lay on the nightstand. The half-finished meal looked like baby food. McCall thought that, since the war, baby food was all Geary had been able to eat.

Slowly, Geary opened his eyes. They were astonishingly bright blue. They were the clear, alert eyes of a much younger man. McCall thought back to the seventeen-year-old boy Cordell had described, the boy who wanted to run, but who had put his faith in Cordell and the relief column that never came.

"Mr. McCall?"

McCall was startled by Austin's voice.

"What, Jim?"

"Remember what they said about his blinking once for no and twice for yes."

"Yeah, I remember."

McCall looked back down at Geary. "Hello, Mr. Geary. I'm Spenser McCall." Spenser thought his voice sounded strange, unnatural. He didn't know how or if Geary would respond to a question. "You are Bobby Jerome Geary?"

The blue eyes stared at McCall for a long moment. Then, very deliberately, they blinked twice.

"Can you speak at all, Mr. Geary?"

The blue eyes immediately blinked once.

McCall looked up at Tony and Austin.

"Mr. Geary, if I asked you to, could you do any writing?"

The eyes stared at McCall for a very long moment. Then, hesitantly, they blinked twice.

McCall looked at the other two men standing several steps back from the bed. He took a deep breath and began.

"I'm here, Mr. Geary, because a friend of ours needs your help. You and he were in the war together. Will you help us?"

McCall noticed that the expression of Geary's face never changed. It was as if the face were made of wax. Only the eyelids seemed to move. They blinked twice.

"Were you with the Five Seventeenth Parachute Regiment, George Company, during the Battle of the Bulge?"

The eyes closed for what seemed like minutes. McCall thought Geary had fallen asleep. When the eyes opened, they were staring past McCall at the ceiling. Geary quickly blinked twice.

"Mr. Geary, this next question is very important to us. Do you remember being at the roadblock near Hotton in Belgium? It was in December of nineteen forty-four. Do you remember being with a Corporal Cordell Jackson on that day?"

Geary's eyes closed for a long moment. When they opened, Geary stared at McCall. Then he tried to roll his eyes to the side to see Austin and Tony.

McCall gestured impatiently to Tony. "Step up closer to the bed. C'mon, dammit, get closer."

Tony leaned over the bed slightly so Geary could see him better.

When the blue eyes focused on Tony, Geary's skin flushed pink. McCall could feel Geary's breath as it rasped in short bursts through the metal tube.

Geary's hand lifted from the bed sheet and fluttered until the long thin fingers could grasp Tony's jacket sleeve. The waxen face seemed to melt as the blue eyes brimmed with tears. Geary's mouth opened and closed, as if he desperately tried to speak. Still grasping tightly to Tony's sleeve, Geary's eyes shifted to McCall. All three men clearly could see Geary's lips, with agonizing deliberateness, silently form the words, "Corporal Jackson."

McCall had difficulty swallowing. The room suddenly became too warm. He reached and gently patted Geary's shoulder. "Mr. Geary, we...ah, we have to leave for a few minutes. We want you to rest. But I promise you that we'll be right back."

McCall and Austin started for the door when they noticed that Geary's hand was still locked on Tony's sleeve. Tony looked helpless, almost frightened.

McCall gently placed his hand on Geary's. "Bobby, I promise you that we'll be back in just a few minutes. We're not going to leave here without talking to you again." McCall could feel Geary reluctantly relax his grip. McCall held Geary's hand for a moment, then gently placed it on the bed sheet.

McCall stepped to the door of the caretaker's office. "We're going outside for a few minutes. We'll be back." The old man nodded.

"Tony, you still have those cigarettes?" McCall asked when they were standing on the driveway.

"Mr. McCall, may I have one?" Austin asked.

"I'm sorry, Jim," McCall said as he handed Austin the pack, "I didn't know you smoked."

"I don't, sir."

Tony nervously walked a few paces then stopped. "I don't understand it...I honest to God don't. How could they permit a human being to live like that for so many years? For all practical purposes, he died on that goddamn road twenty-two years ago."

Tony flung the cigarette he had just lighted to the crumbling blacktop. "Can you believe it, Spense? That man thought I was Corporal Jackson! He thought I was my father. The poor guy's living in a time warp."

Tony moved to the car, resting his arms on its roof. "It's really incredible, you know? My dad buries that day in his gut for all those years, and it takes a punk with a gun to jar it all loose. But that poor bastard in there must think the Battle of the Bulge was yesterday."

McCall placed his hand on Tony's shoulder. "C'mon, we've got a lot of work to do." McCall turned to Austin. "We should have a doctor present before we talk to Geary any more. Jim, find the best doctor in Waycross. Tell him we'll double his fee for the day. Try to get him down here as fast as you can." McCall reached for his wallet and withdrew five one-hundred dollar bills. "Then find a notary public and a court reporter. Try the county courthouse, city hall, a license bureau -- any place you can think of. Pay them what they ask. We'll wait here for you."

When Austin drove off, Tony said, "You know, I've been wondering what my father's reaction will be when he finds out that Bobby is alive?"

"We'll make sure we have the right medical people tell us how to handle that. I guess we should also consider the possibility that the doctor may say it might be best if your dad never learns about Bobby."

Tony nodded, then gestured toward the nursing home. "Suppose that cranky old duffer in there will give us a cup of coffee?"

"If he did, would you really want to drink it?"

Tony laughed. "No, I guess not. Let's see if he's got a Coke machine."

McCall could tell that the caretaker sensed that something important was happening in his nursing home, and his attitude improved considerably. He had Tony and McCall sit in the tattered waiting room while he fetched the cold drinks.

"Mr. Mobley," McCall said, "we're going to have several more visitors to see Mr. Geary. Do you suppose one of your people can put some chairs and a small table in that room?"

"Gosh almighty that man's gotten pop'lar all of a sudden." Mobley started to walk to his office, then stopped. "If you ain't a doctor, then you gotta be a lawyer. Yep, you even look like a lawyer. Has Geary come into a bunch a money?"

McCall smiled and gestured toward Tony. "Mr. Jackson here is the lawyer. He works for the United States Justice Department. He's a government prosecutor. Last year he put more racketeers behind bars than any other U.S. Attorney."

"Well, ain't that somethin'." Mobley, obviously awed, tilted his head, eyeing Tony curiously. "A U-u-nited States prosecutor. Ain't that somethin'. I ain't ever met a Nigra government prosecutor before."

The old man snorted and hawked up phlegm that he spit into a filthy handkerchief. "Well, I can tell you that you ain't gonna prosecute Geary for nothin' because he ain't left that bed for twenty years." Mobley paused, his pale, rheumy eyes narrowing as he looked at Tony. "And if you got somethin' on me, mister prosecutor, I'm saying that I'm doin' the best I can with what they give me." Mobley eyed Tony for a moment more. "I reckon I'll get those chairs myself."

When the caretaker was gone, Tony asked, "What are we going to do with whatever statements Geary gives us?"

"I don't know, yet. As I see it, the first thing we need is to clearly establish that your dad was on that road. We're going to have to depend on Jim Austin's friend, Johnny Parker, to guide us."

Tony added, "And we have to substantiate dad's version of what occurred on that road."

"Right. We also have to prove that Oliver Crawford, Bobby Geary, and your dad were on the same roadblock that day. If we can do all of that, counselor, I think we have a case."

"And what's our case going to prove?"

"Oh, that's easy. We simply have to prove that Secretary of the Army Oliver Wentworth Crawford II -- a former Brigadier General of the U.S. Army and son of the renowned Major General Oliver "Iron Ollie" Wentworth Crawford -- did wrongfully and fraudulently accept a Medal of Honor. And that the aforementioned Medal of Honor rightfully belongs to -- in your words -- the poor old black bastard who shines my shoes for a living."

Tony laughed softly. "There are folks in Washington who will go ballistic."

McCall rose from his chair and walked to the window overlooking the scraggly front yard. He clasped his hands behind his back. "Tony, what we're going to do today may not mean a damn thing to the army -- certainly they won't consider it as conclusive evidence. I'm positive they'll want to do their own investigation. As they properly should."

He turned to face Tony. "But we'll never get anybody's attention until we develop our own evidence. That's why we need everything documented, witnessed, and notarized. I think that's the only way we'll get the right people to listen to us."

"I agree. We should view this as the taking of a legal deposition."

"Okay, you're the lawyer. Let's develop the questions and you interview Geary."

McCall returned to his seat. "One other thing needs to be said. I'm sure you understand that when it hits the fan, it's possible that your career in the Justice Department may be a wash."

"Spense, I'd be lying if I said I hadn't thought of that, especially after how the Arnold thing was botched. But after hearing what my dad went through, and seeing Bobby Geary in that crummy room...well, I guess we'll just see where the chips fall."

They both walked to the window when they heard Austin drive up. McCall checked his watch. Austin had been gone only forty-five minutes. He was accompanied by a distinguished-looking elderly man and a young woman.

Austin ushered the couple into the sitting room. "Mr. McCall, the doctor promised he'd be here within the hour." Austin gestured toward the visitors. "I'd like to introduce Judge Claude Singletary, and this is Melinda Singletary. Judge Singletary is the county judge and a notary. Miss Singletary is a court reporter."

The judge acknowledged the three men, then asked McCall if they could speak privately. When they were away from the others, Singletary said, "Your man offered to pay for our services. He gave me a rough idea of why you need our help. I served as a Naval officer during World War Two and Korea. Melinda is my granddaughter. Her father -- my son -- has been a prisoner in Vietnam for almost three years. We've discussed it and neither she nor I will accept payment to hear Mr. Geary's testimony. We will help you however we can."

McCall nodded. "Thank you, Judge Singletary. Thank you very much."

When they were all seated in the waiting area, McCall related to the judge and Melinda what he wanted to accomplish. He explained what he knew about the events at the roadblock and the role Tony's father had played. McCall made no mention of Oliver Crawford.

"Our intention is to develop enough evidence that the army will consider awarding a citation, perhaps the Medal of Honor, to Cordell Jackson. Mr. Geary witnessed and participated to that action. We feel he also should receive some honor."

The judge slowly shook his head. "Mr. McCall, you must realize how difficult this all will be. So many years have passed. You realize that there must be at least two witnesses to substantiate what Mr. Jackson did that day."

Tony looked at McCall. "I didn't know we need two witnesses."

"Yes," McCall said, "two are required. Jim Austin, here, will explain some other requirements in a moment. But we may have another witness. However, we don't know at this time whether his testimony will be available to us."

Tony, looking quizzically at McCall, started to say something just as McCall turned to Austin.

"Jim is a retired army lieutenant colonel and has researched the requirements for the Medal of Honor. Jim?"

"Well, Mr. Singletary," Austin said, "a petition for the medal must be submitted within two years. Beyond that period, the petition must be directed to the President of the United States. With his endorsement, the petition then goes to Congress. Congress must approve a special statute that authorizes -- in this case the U.S. Army -- to investigate the matter. That, very briefly, is the process we are beginning today."

Melinda Singletary said what some people in the room may have been thinking. "My gosh, that all could take years."

Austin nodded agreement. "Yes, ma'am, it often does."

McCall could see the disappointment infect the group. "Ladies and gentlemen, I can assure you that this process isn't going to take years. Now, I'd suggest that we go into Mr. Geary's room and begin."

"Just a minute, Spense," Tony said. He looked at Melinda and the judge. "Before we go in there, I think they should be told about Geary's physical condition."

When McCall had explained the extent of Geary's injuries, the judge pursed his lips in disappointment. "Considering what you've just said about his condition, I don't see how eye blinks are going to communicate the testimony you need, certainly not with any depth."

The room was quiet for a long moment. Then Melinda asked, "Can he move his hands at all?"

"Yes, but with some difficulty," Tony answered. "We're not sure he'll be able to write."

"Then can I suggest," the young woman continued, "that we use a device, a kind of typewriter that has a special keyboard designed for the handicapped. From what you tell me, I'm sure he can use it." She paused a moment. "But it will be a very slow process. I'd also suggest that we film the interview."

McCall asked, "Do you know where we can get this equipment and can you operate it?"

"Yes, sir. I think I can get it this afternoon. But we'll need someone who can operate the camera equipment."

"Jim, why don't you and Miss Singletary get the equipment and hire the people you need. If you can't rent it, buy it."

When Melinda and Austin had gone, Tony said, "You know, this project could be a lot easier on everyone if we could take Geary some place...any place else."

"Yes, it would," McCall said. "But when that young woman suggested that we film this, it occurred to me that there is a certain person I'd like to see the film. I want him to see that room and this place, and I want him to see Bobby Geary. We've got to do it here. Maybe that will help us get all of the Bobby Gearys out of holes like this."

"Well, it looks like we're going to be a while," Tony said. "I'm going back to see Bobby. We told him we'd be gone only a few minutes."

The doctor's car pulled into the driveway as Tony braced himself for the walk down the hallway.

CHAPTER 9

April 4, 1967
The Times Tower
Chicago
9:10 a.m.

"Tony, the phone call from Spenser was a tad mysterious," Eleanor said. "What's this meeting all about?" She and Tony were seated in her office on two small couches arranged on either side of a low table.

"Well, it involves my dad and a man named Bobby Jerome Geary," Tony said. "Beyond that, I shouldn't say anything until Spense gets here."

Eleanor laughed. "Oh, you've really shed a lot of light on this thing." She reached to the coffee table for a manila folder, opened it, and handed Tony four sheets of paper. "While we're waiting, you may find this interesting."

Tony started to read, looked up at Eleanor, then continued reading. "How in the world did you manage to get this information?" Tony asked when he closed the folder.

"We have a man who's exceptionally good at that sort of thing. We don't plan to run anything just yet. But I want to keep you advised of anything we might uncover."

"I have to ask, Ellie; who wrote this?"

"You know him – our police reporter, Gus Petockis."

"Yeah, I know Gus. I wish he worked for me. Is this the latest information you got from him?"

"Yes. You can see that he filed that just before one o'clock this morning."

"You understand, Ellie, that I've got to let the bureau know about this right away."

"Of course, that's why I gave you the information." Eleanor smiled. "Besides, Petockis has a lead of several hours."

"May I use your phone?"

"Of course."

Tony called the FBI's Chicago office, gave them the information, and suggested that it be relayed to the bureau's Indianapolis office.

When he completed the call, Tony walked slowly back to the couch, his hands thrust deeply into his pockets. "You know, I can't get that girl out of mind. I hope to God they find her and that she's okay."

Tony folded the four sheets of paper and put them into his inside jacket pocket. "Ellie, thanks. That information really helps."

"You can thank Spenser. He asked us to help. I'll continue to supply you with information that we think will lead to Arnold's arrest," Eleanor said. "We don't want to impede the government's investigation in any way." Eleanor leaned forward to emphasize her words. "But, Tony, I'm sure you understand that we will decide what information will be made available to you -- as well as what will be published."

Tony nodded.

While they waited for McCall, Tony examined Eleanor's office and was surprised that it was much more opulent than McCall's. Earth tones, accented by controlled splashes of bright color, dominated the carpeting and furniture. Rich, block paneling covered the longest wall. Expensive and unique crystal and porcelain pieces were displayed about the office with a studied nonchalance. Tony noticed something was missing.

"Ellie, you don't have a desk in here."

"That's where I work," she said, gesturing toward a waist-high table. "I take all of my phone calls while standing. I've found that conversations are shorter, more efficient."

Tony saw that two phones, a leather folder, a miniature pendulum clock, and a pink marble pen holder were the only objects on the table.

"Ellie," Tony said as he looked around the room, "I've got to say that this office is something else."

"Yes, it is very nice, and it drives Spenser crazy. He says it's the kind of office an oil baron should have. But believe it or not, it does serve a purpose, other than for my personal comfort. I do occasionally meet here with some of our major advertisers."

Tony raised his eyebrows. "I would think this would be a turn-off for them."

Eleanor laughed. "Oh, they always grouse about the ad rates. But they're business people and they like to see success."

"I guess I've never thought of the newspaper business as a business -- and I didn't know it could be this good."

"We're been fortunate and, yes, we work smart. Few newspapers do as well as this one." Eleanor smiled. "That's why this office turns the other publishers in this city green with envy."

At that moment McCall came into the room. He leaned over and kissed Eleanor on the cheek.

"Ellie," McCall began, "I really don't know how far this conversation will go. I've never asked you to do this before, but the only way we can discuss it is off the record."

"Spense...I don't know how...I don't know *if* I can agree to that." The room was uncomfortably quiet, and it occurred to McCall that he and Eleanor rarely encountered a situation where the needs and demands of their professions clashed – at least openly.

"Ellie, you know I wouldn't ask unless it was damned important. But I can say this: if there is a story, it will be a very important one, and The *Times* can break it."

"Who decides if there's a story?" she asked.

"Only Tony and I can make that decision."

Eleanor didn't respond for a long moment. Her fingers played lightly over her necklace, the pearls rippling a pinkish-white as they twisted in the light.

"I'm sorry, McCall. That's unacceptable."

Why? Hell, you don't even know what we've got."

"I don't have to know what the story is about." Eleanor's face, McCall noticed, was slightly flushed. "But I know it's big because you're playing this damn silly game."

"Ellie, it's not a silly game. We just--"

"And one other thing." Eleanor's anger was evident now. "I don't like the idea that you think you can tempt me with the promise of an exclusive. Someone tries that almost every day. If there is a story, McCall, The *Times* will get it. I can assure you of that."

"Ellie, damn it, you're being stubborn as hell about this." Spenser's voice was rising.

"Look, Spenser, I made the decision a long time ago that nothing is ever off the record. I've been burned too many times. Now, if that's a problem, I'm sorry. I suggest that you don't tell me anything until the story breaks. That way nobody's nose gets bumped."

McCall sighed. "Damn it, that's no good because we're going to need your help with this thing. We're going to need a helluva lot of help."

The room lapsed into silence. McCall was uncomfortable about arguing with Eleanor with Tony in the room.

"Ah...maybe I can suggest a way to get around this," Tony said, as he sat forward on the couch. "Having worked with the media quite a bit, I appreciate your concerns, Ellie. What we've got is something that can embarrass the hell out of the President and the army brass. The problem is that our case isn't strong enough yet. That's where you can help us, Ellie."

Tony paused as he chose his words carefully. "Now, here's what I suggest: we'll tell you everything we know, and show you what testimony we have -- no holds barred."

McCall did not like the expression on Eleanor's face. "Further, I agree that it's your decision to write the story -- or to hold it -- as you see fit. However, I'm confident you'll see that it's best if you don't go with the story until we nail down the key evidence we need. But that decision is, of course, yours to make."

Eleanor smiled. "Tony, I was wrong about congress. You're a natural for the State Department." She looked at McCall. "Spense?"

"Do you suppose can we get some damn coffee in here?"

"I'm waiting for a response, McCall," Ellie insisted.

"Okay, okay. I can live with what you and your *friend* there want."

Eleanor reached over and placed her hand on Spenser's. "Dearest, it's no wonder that people love you oil barons almost as much as they do used-car dealers." Eleanor rose from her chair. "Now, I'll get your coffee -- and I'll even serve it."

It took more than an hour for Tony and McCall to brief Eleanor. They showed a portion of the film of Geary's interview. After several minutes, Ellie asked that the projector be turned off.

"My God. That poor man."

McCall said, "It took us almost two days to interview him. Jim Austin had that film processed overnight. The doctor said Geary doesn't have a lot of time left. It seems that he's, well, just giving up."

"You're going to have to explain some things to me, guys. I don't understand all of the military stuff or the significance of some of your evidence."

"There were two key things that Bobby Geary gave us, Ellie," Tony said as he got up and began to pace the room. "First, he substantiated that my father was at the roadblock and that he took command of the unit."

Eleanor held up her hand to stop Tony. "And neither your dad nor Geary have seen each other all these years?"

"Right. In fact, they each thought the other had been killed. Bobby spent three years in a hospital. He's had a total of twenty-seven operations. My dad still doesn't know that Bobby's alive. The doctor will advise us whether to tell him."

"Well, what about this lieutenant -- ah, his name is Crawford? -- who was supposed to be in charge? Did he survive?"

"That's the second important piece of evidence that Bobby gave us," Tony said. He then gestured for McCall to pick up the conversation.

"When we read Cordell's version of what happened at that roadblock," McCall said, "he mentioned several times how afraid he and Bobby were. They held onto each other -- as much to give each other courage as warmth. They were waiting for a relief column that was supposed to come up from the town. Cordell said he noticed Bobby constantly looking over his shoulder, hoping to see the column."

"But the column never showed up?" Eleanor said.

"It did, eventually, but too late for most of the guys," McCall said. "But Bobby did see something else. After the first burst of tank fire, nearly half of the Americans were killed or wounded. Bobby told us that he kept looking back down the road, hoping to see American troops." McCall paused. "And that's when he saw the lieutenant run into the woods well behind their position."

"Does that mean he just ran away...that he abandoned his men?"

McCall looked at Tony. "Ellie, that's what we have to be damned sure of. For all we know he was going for help, or even trying to encircle the Germans. Hell, we just don't know."

"What did Cordell say about him?"

"Cordell hasn't said much about the lieutenant," McCall said. "Certainly he didn't say that he ran. But we haven't asked Cordell that question."

Eleanor shook her head in confusion. "Well, didn't you say that Geary was interviewed when this lieutenant was recommended for the Medal of Honor?"

"Yes, we asked Bobby about that," Tony said. "He vaguely remembers being interviewed. What he remembers best about it, though, is that the interviewer got very angry because Bobby couldn't talk. Bobby said he signed some papers, but remembers he had trouble focusing his eyes to read."

The conversation paused when more coffee was brought into the room.

When the secretary closed the door behind her, Eleanor said, "Okay, so what you're telling me is that if anyone got the Medal of Honor for what happened at this roadblock, it should have been Cordell. We have Cordell's version of the story from the interviews with that psychiatrist right after the war. And Cordell's version is substantiated by Bobby Geary. But instead of Cordell getting the medal, this Lieutenant Crawford got it, even though you suspect he abandoned his people. Is that right?"

Tony and Spenser nodded agreement.

"So in order for Cordell to get the medal, you've got to prove that this Crawford shouldn't have gotten it. Right?"

"There's a strong possibility that he lied to get it," Tony said. "We're also checking to see if dad was recommended for a citation which, for whatever reason, was never acted upon. Something else: one of Spenser's people -- Jim Austin -- got a copy of the citation describing the action for which Crawford was awarded the medal. The action described in that citation is nearly identical to what my father said to that army psychiatrist in 1946."

McCall held his hands up to halt the discussion. "Let's remember people, that we're talking *suspicion* here. So far we only have Geary's statement that Crawford ran into the woods. What we don't know is why he did that."

"Well, then. What do you know about Crawford? Do we know if he's alive? Did he receive the medal posthumously?"

McCall noticed early in the discussion that Eleanor didn't recognize Crawford. He realized that he should have told her who Crawford was at the very beginning, but he felt she was a little too smug about the off-the-record business. McCall smiled at Tony.

"Ellie," McCall began, "several days ago your paper ran a page-one story and photo about the appointment of a new Secretary of the Army. The man the President appointed to that position was Oliver Wentworth Crawford." McCall held up a clipping of the article.

Ellie reached for the clipping and read it quickly. "My God."

She looked at McCall, then smiled. "Spenser McCall, you bastard. You could hardly wait to hand me my own damned clipping."

McCall held up his hands. "Now Ellie, no one can expect even you to remember everything that appears in your paper."

Eleanor nodded slowly. Her eyes still on McCall, she said to Tony, "When you become a congressman, one of the first things we're going to do is geld all these damned oil barons."

"Ellie, I told you I'm not running for--"

"There's one more twist to this story, Ellie," McCall said. "I know Crawford. I've met him several times, and I even asked him to join our company when he retired from the army a couple of years ago. I first met him when he was fresh from the academy during the war. I was working for his father at the time.

"Shortly after the war," McCall continued, "I got a phone call from Crawford -- the son. His father died in about 1960. Crawford had met Cordell at the Hilton, where he was shining shoes in the men's room. Crawford asked that I find a job for Cordell. He said they'd served in the same unit -- Crawford's first combat command -- and that he remembered Cordell as a good soldier."

Eleanor nodded slowly. "Guilt?"

"Maybe," McCall said. "Probably. Looking back on it now, it just couldn't have been a coincidence."

Ellie looked at both men. "Okay, now you can explain what kind of help you want from me.

"We need you to go to Washington with us," McCall said.

"Why?"

"To talk to the President."

Tony turned to McCall. "*The* President?"

"Right."

"Why?" Tony asked.

"Because we may not have a lot of time; Bobby Geary may not have a lot of time. So, to get things moving we're going to start at the top. Jim Austin has made arrangements for us. We'll leave tonight and see the President in the morning."

"What actions can the President take," Eleanor asked.

"Two things," McCall said. "First, after so many years, only the President can ask congress for a special statute that authorizes an investigation into whether Cordell deserves the Medal of Honor. Second, we want the President to authorize an investigation into whether Crawford should have received his medal."

"You're not asking for a helluva lot, McCall," Eleanor said. "Has any of that ever been done before?"

"Yes, in the situation where people think they qualify for the medal. In fact, it's fairly common, even years after the war. But very few are ever approved," McCall said. "But I'm not aware of a precedent for an investigation into charges that someone fraudulently received the Medal of Honor."

Eleanor looked at both men. "And in this case we're alleging that the Secretary of Army didn't deserve to receive it. Whew, this is powerful stuff, guys."

"We're not ready to make that allegation yet, Ellie," McCall said.

Eleanor looked suspiciously at McCall. "And why should I go to Washington with you?"

"Because if the President knows that one of the nation's top newspapers has the story, we may get his undivided attention."

"In other words, McCall, the real reason we bumped noses today is that you just want to *use* me?"

Spenser smiled. "As a matter of fact, yes. What we need from you is your writing talent. And we'll need it tonight. When we get to the hotel, I want us to prepare a synopsis of the whole story. We've only got twenty minutes with the President. I suggest we be ready to leave in an hour."

"An *hour!*" Eleanor looked at her watch. "Damn you, Spenser McCall. It'll take me that long to get my makeup together."

April 6, 1967
Namur, Belgium
8:45 a.m.

Oliver Crawford hadn't seen southern Belgium since the war. It was cool and sunny, and he was surprised that the gently rolling countryside was so green. He'd always remembered Belgium as covered by a thick blanket of snow. The traffic was light as he drove southeast from the city of Namur toward Bastogne.

He'd convinced himself that he wanted to see the memorial to the Americans who had held the city while it was surrounded by Nazi tanks and troops during the Bulge fighting. It was a spur-of-the-moment decision.

Crawford had spent the previous three days in Brussels attending his first NATO conference. The night before he'd been the dinner guest of Gen. Clayton Monroe, who commanded U.S. NATO forces. They had reviewed the highlights of the meeting. Then, like most of the officers Crawford had met during his service career, Moore was interested in stories about "Iron Ollie" Crawford -- stories he had heard, and those that only the famous general's son could tell him.

General Moore had invited the Secretary of Army to join him in a round of golf this Sunday morning. Crawford had politely refused, saying he wanted to do some sight-seeing in Brussels and perhaps drive up to Antwerp, cities he had spent time in during the war. The general thoughtfully had provided a pool car.

It was during breakfast when Crawford had decided he'd rather drive to Bastogne. Now he felt a growing uneasiness. He could feel his pulse quicken as the miles passed and his hands gripping the steering wheel were damp. A half-hour or so after he passed through the city of Huffalize, he saw the sign. The town was ahead, perhaps ten kilometers, according to his map. He turned onto the single lane road.

He drove slowly through the small town of Saint-Vith. Crawford was surprised that traffic was so heavy. People apparently were going to church or to restaurants for breakfast. For some reason, he was surprised that they all were dressed so well. There wasn't anything in the town that Crawford could recognize. It had been too long. It had been nearly destroyed and rebuilt.

He paused on the south edge of town and pulled to the curb. Small neat brick homes lined the street. He couldn't remember which house it had been, but he remembered seeing it that morning when he was leading his squad to the roadblock. He always would remember the house.

A heavy artillery barrage had raked the area earlier the morning after the German breakthrough. Many of these homes had been destroyed or badly damaged and several were burning. Crawford remembered that he had been in his jeep, leading the convoy of two trucks when he saw the young boy, who couldn't have been more the seven or eight. The boy, bleeding from a deep gash on his forehead and his clothes covered with dust, was standing looking into the side of a house. An artillery round had peeled away one entire wall of the house, which otherwise didn't appear to be heavily damaged. Crawford told his driver to stop, and he walked up to the boy.

When Crawford followed the boy's eyes, he saw them. They were sitting around the kitchen table, apparently about to have breakfast. There was the middle-aged woman, a much older woman, a teen-aged girl, and the father. One chair was empty. It must have been the boy's. They were all covered with brick and plaster dust. The girl was strikingly attractive. Her blue eyes were open, but they were dulled by the plaster dust that coated her long blond hair. Like the others seated around her, she was sitting upright, her head slightly bowed. It appeared to Crawford that they were saddened by what had been placed on the table.

They were all dead, killed by the concussive blast of the shell that had sucked the life from their lungs. Crawford thought it strange that there was no blood. The bodies appeared to be unmarked, except for the father, who was seated with his back toward the missing wall. His head was gone. His upper torso was leaning far forward. The blood had overfilled the breakfast bowl that had been placed in front of him, and the blood, now gelled by the cold and dusted with plaster, had seeped across the white tablecloth. In the dim morning light, Crawford looked closer. In the center of the table was the father's head.

Could that house have been one of these? Crawford thought as he pulled away from the curb and drove slowly past the small, neat homes. Do the people now living in any of these homes know about the beautiful young girl and the man without a head? Whatever became of the little boy?

Crawford turned east from Hotton onto route 807. He drove a half-mile and pulled to the side of the road. He couldn't see it, but ahead a few kilometers was the German border. There was no way to be absolutely certain, because everything seemed to have changed, but this had to be the spot.

Crawford got out of the car. There was little traffic on this road. He stood in the middle of the road facing east. The sun was warm on his face. The fields and the trees already were green. He could hear birds chirping.

He stepped to the left side of the road when a truck passed. He looked around him. About a hundred yards ahead the road curved to the right. They'd come from that direction, across the border. Yes, he thought, it may have been about here where I'd placed the machine gun crew. Another truck was approaching and the sound of its diesel reminded him of the tank engines. He shuddered. The sounds of German tank engines, he thought, must have been designed to create terror.

Crawford felt his heart beating faster and when the passing truck churned the air he could almost feel that cold December wind and the snow. He pulled up the collar of his light jacket. Yes, he thought, this is where I had the men drag the logs onto the road. On the right, there seemed to be fewer trees than he remembered. But, there, just inside the tree line, was where he placed the bazooka team.

He carefully examined the area. There wasn't a mark, no indication, of what had occurred here. How sad, he thought, that so many lives ended so violently on this small piece of road and there is no trace of any of it.

Crawford walked back several paces, perhaps twenty feet. He looked into the ditch for a very long moment. The horrible thing wasn't there now; he hadn't really expected to find it. But he remembered. He remembered every detail, and the memory of it gripped his throat like a powerful hand.

Crawford looked up as a car came around the bend. The car slowed, then pulled to the side of the road and stopped. A young couple was in the front seat. There was a young boy in the back seat with a dog. The driver rolled down the window, smiled, and said something in what to

Crawford sounded like German. Crawford shook his head, indicating that he didn't understand.

The man smiled and nodded patiently. He pointed to Crawford's car and asked haltingly, "Send help?"

Crawford looked at the man, at the woman, and at the small boy playing with the dog. Then he looked at the road, toward the bend. Crawford shook his head quickly and stepped away from the car. The driver looked at Crawford warily, shrugged, then rolled up his window and drove away.

Crawford watched the car as it headed toward the town of Hotton. He smiled as he turned toward his car. *The man wants to know if he can "send help?"* Crawford laughed as he got behind the wheel. *That may be the funniest thing anyone has ever said to me.*

Crawford didn't start the engine. He sat behind the wheel, staring down the road toward the bend. The laughter came from deep within him. *Of all the spots in the world that a German might offer to help me, he picks this spot.*

Then, instantly, the humor was replaced by intense anger and Crawford shoved his car door open and sprinted down the road after the German car, which long since had disappeared around another bend.

"You dumb sonofa*bitch*!" he yelled, shaking his fist. "You can send help to bring back the men who died here." Crawford stopped running when the road became blurred through his tears. He sat down at the side of the road. In little more than a whisper, he said, "And send help for that beautiful young girl, and for that little boy who saw his father's head blown off."

Crawford couldn't help but look into the ditch again as he walked slowly back to his car. "And, god dammit, send help for me."

CHAPTER 10

April 8, 1967
Camp David, Maryland
10:35 a.m.

The Presidential Sikorsky H-34 helicopter was plush, at least by helicopter standards. The whump-whump of the rotor blades reverberated in the cool air as the Marine Corps pilot flew northwest over Maryland. McCall decided that the President's helicopter wasn't nearly as plush, or as quiet, as the Horizon Corporation Saberliner that had brought them the night before to Washington's National Airport.

McCall had to raise his voice over the sound of the twin turbine engines as he reminded Eleanor and Tony that he had not said that they were meeting the President in the White House. "I merely said we were going to Washington."

Eleanor made a face, then leaned close to McCall. "But if you would have told me we were meeting him at Camp David I would have worn something much more casual."

"Don't worry," McCall laughed, "this ain't no a summer camp."

McCall looked out of the window at the countryside rolling up to the Catoctin Mountains. The presidential retreat, only seventy miles from Washington, was surrounded by a ten-thousand-acre national park.

A limousine driven by a Secret Service agent had picked them up at the Horizon apartments. When the agent took them to the White House helipad, both Eleanor and Tony reacted with apparent indifference when they found out where they were going. But McCall, as the helicopter was making its approach to Camp David, could tell that they both were doing a lousy job of covering their excitement.

They had to wait ten minutes before they could see the President in Aspen Lodge, his personal quarters on the 143-acre compound. When it was their turn, they saw that the President was wearing a loud, flower-patterned shirt. He smiled broadly as they walked into the room.

"Spenser, it's good to see you. How've you been?" The President firmly clasped McCall's hand. With his left hand, the President gripped McCall's right elbow, then moved his hand up to McCall's bicep, squeezing it firmly.

"Fine, Mr. President. It's good to see you."

Johnson then stepped in front of Eleanor, his head tilted as he looked down at her, his hands resting on her shoulders. "Honey, you and Lady Bird are still the best looking women in Washington." The President gathered Eleanor into his arms and held her close -- too close, McCall thought.

Eleanor smiled, her face slightly flushed. "I'm pleased that you're still talking to me, Mr. President, considering the position our paper took in the last election."

"Honey, that's just politics. We've known each other too many years to let a couple editorials get between us. Besides, I know I can get you to come over to our side of the fence for the next election." Eleanor and McCall knew that Johnson had been furious over the editorials.

McCall gestured toward Tony. "Mr. President, this is Tony Jackson. He's an assistant U.S. attorney for the Northern District of Indiana.

Johnson's eyes narrowed in thought as he grasped Tony's hand. "Yes, I remember hearing about you, Jackson. You did something that got J. Edgar feeling warm all over. Didn't you put a bunch of them Midwest racketeers behind bars?"

Tony nodded. "It's a pleasure to meet you, Mr. President."

Johnson looked at all three of them, obviously curious about the meeting. "Well, let's all sit down and you can tell me what we're going to talk about." His long arm gestured toward a chair next to his. "Ellie, you sit right here, next to me."

When they were seated, McCall withdrew the envelope from an inside pocket. It contained the synopsis they had written the night before in McCall's suite.

"Mr. President," McCall began, "if you will read the two pages in this envelope before our discussion, I'm sure your time with us will be used more efficiently."

The President smiled at Eleanor, then reached for his half-glasses. "Well, let me have the thing and we'll get started."

The room was very quiet. Several times, as the President read, he looked over his glasses at McCall.

When he was finished, he folded the papers very deliberately and placed them on the low table between them.

"First, tell me about this Cordell Jackson." There was an edge to the President's voice and his eyes, no longer friendly, lingered on Tony. "I gather he's some kin of yours?"

"Cordell Jackson is my father, sir."

Johnson picked up the folded sheets of paper again, but he didn't open them. Instead, he tapped them against his trouser leg while he surveyed the three people sitting around him.

"And *who* is your father, Mr. Jackson?"

"Well, Mr. President, he's one of the most decent men I've ever known. But according to the way Washington measures the worth of people, I guess he's not anybody special."

"He shines my shoes."

Johnson's head snapped toward McCall, apparently wondering if he were being flippant.

"He shines my shoes, and those of a good number of our other employees. He pushes a shoe-shine cart around our building. It's the way he's made his living for the last twenty years or more."

Johnson nodded, and McCall could tell that he was fighting to control his temper. The President smiled at Eleanor, but the smile lacked warmth. "And I suppose you're here, Ellie, to help stir this chili pot."

Eleanor didn't answer. Johnson got up and fixed himself a drink. He held his glass toward the others. "Anyone?" No one accepted the offer and he returned to his chair.

"Well, just what is it you folks want me to do?"

McCall cleared his throat. "We would like the Army to examine our evidence, Mr. President. We believe another review should be held to consider Cordell Jackson as a candidate for the Medal of Honor."

McCall turned to Eleanor. She nodded and began. "Mr. President, The *Times* has copies of the testimony and a film of Mr. Geary. I've agreed not to publish anything until you've had a chance to deal with this matter."

"Yeah," Johnson said sarcastically, "as long as I deal with it *your* way."

"Mr. Presid*ent*," she said, "There is strong evidence that the medal went to the wrong man. At the very least, Cordell Jackson was overlooked by the military for the role he played in the fighting. I'm suggesting that if an error has been made, we are obligated to correct it."

"Do you people fully understand what you're asking me to do? What it all would involve?"

The room was silent. Johnson turned toward a window through which McCall could see the woods that surrounded Camp David.

Finally, gesturing toward Eleanor and Tony, he said, "I want to talk to Spenser privately for a few minutes."

Eleanor and Tony quickly left the room. Johnson refilled his glass. When he returned to his chair, he slammed the glass onto the low table, the whiskey splashing onto the polished wood.

"*Christ*, Spense! You're supposed to be inside my tent pissin' out, instead of outside pissin' in. You did a helluva job for me in the last election, and I need you again." The President ran his huge hand over his face. "It's gonna be a damn circus -- Wallace, and Bobby Kennedy and McCarthy and who knows who the hell else. But whoever wins is gonna have to whip Nixon's ass. And I'm the only man big enough to do that."

Johnson sighed. "Look, Spense, you sure as hell don't expect me to fire my goddamn Secretary of the Army when he hasn't been on the job for a goddamn *week?*" He shook his head. "My God, man, that'll make me look like a horse's ass -- the investigation alone would do that."

"No, Mr. President, our intention is not to get him fired, although I realize that could be the result of an investigation. Our only intention is to make sure he didn't get the medal that rightfully belongs to Cordell Jackson. I'm sure the review can be done quietly."

"*Bullshit!* You ought to know that nothing is done quietly in this town. Every pointy-headed bureaucrat in this city will know about it damn near the minute it starts."

McCall pursed his lips. "Mr. President, I've thought very carefully about the problems this can cause for you. But the simple fact is that if Crawford lied to get his medal, he doesn't deserve to be Secretary of the Army."

"Dammit, Spense, there are no *simple* facts. You're being naive as hell!"

"Mr. President, based on what Geary said, there's a strong possibility that Crawford abandoned his unit -- at least for a while when the fighting became the heaviest, when it looked like they were going to be overrun."

"Then why the hell didn't Geary say that twenty goddamn years ago?" The President nearly shouted the question.

"We asked him that," McCall said, struggling to keep his voice low and neutral. "He was very badly wounded. The investigators read prepared statements to him. Hell, to this day he can't even nod his head. So all he could do was blink his eyes -- once for no and twice for yes. He did sign his name to the statements. His wounds made even that very difficult."

"Did Geary mention Cordell Jackson to them?"

"He said that at one point he wrote 'Corporal Jackson' on a piece of paper. But his handwriting was bad, and he could tell they were losing patience with him because the interview was taking so long. He said they seemed intent on qualifying Crawford for the medal. Geary also said it was clear to him that they didn't want any delays because they were concerned that he was about to die."

The President reflected on what McCall had said. "What about the other witness, this Private Wilcox? He didn't say anything about Crawford hauling-ass, did he?"

"Wilcox was one of the machine gunners. Crawford fought at his position when the attack began. That gun was knocked out early on, and Wilcox was seriously wounded. The record shows that he died in a London hospital less than a month later. He simply may not have seen Crawford running into the woods."

Johnson started to say something when there was a knock at the door.

"*What?*" the President shouted.

A young secretary stepped into the room. "Mr. President, your next appointment is waiting."

"Let him *wait*. Can't you see I'm not finished yet?" The secretary quickly turned and left.

Eleanor and Tony, who were standing on the porch, could hear the President's voice boom inside the small cottage. "We're cooling our heels out here," Tony said, "while Spense is getting reamed in there."

"Don't worry," Eleanor said softly. "The oil baron knows how to take care of himself."

When the secretary left the room, the President said, "Spense, I'm also disappointed that you brought that newspaper woman with you. What the hell you trying to do, put a kink in my pecker?"

McCall hesitated. "Yes, sir, I suppose I am. I felt it would get your attention."

"Well, it sure as *hell* did *that.* Considering what she said about me in the last primary, I know damn well she's gonna support Kennedy. Hell, when I heard she was coming with you I was hoping you'd managed to turn her to our side. And that Jackson -- you figured I'd have to do something about all this because him and his daddy are Nigras. Right?"

McCall didn't respond.

"You're goddamn *right* I'm right!"

Johnson leaned back in his chair, propping his feet up on the low table. He swirled the sour mash whiskey in his glass several times, then smiled at McCall. The President respected power politics because he was a master of the game. He knew that his success was linked to his skill of knowing when and how to compromise or, more effectively, how to create the perception of a compromise. It was a matter of timing and finesse. Johnson knew that McCall probably wouldn't buy what he would propose next. But he hoped it would give him enough time to work out a solution.

"Look, Spense. Why don't we see about getting this Cordell Jackson another medal -- the Silver Star or even the Distinguished Service Cross? That way everybody comes out with something. Then you and I can sit down and talk about you going to the Middle East for me and about the next election."

Johnson's enthusiasm was building and he leaned forward in his chair. "I've also asked you twice to go to Iran. This administration needs you, Spense. I need you."

McCall shook his head slowly. "I'm sorry, Mr. President. I haven't made a decision about that, but I will soon."

When Jim Austin had made the arrangements with the President's appointments secretary, he asked that a film projector be made available.

McCall took the metal film canister from his briefcase and walked to the machine. He loaded the film and pulled the room's curtains closed.

"I'd like you to see a few minutes of this film, Mr. President. It was taken during our interview with Bobby Jerome Geary."

Johnson watched as an exterior shot of the nursing home flickered onto the screen. The scene shifted to Bobby's room. The voices on the sound track sounded tinny and hollow as they echoed in the small room. A wide shot showed Judge Singletary at the foot of the bed. Melinda was seated next to him, her court reporter's machine -- which looked like an adding machine -- on a small stand in front of her. Tony was standing nearest to Bobby, asking questions. The lens zoomed in on Bobby's face as he blinked. The scars on the side of his head and his throat were clearly visible. Then the film showed the index finger of Bobby's right hand moving over the large keyboard as he typed out answers, a letter at a time, with agonizing slowness. After six or seven minutes, McCall turned the machine off and took his seat.

"That man, Mr. President, despite an almost overwhelming fear, stayed on that road with Cordell Jackson. Crawford's citation gives Crawford credit for the thirty-two enemy dead found on the road by the relief column."

McCall reached for the typed copy of Geary's testimony and held it up. "The evidence, Mr. President, is that Jackson took over leadership responsibilities for holding that road, and that Jackson and Geary killed most of those SS troops. If anyone gets the Silver Star or the Distinguished Service Cross, it should be Bobby Geary."

McCall placed the film canister and Melinda's typed record of the interview on the low table. "There must be an investigation," McCall said, "because our evidence indicates that Crawford may have taken credit for what Jackson and Geary did."

McCall stood in front of the low table, looking down at the President. "In fact, Mr. President, Geary's testimony suggests that the Secretary of the Army may have abandoned his men under fire -- that he may have been a coward."

Johnson, moved by what he had seen and heard, nodded his head slowly. His enthusiasm had evaporated. He seemed weary. "All right, Spense. Johnson rose and walked to the bar. He started to pour another drink, then stopped. He turned to face McCall.

"All right. Here's what I'm prepared to offer. I'll look into it, as soon as I can. You have my word. In return, I want you to see Hussein, as soon as you can get there."

"What does 'looking into it' mean, Mr. President?"

"Goddammit, it means just what it says. I'll have the records checked."

"And what if we're right about Crawford?"

"Don't push this too hard, McCall." Johnson's eyes flashed with anger. "All I'm prepared to give you is I'll check the damn record."

"With respect, sir, that's not good enough."

Johnson threw up his hands in frustration. "Jesus H *Chris*t, Spense, if you're looking for a iron-clad commitment right at this moment that I'm going to trash my Secretary of the Army and give your Nigra friend the Medal of Honor, you're not being realistic."

"All I'm asking is that if the evidence is clear that Jackson deserves the medal he should get it; if the evidence is clear that Crawford lied, then that fact should be made known and appropriate action be taken."

Johnson was silent a long moment, his eyes locked with Spenser's. Finally, he began to nod slowly. "Okay. You've got that. You'll leave for Jordan as soon as possible?"

"Just as soon as I can, probably in week or so."

"Okay. Good. Now, there's one more piece to this deal. There's someone I want to go with you, someone who can be a lot of help in assessing the situation."

McCall didn't respond for a moment. He knew that LBJ's personality wouldn't permit McCall to have the final word. "Who would that person be?"

"Ollie Crawford."

"Why? What possible reason could you have for sending us there together?"

Johnson sat across from McCall, then scooted his chair as close as possible to McCall's. "I want him to talk to the Israelis to see how prepared they are for a fight. Maybe he'll get some intelligence about if or when they plan to attack. He'll join you in Tel Aviv. He'll only be there a day or so, and I want you both to keep your presence there quiet -- I sure as hell don't want to read about it in the damn newspapers."

"What will be his assignment in Israel?"

"Strictly to assess the military; he has good contacts in the Israeli military. But I also want you two to be together so you can find out for yourself that he's a good man. What I know you're going find out is that he's not the kind of man who would lie to get the Medal of Honor, no matter what your Nigra friend did during the war."

When McCall walked onto the porch, Eleanor could tell immediately that he was furious. She had never seen him so angry.

April 10, 1967
Wesley Memorial Hospital
Chicago
1:15 p.m.

When Tony and McCall walked into Cordell's room, Tony could tell that his father was surprised. Cordell, wearing a dark blue robe over his pajamas, was sitting in a wheel chair next to the window. He'd apparently been looking down at the street from his third floor window.

"Hi, Pop," Tony said as he reached down and gently hugged the old man. "They say you're doing well enough to come home in a day or so. Isn't that good news?"

Cordell smiled and nodded agreement, but his eyes were on McCall. "Mr. McCall," the old man said, his voice soft and low, "thank you for taking the time to come visit me."

McCall shook Cordell's hand. "We're waiting for you to come back, Cordell. The place just isn't the same for me without our daily talks. We all miss you."

Earlier, the doctor had told McCall and Tony that they could tell Cordell about Bobby.

McCall and Tony pulled chairs close to Cordell's wheelchair, and for several minutes the three men exchanged the kind of small talk typical between hospital visitors and patients.

Then McCall began. "Cordell, do you remember much about the night you were hurt?"

"Yes, at least some of it. A couple of weeks ago I told a policeman all that I could remember." Cordell looked down into his lap, straightening the folds of his robe. "I remember shooting that boy, if that's what you're asking me."

McCall leaned forward, closer to the old man. "Cordell, you did what had to be done that night. Some of what happened was beyond your control."

Cordell looked into McCall's eyes. "I still didn't have to shoot that boy. It's okay if they're going to send me to jail for that."

Tony reached out and put his hand on his father's forearm. "Dad, you're not going to jail. We -- Mr. McCall and I -- talked to some doctors and some other people, and we're here to explain a little of what happened that night. The important thing for you to know is that it wasn't your fault. You did the only thing you could."

Cordell looked at his son, then patted his hand.

McCall waited a few moments, then asked, "Cordell, when that shooting occurred, do you remember saying anything?"

"No." Cordell shook his head slowly. "I told the police that I don't remember anything about that."

"Cordell, does the name Bobby Jerome Geary mean anything to you?"

The old man tilted his head as he looked first at McCall, then at his son. "I...I know the name, but..." Cordell moved his right hand as if he were trying to express a thought, then his hand fell back into his lap.

McCall looked at Tony, who seemed to be holding his breath. Then, in almost a whisper, McCall said, "Think back to the war, Cordell, when you were hurt. There was a young white man, a boy, whose name was Bobby. He was with you when you were at that roadblock. Do you remember him now?"

McCall watched as Cordell brought his hands together, tightly interlocking his fingers over his chest, his eyes again lowered to his lap. "Cordell, we've found Bobby. He's alive."

It seemed as if minutes passed before Cordell looked up.

"No, Mr. McCall. You must be wrong. Bobby can't be alive." Cordell shook his head quickly. "No...that can't be. He was hurt too bad. No," he said more firmly, "Bobby died on that awful road, along with all those other boys."

"We've seen him, Cordell. We've talked to him. Tony and I were with him, and he remembers you."

Tony moved from his chair and knelt in front of his father. "Dad, it's true. I've met him -- I've met Bobby. He's a very sick man. When you're a little stronger, we'll take you to see him. He very much wants to see you."

Cordell, his eyes welling with tears, looked up at McCall. "How can that be, Mr. McCall? How can Bobby be alive? I saw him in that ditch, covered with so much blood."

Cordell shook his head slowly, as if he were afraid to accept McCall's words. His voice was low and raspy with emotion.

"For a long time I'd see Bobby in my dreams that way, covered with blood that was beginning to fill up the ditch, the blood running from Bobby and all the other dead. I'd dream that he'd always ask, *Can we leave now, Corporal Jackson?* And I would say, *We can't leave until we get relief, because that's what the lieutenant said.* And I could see the fear in Bobby's eyes as he saw the blood getting deeper and deeper and he would say, *But Corporal Jackson, if we stay here we're all going to die.*

"I'd tell him that I wouldn't let him die. That's what I told him, but even in that dream I knew we were all going to die, because the ditch was filling up with blood until it became a river. I could see that terrible river carrying the American and German boys past me, then Bobby came swirling past, drowning in that blood, and then all I could see was Bobby's hand sticking up out of the blood, waiting for me to grab it."

Cordell held out his hand, his fingers curled, grasping, as if he were reaching back into his dream for Bobby. "I was trying to close my hand over Bobby's, and just when I almost had him, just when our fingers were touching, I saw my leg float past and I tried to reach out for it." Cordell's voice broke with emotion. "But I could only grab one of them -- my leg or Bobby's hand -- and, God forgive me, I didn't know which to grab. I wanted them both."

Cordell's arm collapsed into his lap. His face was a sheen of perspiration. "But I waited too long to decide and I lost them both. They just sank into the blood and were carried away."

Cordell looked out of his window, down into the street. "That's the dream I've had all these years. I wish God would explain to me why I was so selfish to let Bobby die just so I could try to save that old worthless leg."

Cordell turned to face McCall. "Now you're telling me that he didn't die," Cordell sobbed. "I just don't know how the good Lord managed to find enough left of that poor boy to save."

Cordell lowered his head until his chin rested on his chest, his hands clenched in his lap. The old man's shoulders shuddered rhythmically.

McCall quietly rose from his chair and walked to the door. He paused and looked back. Tony was kneeling in front of the wheelchair, his head bowed, covering his father's clenched hands with his own.

When McCall stepped into the corridor, he was surprised to see Eleanor standing near the door. "What are you doing here?" he asked.

"You didn't think I'd let you handle this alone, did you?" Eleanor stepped close to him. She looked into his eyes as she gently placed her hand alongside his face. "You okay, McCall?"

"Yes. I think it went okay. He had a little trouble believing that Bobby's alive. But, yes. I'm fine. Really."

Eleanor smiled. "Yes, I can see that." She slipped her arm inside his and gently tugged him toward the elevators. "Let's see if this place has a restaurant. I'll spring for the coffee. You look like you can use it, tough guy."

When they boarded the empty elevator and doors hissed closed, McCall suddenly drew Eleanor into his arms, holding her tightly. He felt an immense sense of security when her arms encircled him and she kissed him tenderly on the cheek. They held each other, silently, unaware when the doors opened at the lobby. Eleanor and Spenser chuckled without embarrassment when they realized that at least a half-dozen people waiting to board the car were staring at them.

"Excuse us, please," McCall said as they passed through the group. One young man, his hair down to his shoulders, looked appreciatively at Eleanor. He smiled at McCall. "Way to go, Pops."

Eleanor laughed and paused to pat the young man's cheek. She leaned close and said in a stage whisper, "And Pops handles it very well."

April 12, 1967
Horizon Building
Chicago
11:22 a.m.

McCall was a creature of the corporate culture. He understood the system's strengths and weaknesses. Whatever the outcome, he had years earlier made the decision that he would live within the system.

When McCall's secretary called on the intercom to tell him that Larry Thompkins, the vice chairman, wanted to see him in ten minutes, McCall instinctively knew that the system was about to change his life.

McCall had learned early in his career that the hierarchy of an American corporation is not a textbook example of the democratic process. As Horizon's president and chairman of the board of directors, McCall had for nearly two decades effectively "controlled" his board by his superior performance. Board members are usually the top officers of other corporations whose businesses are not directly linked to the company on whose board they are serving, which means they often lack intimate knowledge of the oil business. Their primary expertise and interest is the bottom line.

McCall had always enjoyed a good relationship with his board. Most of the board members recognized his talent, saw the company grow and, therefore, were reluctant to suggest views that conflicted with McCall's.

But the one-and-a-half billion dollars that McCall wanted for the production of carbon dioxide to rejuvenate aging oil fields appeared very risky to most of the board members. No other oil company had embarked on such a project. Besides, domestic oil was still cheap and plentiful, selling for a little more than three dollars a barrel. Imported oil, primarily from the Middle East, was about a dollar and fifty cents a barrel.

Only four of the board members supported McCall's concerns that the United States would, within less than a decade -- perhaps sooner -- become dangerously addicted to cheap oil from a politically unstable part of the world.

When Thompkins walked into McCall's office, he sat in one of the chairs in front of McCall's desk. McCall thought that Thompkins was working too hard to appear relaxed.

"Spenser, I wanted you to hear this from me, rather than from someone else. The board has voted to scuttle the carbon dioxide project. They feel that the project can't be justified with oil prices so low."

McCall was stunned that the board voted without his being present. "Do you agree with them, Larry -- about the project, I mean?"

"I agree that it's too much money to spend now. But I also agree with you, Spense, that there is some risk of being trapped by our dependence on cheap foreign oil."

McCall smiled. “It’ll be interesting to see how, as chairman, you’re going to straddle those two lines.”

“Spense, you’re just ahead of your time. In a few years the price of crude will be more realistic and we can give serious consideration to going back to those old fields with carbon dioxide. But not at current oil prices. The economics just aren’t there.”

McCall leaned forward, resting his elbows on his desk. “Larry, I’ll tell you how the price of oil is going to become more realistic. The Arabs will get their act together and, when we’re hooked on their oil, they’ll cut us off, probably because of our position on Israel, or maybe just to tweak our noses.”

Thompkins shook his head. “Spense, we’ve got an ambitious drilling program and I’m sure we’ll find the oil we need.”

“That’s bullshit, and you know it. Most of the easy oil in this country has been found. The environmentalists are getting tougher, and it won’t be long before they’ll stop you from drilling in areas they consider sensitive. Even if you find some big fields it takes six to eight years to get that oil to market. If the Arabs cut us off in the next five years, the American government will panic and climb all over you when oil prices soar. If you won’t be able to supply gasoline at reasonable prices -- prices the people of this country think are reasonable -- they’ll want your head.”

“That’s a pretty grim view, Spense. What you’re overlooking is that the Arabs are too dependent on their oil money. They’d be cutting their own throats.”

McCall leaned back in his chair and rubbed his eyes. “Okay, Larry. But promise me you won’t deep-six all of the work we’ve done on CO2. Keep some research going. At least mothball the project, don’t kill it. When the flow of oil stops, you’re going to be scrambling asses over elbows to get this project going again, because I guarantee that the price of oil will be higher than you ever dreamed it would be.”

Thompkins rose from his chair. “Well, Spense, I guess only time will tell which of us is right. In any case, because of our years together, I wanted to personally tell you about the board’s decision.”

“Larry...” McCall paused, his face flushing with anger... “when you report this conversation to them -- and I know you will -- tell them that I think they’re gutless bastards for scuttling the project and for not telling me personally. It looks like you'd better get accustomed to doing their dirty work."

Thompkins grimaced. "Spense, I can't--"

"I'm well aware of what you're incapable of doing, Larry. But you know in your gut that I'm right about this project. Hell, a year ago you admitted as much." McCall paused and locked eyes with Thompkins. "You've sold your ass for this damned desk. Haven't you?"

"I hadn't planned to tell you this, Spense -- even though they asked me to -- but it's more than just the New Mexico project. The directors were willing to consider a scaled down -- considerably scaled down -- version of what you wanted. But there are situations developing that have eroded their confidence in you."

"What situations?" McCall demanded belligerently.

"That woman, for one thing -- the publisher of that liberal rag. She's been critical of our industry ever since she took over as publisher. Hell, she's worse than her husband was."

McCall rose slowly from his chair and leaned his clenched fists on his desk. "Which one of those bastards brought that up?"

Thompkins held up his hands. "There was something else that was only alluded to, something that you're up to that has some very important people in Washington concerned."

"What?"

"There wasn't any discussion about it. I honestly don't know what it's about, but I was directed by the board to relay two words to you -- back off. They said you'd understand."

McCall tried, but couldn't conceal the fury in his voice. "Those are private matters, Larry, that have nothing to do with the company. What the hell business is it of theirs?"

"That's the point, Spense. Your private life is getting in the way of your responsibilities to this corporation."

Thompkins rose and stood, facing McCall across the desk. "The bottom line, Spense, is that your project has been axed and you will retire as scheduled. Unless you back off as ordered, your retirement date will be moved up. In other words, from this moment, you could be asked to leave at any time. You have only yourself to blame."

Thompkins didn't wait for a response. He turned and walked quickly from the room.

McCall remained standing at his desk. The fury he felt was pounding in his temples.

'Back off,' is what they said. It had to be the business with Crawford. How could they have found out so soon? Only a handful of people know about it, and none of them has a connection to the board. Who could have told the board?

Then McCall almost collapsed into his chair when he realized that Thompkins was wrong when he said *some very important people in Washington are concerned.*

There was only *one* very important man in Washington who had cause for concern.

CHAPTER 11

April 14, 1967
640 North Michigan Avenue
Chicago
9:40 p.m.

"So it's over." Eleanor said the words softly, with finality, looking down at the corner of the linen napkin she had wound around her forefinger. McCall's housekeeper had cleared away the dishes and refilled their wine glasses while he and Eleanor lingered at the dining room table.

"Yeah, I suppose it is -- or will be in less than ten months, with vacation time. Fitz called before I left the office. He'd heard. He said he'd stay as long as I wanted him to. I told him that I appreciated the offer, but that he ought to bail out whenever he's ready." McCall chuckled. "He sounded relieved. He said he'll announce his retirement in June. He wants to hang around for a couple of months to make sure his people are taken care of."

"I just wish there were something I could say."

McCall reached across and held her hand. He hadn't told her about the board's criticism of their relationship. "There's nothing to say, really. I guess what I've got to decide is whether I want to fight it."

Eleanor shook her head. "Spense, I'm not sure that's such a good idea."

"Why not? The financial analysts and the stockholders have always been complimentary about the way I've run the company; they've said many times that our real strength is superior management."

"Spense, they've got the bulge on you," Eleanor said. "What options do you have? A proxy fight? Are you going to go to the media?" Eleanor grimaced. "No, we've both seen that kind of thing get very ugly and ends up dragging both sides into the gutter."

"I'm just supposed to roll over, huh? Is that the way you'd do it?"

"Think about this scenario, Spense: You decide to fight to stay on as CEO. They trot out the big numbers for the CO2 project -- big bucks you want to spend when, according to you, the price of oil isn't high enough to replace your reserves now.

"Then, when things get down and dirty, they'll probably find a way to criticize you -- and it won't be difficult -- for bumping noses with LBJ over the Crawford matter. Then, finally, when they're desperate, they'll bring in your personal life -- things like your penchant for a certain liberal newspaper woman who's been critical of your industry and your company, and whose father some said was a socialist.

"One more thing that's most important of all. When they start digging around in the McCall closet, anything they find is fair game. Your son, for instance."

"You mean the fact that we don't get along? That I don't like some of the projects he gets involved in? That's a tragedy for me, but who the hell else would care?"

Eleanor shook her head. "McCall, you can be naive as hell. I didn't say their charges and allegations would be true. To them, truth and fiction are commodities; they are the means they use to justify the ends. Spense, if you fight them, you'll simply be a hunk of raw meat for the vultures to pick at."

"Ellie, a lot of what you're saying is based on that jaded view you liberals have of the corporate management system." He looked at her. "A hunk of raw meat, huh? Thanks a helluva lot for your vote of confidence."

Eleanor rose from her chair and stepped behind McCall's. She leaned over and wrapped her arms around him, her lips close to his right ear.

"Spenser McCall," she said softly so the housekeeper couldn't hear, "I have intimate knowledge of your manhood. I know you're right. Fitz and most of the others know it. You don't have to prove anything to yourself, and you sure as hell don't have to prove anything to me. Anyone else doesn't count worth a damn. Let it go, McCall. Let it *go*."

McCall reached up to take both of Eleanor's hands and brought them to his lips. She kissed the lobe of his ear.

"Damn you, Spenser McCall. My father must be spinning in his grave. Like him, I hate your politics; like him, I hate big oil corporations. But if he knew that I'm hopelessly in love with a damned oil baron, he'd find a way to come back."

McCall stood and gathered Eleanor into his arms. "Don't worry," he said. "When he hears that I'm about to be busted back to ordinary civilian, he'll rest easy."

McCall looked into Eleanor's gray-green eyes for a long moment, then kissed her with passion and emotion. They held each other, swaying gently, for a long moment.

When the phone rang, McCall was reluctant to move. Finally, he kissed the tip of her nose. "I suppose I'd better answer the damn thing."

Holding hands, they walked into the living room. He reached for the phone next to the couch.

"This is McCall."

"Spense?"

"Yes, Mr. President." McCall turned on the speaker phone and looked at Eleanor, his finger to his lips.

"I'll tell you up-front, old friend. What I've got to say you don't want to hear. Crawford says he can document how he got his medal. In fact, he was highly pissed -- at least as pissed as a guy like Ollie can get. I've got to say that I believe him."

"Did you mention Geary or Jackson or show him any of the evidence?"

"I didn't show him the film...hell, I can't look at that damn thing again. But I showed him your letter -- that synopsis -- and told him to read Geary's testimony, and he read Jackson's interview with that head doctor."

"How did he react to all that?"

"He said he didn't have to read a version written more than twenty years after the fact. He discounted Jackson's version. He says the man obviously was disturbed, which he says is substantiated by the fact that just a few weeks ago he shot and killed a fifteen-year-old kid."

"Mr. President, excuse me, but that's bullshit."

"Spense, you're not getting the message. It doesn't make any difference if it's bullshit. The bottom line is that when you stand those two men up in front of the public, who do you think is going to make the best impression? Which one of them is going to look and sound like he's got the bonifides to be a damned war hero?"

McCall didn't respond. He was thinking of what Eleanor had said moments earlier about truth and fiction and perception.

"I also had someone dig up those original reports by the review committee that approved Crawford's medal," Johnson said. "Based on what Crawford says and what I read in those accounts, I don't see that I've got any other choice but to stand with Crawford."

"Okay, let's forget Crawford for the moment. How about the Medal of Honor for Cordell Jackson?" McCall asked. "Will you take the matter up with congress? You've got to agree that the evidence shows he deserves it."

"Hell, yes I will, Spense. You've got my word on that -- but not before the election."

"What does the election have to do with it?"

"Come on now, Spenser. Use your head. You know I can't take the chance that one of the goddamn pepperpots may dig into this thing too deeply and come up with some half-assed conclusions. That'd be too risky for Crawford."

"And for you."

"Now, don't get contrary with me; remember who the hell you're talking to. I'm thinking of what something like this might do to the country, and to my plans to get Vietnam squared away. You've got to understand that my top priority isn't to get medals for old soldiers who fought in a war most people have forgotten. That's history. My number one job is today, and the future. I've got to get this country rolling again."

McCall could visualize the President's arms swinging like windmills as he talked. "So that's where you're going to leave it?"

"Dammit, Spense, you really are a hard-ass. You can't expect me to go balls-out on this thing with the primary coming up, do you? Hell, I promised you I'd take a long hard look at the Crawford business after the election...and you have my word that first thing after the election Jackson will get whatever the hell medal you want for him. Deal?"

"I'm sorry. We can't wait until then. The investigators have to talk to Bobby Geary now. The doctors say he doesn't have much time."

The President sighed. "Hell, Spense, I'm choppin' and no chips are flyin'. I've *already* explained why I don't want to do anything now."

McCall looked at Eleanor, then closed his eyes. "Mr. President, what if I were to offer a compromise."

The line was silent for a moment, then McCall heard a brusque, "Let's hear it."

"What if we back off on Crawford? Nothing more will ever be said about him, at least not by us. In exchange for that, you pull out all the stops to get Cordell the Medal of Honor. Now."

Johnson's voice was sober, edged. "McCall, that sounds like you're trying to blackmail the President of the United States."

"I prefer not to think of it as blackmail."

"I damn well imagine you do." McCall could hear the President moving about as he talked. The President asked, "Why the hell are you pushing this thing so hard? What's so special about this Nigra for you, Spense?"

McCall glanced at Eleanor. His words were soft, thoughtful. "I don't have the whole answer to that, Mr. President. I honestly don't know. What I do know is that the contributions he made to his country, and the sacrifice he made for it, have been totally ignored. However you cut it, that just isn't right."

McCall heard Johnson grunt, apparently as he sat heavily into a chair. "Spenser, let me tell you a little story that'll reveal something about me I thought you knew. I know you met Ev Dirkson, one of your Illinois Republican buddies who's a powerhouse in the Senate. A couple years ago I had a phone put into my car. I made a habit of calling Ev from my car and I'd say, 'Ev, guess where I'm calling you from?' Then I'd tell him I was calling from my new car phone. Well, it wasn't long before I heard Ev had his own car phone. On the first day he had it he called from his car to mine. 'Lyndon,' he says, 'guess where I'm calling you from?' You know what I told him? I said, 'I can't talk now, Ev. My other line is ringing'"

McCall looked quizzically at Eleanor. Her eyes were narrowed, her head nodding slowly in understanding.

"The point of that story, Spense, is that Ev thought it was a harmless little game of one-upmanship. I didn't. Nobody gets one-up on me. Later, whenever Ev and I would go head-to-head in the Senate, I knew that in the back of his mind he'd remember that I always win, even the harmless little games. That's something I want you to remember, Spenser. I never like to lose. Anything."

The President sighed. "But I guess a stubborn old coot like you is going to charge ahead anyway, right?"

"I don't see how I can back away from it. I guess I'm in too deep."

"You've got that part right, son. But as long as we're talking compromise, let me offer you one. If you drop the Crawford business right now, this minute, I'll do two things for you. As I promised, Jackson will get his medal after the election -- if he really qualifies, the Medal of Honor. And you get to start that damn New Mexico project you've been breathing heavy about. I'll give you eighteen months from tomorrow morning to kick all the ass you need to make it hum. Then, my friend, your ass is mine and you come to work for me."

McCall heard Eleanor's sharp intake of breath. "How can you do that?" McCall asked, "I mean how can you get the board to approve it?"

"Jesus H. Christ, Spense. I'm President of these United States. I can do something like that with my left hand during lunch."

McCall wanted to ask the President if he'd already exercised his 'left hand' on Horizon's board of directors. He glanced at Eleanor and saw her emphatically shaking her head. She must know what I'm thinking, he thought.

"Spense, talk to me."

McCall visualized Larry Thompkins' face if he were told that McCall would be staying on as CEO and that the CO2 project had been approved. He visualized calling Fitzsimmons and asking him to stay, and to start cranking up the drilling for CO2 in New Mexico. He visualized all that while he looked into Eleanor's eyes. He looked to her for some message, some hint of what she wanted him to do.

"Goddammit, Spense. You still there?"

"Yes, Mr. President. I'm sorry. I'm very sorry. But no deal."

"Okay," the President said immediately. "You called it. I hope the hell you realize what you let slip through your fingers. Now, I suppose Ellie's going to run the story?"

"I don't know. That's her decision."

"Well, I know she will, but I figure I can take the heat this early in the race."

"I sincerely hope so, Mr. President. It was never our intention to cause *you* any embarrassment. I hope you believe that."

"Hell, Spense, I don't like bumping heads with you. We go back too many years for me to think anything like that. It's just that I need Crawford, at least till I can make things happen over there in Vietnam. Christ, that sorry-ass country is pulling us apart. The last damn thing I need right now is a flap about the medal he got."

"I don't know what more to say."

"Look, like I said, after the election I'll personally dig into this thing till we find out whether Crawford is a hero or a bald-assed liar. Okay?"

"I'm sorry. I'm not trying to be stubborn about this."

The disappointment was evident in the President's voice. "Spense, old friend, you're putting me between two hard places."

"Again, I'm sorry. I don't know what we're going to do next, but we've got to pursue it."

"Well, then, I guess that's it. But I'll give you this, Spense: if you come up with anything that clearly makes Crawford out a liar, then I'll personally throw his ass out. Otherwise, I guess I'll wait to hear whether you want to be ambassador to Iran. I guess I can still count on you to help with the campaign?"

"Of course."

"Good. Very good. I knew I could count on you, despite this other business." There was a short pause. "Give some more thought to the compromise I just offered. Sleep on it. It's the best deal you're going to get. Good night, Spense."

"Good night."

"Well," Eleanor said, "that's the most interesting civics lesson I've ever had." She had been standing in the middle of the room, her hands on her hips. She walked to McCall and kissed him, holding his face in her hands. "Spenser McCall," she said softly, "I've never been more proud of you than I am at this moment."

McCall felt the urge to pace, and he walked to the window. He pulled the drape back and looked down onto Michigan Avenue. He wondered if he'd ever regret the answer he gave to the President.

He turned away from the window. "Well, I guess the ball's back in our court."

"Spenser, what strings can he pull on your board?"

McCall shook his head. "I don't know, but like he said, he's President. A few phone calls from the White House can work magic."

"I'd give a lot to know more about what Crawford said to Johnson," Eleanor said.

"I don't think Johnson based his decision just on what Crawford said. Remember that Johnson said he also read the review committee's report that endorsed the recommendation for Crawford's medal. Jim Austin's Washington contact has a copy of the report. I'll have Jim get it for us."

McCall took the wine bottle and glasses from the table and he and Eleanor moved to the couch. She sat at one end, while McCall stretched out, resting his head on her lap. "It's clear," he said, "that he's worried about the primary and what Vietnam is going to do to him in the election. You heard him admit that. I also think he's convinced that Crawford is telling the truth."

"We both know the first reason may, in fact, be a legitimate concern, but the second reason is crap. I don't think he cares whether Crawford is lying or telling truth – he just doesn't want to deal with it until after the election." She gently rubbed McCall's forehead. "Do you think he'll change his mind about Cordell's medal?"

McCall shook his head. "Ellie, what I honestly believe is that the man just doesn't have the time to screw with it. My God, think of the problems he's juggling."

"Spenser McCall, it sounds like your making excuses for your old hunting buddy."

McCall smiled and shook his head. "No, I can't say that we've ever been really close friends. But I've seen him operate for a lot of years and, in many ways, I have a great deal of respect for him."

"Well, it has been evident to me," Eleanor said gently, "that he respects you very much." Eleanor shrugged. "What now?"

"I don't know. You heard him say he knows you're going to run the story."

"Yes, and I also heard him say it probably won't hurt him this early in the campaign. I guess we'll just see about that, won't we?"

"Does that mean you're going to run it?"

"Oh, I'm going to run it, all right. I'm just not sure when. I'd like to ask Tony about it first. When will he be back?"

"Tomorrow night, I guess. He wanted to spend a couple of days with his family."

"You still haven't said what you're going to do," Eleanor said.

McCall reached for the wine bottle to top off their glasses.

"McCall, whenever you pour wine before you answer one of my questions, I know you're evading the question. Once more -- what are you going to do?"

"There's only one thing left to do, as I see it. Meet with Crawford. Confront him with what we've got. And I think it's best if I meet with him alone."

"Spenser, is that smart?"

"We've got nothing to lose, as far as I can see. Now that Johnson has talked to him, he knows we're on to him."

"Then why meet with him? And why alone?"

Spenser smiled. "C'mon, Ellie, aren't you going to let me fight with anybody?"

Eleanor nodded understanding. "Oh, I see. You just want to spar with him. Measure him, the way boxers do. You want to see what kind of a man he is -- how much of man he is."

"Ellie, we've got to know what kind of guy we're up against. I want him to know that we're not giving up on this thing."

Eleanor laughed. "If I live another thirty-nine-plus years, I'll never understand men."

CHAPTER 12

April 16, 1967
Helmsly Palace
New York
4:30 p.m.

The limousine carrying Secretary of Army Oliver W. Crawford pulled up to the canopy. The car had picked him up Crawford at LaGuardia, where he had landed on the TWA flight from Brussels. He had attended his first meeting at NATO headquarters, and it had gone well, so well that he wasn't really concerned about the meeting scheduled for seven o'clock in his suite. In fact, despite a mild case of jet lag, he was anxious to have the meeting.

A doorman, whose uniform Crawford thought would be the envy of one of his generals, opened the Lincoln Continental's door. "Good evening, Mr. Crawford, and welcome to the Helmsly Palace." The doorman gestured to a porter. "Charles will take your bags and escort you directly to your rooms."

The porter led Crawford through the lobby, past the crowded registration desk, directly to the bank of elevators.

A basket of fruit and a bottle of wine were on the coffee table when Crawford entered the suite. He tipped the porter with the wine and a twenty-dollar bill and asked him to bring up a bottle of scotch. He thought of ordering a sandwich, but decided to wait for his guest. Yes, it would be a nice touch to offer dinner to his guest, he thought. It would show that he was in control, that he wasn't concerned.

Crawford unzipped his carryon bag and hung a fresh shirt and suit in the closet. When the porter delivered the scotch, Crawford poured two fingers into a glass containing a single ice cube, then added a dash of tap water. He downed it quickly and poured another, turned on the television, and sat on the couch. He held the cool glass briefly to his forehead, then reached for the phone to call Julie.

"Hi, honey. I'm in New York. Yes, it was a good flight, and the meetings went very well. I'll tell you about it tomorrow. Tonight's meeting? Nothing very important, and it won't take long. I'll catch the shuttle and should be home before noon.

"Love you, too, sweetheart. Good night."

To pass the time, Crawford opened his briefcase and reached for the blue folder, stamped classified, to review his notes of the Brussels meeting. Under the folder, he noticed the Michelin map of Belgium. He picked it up and unfolded it to the section where he had marked the route in red ink from Brussels to Bastogne. Without thinking about it, he took a ballpoint pen from the briefcase and drew a circle around the town of Hotton, just east of highway N4.

He stared at the map for several minutes, which is why Crawford didn't immediately recognize the sound. He'd forgotten that the suite had a door chime. He glanced at his watch. It was time. He quickly put the map and other documents into his brief case, closed and locked it, and moved quickly to the door.

"Hello, Ollie. Thanks for making the time available to see me."

"It's been a long time, Spenser. Here, I'll take your coat."

When they were seated, Crawford said, "I'm glad you asked for this meeting, Spenser. I'm anxious to clear the air. Let me say that I also appreciate the effort you've made to avoid having the media involved in any of this."

"I don't know how much longer we can avoid the media," McCall said. "Did the President tell you that a Chicago paper plans to run something?"

Crawford nodded. "Yes. But he expressed the hope that you might be inclined to use your influence to prevent it."

"I'm sorry, Ollie. I don't have that kind of influence."

"When will it run?"

"I don't know, but I would presume any day."

McCall was expecting, but didn't see any reaction.

"After so many years, Spenser, why are you so intent on dredging this all up? Let's lay out our cards -- is there something about me personally that you dislike?"

McCall shook his head. "No, Ollie, but there is a question in my mind whether you deserved the Medal of Honor."

Crawford shook his head slowly, as if he disbelieved McCall. Do you realize what you're saying? You're accusing me of having lied. Don't you realize that the awarding of the medal is based on careful documentation? That witnesses were interviewed? That the scene of the fighting was carefully examined by investigators?"

McCall nodded patiently. "What I'm saying is that, based on the evidence I have, you took credit for what another man did."

Crawford's expression didn't change. He asked softly, "And you're telling me that you believe it?"

McCall paused for a long moment, then said evenly, "You were seen running into the woods before the final attack."

Crawford smiled. "Spense, I can't believe that someone like you would think that kind of allegation would have any credibility. I was on the road when the relief column arrived – all the evidence proves it."

"As Cordell and Bobby Geary described it, they were the only two men fighting at that roadblock toward the end of the fighting. If you were there, one of them would have mentioned it."

Crawford leaned forward in his chair, "Don't you realize what you're saying? Never in the one-hundred-year history of the medal has anyone charged that a recipient lied to get it. It's just not possible for that to happen."

"We have testimony from--"

Crawford, smiling, held up hand to stop McCall. "Spense, we go back too many years to argue over this. You know that I respect you, as did my father." Crawford leaned back in his chair. "If you feel compelled to pursue this, then by all means do so."

"You're serious?"

"Of course," Crawford said, "and even though the President supports me in this matter, I will agree to cooperate with you however I can."

McCall was surprised. He wanted this meeting to be confrontational, an alley fight. *Either Crawford is a consummate poker player,"* he thought, *"or he really does believe he deserves the damn medal.*

"Well, then, I suppose that's it," McCall said, searching for options. "I'm leaving for Jordan on the June 3. I'm meeting the king on June 4. When will you be in Tel Aviv?"

"I'm leaving tomorrow. The military has agreed to meet with me, but I really don't think they're going to give me anything we don't know. They've got a lid on their operations."

McCall rose from the chair and stepped toward the door. Crawford followed McCall to the closet where he got his coat.

At the door, McCall looked at Crawford for a long moment. *He seems absolutely confident. Could we be wrong about him? Have I put all my chips on the table without seeing the hole card?*

"I understand you're staying at the Metropolitan in Tel Aviv. I have a feeling Hussein won't need a lot to time to tell me what he plans to tell me, so why don't we meet there on June 2 to compare notes."

Crawford patted McCall's shoulder. "Sounds like a plan. I look forward to seeing you."

McCall opened the door, then paused. "I'll give you this: I guess I'm not absolutely convinced that you lied. Perhaps there's more to this story than I know at the moment. But I'm going to dig out the truth." McCall closed the door.

Crawford stood by the closed door. He thought of his father. If he were here, Crawford thought, what would he say? No, he realized, he wouldn't have been able to discuss it with his father. The general certainly wouldn't understand. No man could understand unless he'd been there, unless he'd seen that awful thing in the ditch.

Julie. Yes, she would understand. She always did. If I hurry to the airport I can catch the shuttle and be home well before midnight. Then I can tell Julie. She'll help me. She always has.

May 2, 1967
Central Intelligence Agency
Langley, Virginia
9:30 a.m.

McCall had to admit that he was impressed. An assistant director and several staff members were seated around a large conference table. McCall thought the CIA representatives were more corporate-looking than his own people. What struck McCall about the very polished and apparently comprehensive presentation was that it was so low key. He couldn't help but compare it to the countless presentations made to him by managers seeking approval for routine requests for plant additions or drilling programs. Certainly, he thought, these people don't act or sound like war is about to break out.

The assistant director was tall, distinguished and seemed to have a slight British accent. He also was clearly less than enthusiastic about McCall's mission. McCall presumed that the assistant director found distasteful the thought that the President would give such an assignment to an "amateur."

A member of the upper electorate was not at the lectern. As the presenter talked, he periodically stabbed at a large map attached to the easel. For the last ten minutes he discussed the balance of power between the Arab states and Israel.

"...and we and the Brits have been supplying Hussein with arms. Last January we airlifted in supplies and our cargo ships off-loaded tanks at the port of Aquaba."

He pointed so quickly at the map that McCall couldn't see the port. "At the moment, he has twenty-two British Hunter fighter bombers, although six of his pilots are in the States receiving advanced training. He can field one-hundred-twenty-six tanks, all U.S Pattons and Super Shermans, except for a detachment of British Centurions. He has about sixty thousand troops."

"How good are his troops?" McCall asked.

"His soldiers can fight, but man-for-man they're no match for the Israelis, with one exception: the Arab Legion, which is the iron core of Hussein's army."

"Tell me why the Arab Legion is so good."

"They're primarily Bedouin," the presenter said, "who are fiercely – perhaps fanatically – loyal to Hussein because he is one of their own. Hussein wouldn't have survived to this point without them."

"I know they're tough, but will they fight effectively?"

The presenter nodded, "Yes, that is the key question. The Arab Legion won't hesitate to charge into the muzzle of a cannon, but they don't do a good job of maintenance and administration – a problem that can be fatal in any war, especially a desert war."

"Where will the Legion fight?"

The presenter flipped the large-scale map over the back of the easel, revealing a detailed map of Jerusalem. “Primarily here, in the Old City. Any fighting here will be the Legion’s kind of war. Neither side will want to use artillery because of the historic significance of the part of the city – especially here.” The pointer scribed a tight circle around one spot in the Old City.

“It’s the Wailing Wall. There is no holier place for the Jew than the Wall. They’ve waited almost two thousand years to reclaim it.”

“How about aircraft – how many can the Israelis put up?” McCall asked.

“More than two hundred. However, a more critical factor is that Israeli pilots are probably the best in the world. It will be no contest. We estimate that Arab air power will be virtually destroyed in the first few hours.”

McCall held up his hand to stop the presenter. “Summarize for me, please, what you believe to be the root cause of the current tension between the Israelis and Arabs.”

The presenter nodded briskly. Without referring to notes, he walked to the map. “Hussein is between two hard places. In the fifty-six war, he sat on the sidelines. He doesn’t want to fight now. In fact, he’d like to reach some accommodation with Israel, but he knows that if he did the other Arab nations would be at his throat. There also would be serious risk of civil war in Jordan. The problem that’s generating most of the heat now involves the attacks by Fatah, the Palestine Liberation Movement across the Jordanian border into Israel.

“Has Hussein tried to stop them?”

“Yes, sir. We know of at least one Palestinian commando who was killed by Hussein’s troops when he was returning from a raid. Last year Hussein said the Palestinians no longer are a movement for liberation. He said they were under the influence of communism and had become, in his words, ‘a melting pot for all the discordant and displaced elements of the Arab world.’”

The presenter flashed a slide onto the screen. I was a color photo of a small, round, bristly-faced, very unattractive man. “This is the man who is the leader of the Fatah guerrillas. His name is Yasser Arafat.”

McCall asked, “If Jordan stays out of the fighting, will that make a difference as to whether the other Arab nations fight?”

"Mr. McCall, it is our opinion that the Israelis have been so aroused by the Fatah raids that they will retaliate with a powerful attack. Last November the Israelis hit the village of Samu just across the border – about here – which was a Fatah stronghold. The Israelis tell us they had not intended for the raid to embarrass Hussein. They actually hoped the attack would give him the opportunity to suppress guerrilla activity on the grounds that the raids were a threat to peace. However, it backfired, triggering mass demonstrations led by the Palestinians in Jordan, who charged that Hussein was unwilling or unable to defend them against Israel. Hussein called the demonstrations a communist plot. The reality, Mr. McCall, is that the Arabs will fight, and it's very likely that Hussein will have little choice but to support them."

"Is it possible for Hussein to fight, to save face, but for his army to escape destruction?"

The presenter glanced at the assistant director, then said, "I don't see how that would be possible, sir."

McCall now began to seriously consider whether LBJ had given him an impossible mission. He placed the palms of both hands on the highly polished table, as if he were going to stand. "Gentlemen, the President has asked that I talk to Hussein, to convince him to stay out of the fighting. As in incentive, I have been authorized to promise considerable aid to bolster the Jordanian economy. But what I've heard this morning leads me to believe that I'll be wasting my time.

The assistant director cleared his throat. "Mr. McCall, we view Hussein as a moderating influence in the Middle East." McCall noticed that the eyes of each staff member were locked on the assistant director. "The Russians virtually control Nasser, who is trying to assume the leadership of the Arab world. The Syrian militants – the left wing of the Ba'ath party – have seized power and are passionate believers in radical socialism. The Syrians and Nasser are trying to outdo each other in their support for the Palestinians. Hussein has not only opposed the terrorism, but he is viewed by the radicals as an obstacle to socialism."

The assistant director paused to straighten the papers in front of him. "We know the President doesn't want to see a war in the Middle East. If war is inevitable, he would like to see it concluded as quickly as possible, hopefully no longer than a month. As you have indicated, the President will promise Hussein economic and military aid." The assistant director passed a document to McCall that outlined the details of the aid program.

"We know that you have a personal relationship with the king," the assistant director said. McCall suddenly wondered what other information about him was contained in the CIA's files. No doubt they have a file on Ellie, he thought.

"The President hopes you can meet privately with the king to make the offer." McCall thought the assistant director's smile was almost frosty. The assistant director continued, "Depending on the king's reaction, any. following discussion will move through more conventional diplomatic channels."

McCall glanced at the briefing paper, then slid it across the table to the assistant director. "I've committed the essentials of the aid offer to memory, and the President gave me a copy for the king."

McCall rose and rolled the padded leather chair to the table. He looked at the assistant director, hoping his smile was equally cool.

"Thank you for the briefing, gentlemen. It was everything I anticipated it would be."

The assistant director also rose to his feet. "I hope you appreciate, Mr. McCall, that war can break out at any moment. Once you are in-country, there is little we can do to ensure your safety under those circumstances."

"Thank you for the advice. However, I've gotten along very well in the Mideast without the involvement of the CIA."

The assistant director smiled. "You are presuming, Mr. McCall, that you have functioned in the Middle East and developed a relationship with Hussein without the involvement of the CIA."

McCall felt a surge of anger. "Are you saying you people had something to do with all that?"

The assistant director held up his hands, palms outward. "All I can say is there were some people in Washington who thought it would be strategically beneficial to help make it possible for you to do business in the Middle East, particularly in Jordan and Iran." The assistant director smiled again. "I will admit that you developed your relationship with Hussein on your own. All we did is make sure that he noticed you."

Although he was seething, McCall knew he couldn't afford to lose his temper. *If what this man is saying is true, I have no doubt that Johnson had something to do with it. He somehow knew that one day he would need someone with connections in the Middle East. Now I suppose he's cashing in his investment.*

"The fact is," McCall said evenly, "I neither want nor need any help from you or your operatives. If I even suspect that you people are involved, in any way, I will inform the President that I will not continue the mission. Is that clear?"

Without waiting for a response, McCall left the room.

CHAPTER 13

May 22, 1967
Hummar, Jordan
9:15 a.m.

McCall knew he previously had met the tall, powerfully-built lieutenant colonel who greeted him at the helicopter landing pad, but he couldn't think of his name. The colonel, who McCall judged to be in his early forties, wore a tan summer uniform and a Webley revolver in a British holster. The colonel didn't try to speak over the whine of the engines and whumping of the blades. He gestured for McCall to follow him. When they had stepped clear of the pad, the helicopter's twin turbine engines spooled up to a throaty roar. The machine lifted, then turned to the east, nose-down as it gathered speed before climbing, the blades throbbing as they bit into the hot, thin air.

They walked through a garden toward the villa. When the engine noise faded, the colonel paused and offered his hand. "Good to see you again, Mr. McCall. I am Ali Abu Hashim."

McCall instantly remembered the name. "Of course, we met when I was here in November." McCall, who also now remembered that Hashim had recently been named head of the king's personal guards, noticed the colonel was looking at the small leather brief case he carried. McCall saw that the colonel wore the badges of the Arab Legion. That, plus the fact that he was one of the king's personal bodyguards, meant he most certainly was a Bedouin.

McCall smiled and unzipped the brief case and held it out to the officer. The colonel took the brief case, weighed it in one hand without looking into it, than handed it back. "Thank you, Mr. McCall," the colonel said. "Please wait here. His majesty is in his office. He will be with you soon."

McCall looked around the room. He lingered at a photo of the king and his two daughters – Zein, named for his mother, and Aisha. The photo was taken at what looked like their third or fourth birthday party.

Although McCall had never drilled for oil in Jordan, he first met Hussein in 1959, when Horizon had contracted to sell Jordan crude oil produced elsewhere in the Mideast. The king invited McCall to attend an informal party at the Shuna Palace in the Jordan Valley. At the party, McCall noticed there were as many foreigners as Jordanians. The party ended the next morning with a picnic breakfast on the shores of the Dead Sea. The Arab king and the American oil executive became close friends. McCall became one of the few who could address the king as "Abby," short for Abdullah, the name of his grandfather and his son, both of whom he loved deeply.

McCall was especially fond of Hussein's wife, Princess Muna, formerly Toni Gardiner, the daughter of an RAF colonel attached to the British military mission in Jordan. She had chosen the Arabic name Muna al Hussein, which translates to "Hussein's wish." McCall recalled the discussion he'd had with the king before the marriage in 1961, which was openly opposed by the British government and most of Hussein's own key ministers. The British were concerned about being accused of engineering the marriage to cement the colonialist relationship between the two countries. His critics were saying that he "turned to the West to solve his family problems as he always did when seeking the solution to other problems." But Hussein did have the support of his mother, Queen Zein.

Hussein told McCall that among the reasons he was attracted to Toni Gardiner was her British detachment from all the Arab feminine inhibitions and complexes. There was much about the British that Hussein admired. He had been educated in England, and had received his military training at Sandhurst.

When McCall met Toni, he understood why Hussein was attracted to her. Princess Muna had made it clear that she wanted nothing to do with the political role of a king's wife. She remained quietly in the background, refusing to consider any claim to the title of queen. Her only wish was to provide the kind of family life that she and Hussein craved.

"Spenser McCall!"

McCall turned to see King Hussein bin Talal enter the sitting room.

He was wearing his military uniform, adorned only with red and gold collar tabs and his pilot's wings. McCall thought he looked tired. The king embraced McCall, then stepped back to look at him as he gripped McCall's shoulders. "It is good to see you, my good friend. Come into the study."

The king sat in one stuffed chair and motioned for McCall to sit in the other. "Would you like some tea?" When McCall nodded, Hussein looked at an aide.

When the tea was served and they were alone, Hussein said, "Well, my friend, I have been told that you will be meeting with Secretary Crawford tomorrow in Tel Aviv. Does that mean you have been demoted to the role of an official representative of your country?" Hussein was smiling, but McCall knew the king must be concerned about the purpose of today's meeting, and the one with Crawford. McCall wondered how the king knew about Crawford's presence in Israel and that he was scheduled to meet him. Did Hussein's intelligence people discover that? Or did our own embassy people, for some reason, tell him? McCall recalled the President's demand that the meetings be kept confidential.

"No, not at all -- I mean about being an official representative of my country." McCall suddenly felt the weight of the long hours in the unmarked U.S. Air Force Boeing 727. "Abby, I've got to apologize. This meeting has nothing to do with official diplomacy. The only reason I'm here is because of our friendship. The President wanted to make use of our friendship, and I agreed. For that, I apologize."

Hussein nodded with understanding. He leaned back in his chair, brushing his thinning hair back with his hand. "I see," he said wearily. "Johnson is worried about Israel."

"No...well, yes. He's worried about Israel, but he's worried about the entire Middle East. He doesn't want war."

"He thinks *I* do?" Hussein asked, his eyes wide in surprise, "Does he really think I can stop it?"

McCall sighed. "I guess I don't know what he really thinks. The President asked that I urge you not to become involved in the fighting. He said Jordan is the only Arab country that, in his words, has the realistic view that some kind of accommodation must be made with Israel."

Hussein held out his hand to stop McCall. "The President said I should *avoid* becoming involved?" Hussein shook his head. "He doesn't have a very realistic view of how Jordan must accommodate the other Arab nations."

McCall felt the king's frustration, as well as his own. McCall reached for his brief case. "Here is what the President proposes in the way of an aid program if Jordan avoids participating in any fighting that may occur." McCall didn't like the sound of the words he'd just uttered. He handed Hussein the document outlining the aid program.

Hussein locked eyes with McCall as he took the document. He held it for a moment, then tossed it onto his desk without looking at it.

"Spenser, the aid Jordan now receives from the U.S. and Britain is vital to Jordan's economy. But that," he said, pointing to the document, "is nothing more than blackmail."

McCall knew that the king was an emotional man, at times even irrational. But McCall never doubted his bravery or his dedication to his people.

Hussein rose quickly from his chair, paced for a moment, then turned to face McCall. "Spenser, if there is a war, it will be disastrous for the Arabs. We're not ready. There is no central command to coordinate our forces. For all practical purposes, there is no alliance between the Arab nations -- relations between Jordan and Syria are virtually extinct."

The room was silent for a long moment. "The Israelis want Palestine," Hussein said, "and Jordan rules part of Palestine." With finality, he said, "If there is war, Jordan will have no choice but to fight, and we will fight bravely and with honor." He paced again, then paused. "Does Johnson really expect me to give up Palestine without a fight? To just sit back and let the Israeli tanks roll through it?"

"Not necessarily," Abby. "He just doesn't want war." McCall felt in his gut how trite the words sounded.

Hussein sighed, then pointed to the document on his desk. "Tell the President that I cannot accept his offer, and I am very disappointed that he thought I would even consider it."

Hussein's lips were pressed tightly together. "I have some matters to attend to. You can wait here. Muna will be down in a few minutes to have lunch with us."

The king turned to leave, then paused at the door. "Spenser?"

"Yes?"

"You were right, my friend. You are no diplomat. I don't believe that a man of principle can be a good one."

Later that afternoon, the king's helicopter carried McCall to Amman, where a car drove him to the American embassy. The White House had advised the embassy that McCall would be reporting directly to the President.

The streets of Amman were crowded with military traffic. While McCall waited for a convoy of halftracks and Patton tanks to pass, he wondered again whether Johnson was sending him on a wild goose chase. *Is he trying to buy time so he can build a defense for Crawford? Or did he get me out of the country to give Larry Thompkins time to convince the board to get rid of me. Christ, I am getting paranoid.*

McCall also had time to replay the lunch with Hussein and Princess Muna. When lunch began, the king's demeanor still was cool. But Princess Muna had a calming effect on the king, and his mood improved as they lingered after the meal.

"What I suggest, Spenser," Hussein said, "is that you go to Israel and convince them not to attack. If you can accomplish that, my friend, you will have achieved the mission you have been assigned by your President."

"If I go to Israel," McCall had said, "can I tell them that you have agreed to meet with Israel to discuss the Palestinian question, whether or not the other Arab nations agree?"

With only a moment's hesitation, Hussein said, "I will agree to consider the possibility of such discussions. But I will not do so publicly."

McCall leaned close to the king, folding his hands on the table. "Abby, that's not good enough, and you know it. You know that I can't go the President or the Israelis with something that thin."

Hussein smiled. "You are learning quickly, Spenser. Your CIA may be aware of it, but I've held such meetings in the past with Golda Meir. We met in the desert in an air-conditioned car. We each wore disguises." He chuckled. "She was dressed as an Arab woman."

McCall knew that Hussein reveled in that kind of intrigue. Once he had posed as an Amman taxi driver. He asked each of his passengers what they thought of their king, and he was generally pleased with the results of his informal survey.

"I'm afraid that it's too late for talk, my friend," Hussein said. "But talk to the Israelis; talk to your President. If you see some hope, then you and I will talk again. If they fail to appreciate my position, then I suggest that, for your own safety, you leave the Middle East as soon as possible."

When McCall entered the embassy's communication center, he was shown to what looked like the kind of soundproof booth used for hearing tests.

"What is this thing?" McCall asked the embassy official.

"Sir, the ambassador uses this for White House communications. One like it is used in Saigon and a few other locations. I can assure you that it's totally secure. You just have to sit inside and talk. When you've completed your call, just press that button to open the door.

"You mean the Arabs are capable of intercepting our calls?"

''No, we don't think they can," the embassy official said. "But we know the Russians have the capability. Certainly the Israelis do?"

"I thought Israel was on our side."

The embassy official smiled. "They are, but let's just say they like to keep on top of things." A red light began to blink. "Your call's coming through now, sir. You can start to talk when the light stops blinking."

McCall sat in the booth and the door was closed. All he could hear was the phone line clicking as the connection was completed. Then the red light stopped blinking and a voice boomed through the speaker. "Talk to me, Spenser McCall. You there?"

McCall winced at the speaker volume, then cleared his throat "I'm here, Mr. President."

"Where the hell have you been, Spense? I've been waiting for you to call me."

"I've met with the king, sir."

"Well, dammit, what'd he say?"

McCall hesitated, trying to decide what kind of net impression about Hussein he wanted to give the President. "He's royally pissed, Mr. President."

"Everybody in the world is pissed about something, Spense. The whole Middle East is especially pissed. What's he pissed about in particular?"

"He said that your request to stay out of the fighting doesn't recognize what kind of trouble that will cause for him with the rest of the Arab nations, or even his own people."

"I know damn well the Syrians and the Egyptians aren't gonna send him roses and candy," Johnson said, the speaker booming even more loudly. "But he's got the balls to do it. If he backs away, maybe the others will, too."

"It's Palestine, Mr. President. He knows the Israelis want it, and he said he's going to fight to keep Jordan's part of it. He said he has no choice; it's a matter of honor. If he doesn't fight, his own people will probably overthrow him."

The speaker hummed for a long moment, then Johnson asked, "What did he say about the aid package?"

"He didn't even read it."

"What did you say, Spense? I didn't hear you."

"I said he wouldn't read it. He told me to give it back to you and to tell you that he was disappointed that you would think he'd even consider it. He said you were trying to blackmail him."

"I don't give a good goddamn whether he's got his royal bowels in an uproar about me. I just want him to stay out of the fighting. The Russians are the wild card in all this. What are they going to do if Israel attacks? Then how are we going to react to whatever the Russians do?"

"Mr. President, he asked that I talk to the Israelis. He indicated that he might be willing to talk to them — if they'll talk to him, and if the talks can be held in absolute secrecy."

Again the line hummed for a long moment

"Okay, Spense, if he wants you to go to Israel, then go there. That was part of the plan anyway. I'll have someone call the embassy and tell them that you'll brief them. How soon can you get there?"

"Probably first thing in the morning."

"No, dammit, I want you to leave right away. You just brief our people. Let them talk to the Israelis. I'll have Crawford meet you at the embassy or at your hotel."

"How long do you want me to stay in Israel?"

"How the hell would I know? Depending on what the Israelis say, you may have to go back to Jordan. If there's an agreement to meet, Levi Eshkol, the prime minister, will probably want to personally talk to Hussein. But I want you with Hussein if there's a meeting; I want your version of what the hell is said."

"That presumes the king will want me to tag along."

"You'll handle it. Get it done, Spense. I want you there."

"Mr. President, I saw a lot of armor and troops moving up toward the border. I think it's probably too late for diplomacy."

""I just want your eyes and that high-priced brain, Spense. I know you're no diplomat."

McCall felt a surge of anger. "You're the second person that's told me that today. And that makes me wonder, Mr. President, just what the hell I'm doing here. Did this assignment ever stand a chance of succeeding?"

"McCall, do you think you're the only one I've got over there talking to the Jews and A-rabs? I'm pressing all the buttons I've got." Johnson paused, then said very softly, "Hell, Spense, I don't know if it'll work, but we sure as hell have to try."

Despite the fact that McCall could clearly feel the President's own frustration and anger, he couldn't deny his suspicion about Johnson's real motive for the assignment. "I've got to ask this, Mr. President: did you send me here to just keep me quiet about the Crawford business?"

"I want you to remember who the hell you're talking to, McCall." The angry words bristled over the speaker. There was several seconds of silence, then McCall heard the President sigh.

'Jeezus H. *Christ,* McCall, I'm standing in front of the whole world with my fly unzipped, and you're still working up a lather about that old Nigra and his damn medal?"

"You remember our deal," McCall said. "I agreed to come here if you'd check the records about how Crawford got the medal."

"1 know what the hell I agreed to," the President said. "Dammit, Spense, here I am, ready to kiss an A-rab's ass -- and Ho Chi Minh's, if I have to — at high noon in the middle of goddamn Mohammed Boulevard." McCall could see the President pacing, as if on a stage, his long arms swinging in cadence with his words. "All I want is to stop all this damn fighting so I can get on with what I promised the American people I'd do. And all you're worried about is something that happened more than twenty years ago, something that most people wouldn't give a cow plop to know about."

In the booth's sterile environment, the President sounded wounded, aggrieved. The world was conspiring against him, and his Great Society was slipping through his fingers. It was the Alamo again, and Lyndon Johnson was dodging bullets and shells to protect the nation against impossible odds. McCall knew the performance was both real and manipulative. Despite the knowledge of it, he felt the guilt.

"Like I said, Mr. President, I had to ask. I'll meet Crawford tonight in Jerusalem, if that's what you want, but only if I have your word that you'll check the records."

"Okay, you've got my word. You win, but I want you to get over there and talk to the Jews as soon as you can. McCall, this is the most important job you've ever had. I need your help; your country needs you. And one more thing."

McCall waited without responding.

"You know, Spense, you really are a stubborn sumbitch, but do me a favor, will ya'? Keep your ass covered while you're out there. You're one of those people who keeps my blood pumping."

McCall heard the click when the line was abruptly disconnected. Deep in thought, it was several moments before he noticed the embassy official motioning for him to open the booth's door.

CHAPTER 14

June 2, 1967
South Bend, Indiana
9 p.m.

What did they say?" Valerie Jackson, obviously worried, sat across the kitchen table from Tony.

"Oh, they didn't say it straight out," Tony answered. "They don't do it that way. There were just hints about the case load and the suggestion that I've been gone a lot. But I know they're catching hell because Izzy is still free, and I guess they blame me for it."

Tony was thoughtful. "On the other hand, they don't want to appear that they're getting heavy about it, so they said to take whatever time I need to make sure my father's okay."

"Tony, I don't understand what you're saying. I can't understand why they continue to blame you for the death of the FBI agent and that undercover guy. You weren't even in the alley when Arnold killed those men."

"Dammit, Val, I know that. But maybe I pushed too hard to make the arrest that night. I wanted Arnold because of the way he killed Pinkins, that ATF agent, and left him on the hood of his own car. And, yes, maybe I especially wanted Arnold because I know damned well he killed Pinkins that way because he was black. It was a message, like the old days when they'd leave a black man hanging from a tree to keep the other blacks in line."

"Was Arnold sending the message to you?" Valerie asked.

"Maybe. Maybe he didn't like the idea that I got all that publicity about the ITAR cases. Maybe he knew that sooner or later he and I would cross paths. Maybe he *wanted* us to cross paths so he could show everybody that the hot-shot assistant U.S. attorney wasn't such hot shit -- that he was just another uppity coon."

"Tony, stop that," Valerie said without anger. She reached for the coffee pot and refilled their cups. Then she shook her head. "Tony, I think you're reaching. Maybe Arnold did leave a message with that dead man. But I don't think you're reading the message right. I think Arnold's message is that he doesn't give a damn about the law, and he doesn't want the cops or the feds screwing with him. I'll bet that's the way you would have read the message if Pinkins had been a white agent."

"Val, it isn't that simple."

"Okay, maybe it isn't. Let's look at the worst case. What if he did kill Pinkins that way because he was black? What if Arnold is a racist? What the hell would you expect from a man called Izzy The Animal?"

"The problem, Val, is that all racists aren't killers, drug pushers, and gun runners. It can be a lot more subtle than that. You and I deal with it every day. Why do you think dad never got a medal because of what he did in the war? I'll tell you why: because he was just a dumb nigger to the army brass, to the government, and to people like Crawford. That's why. They're the worst kind, Val, because they hide their racism behind their good schools, and money, and power. It's a barrier that blacks can't cross."

"Do you think Spenser McCall is a racist?" Valerie asked. "Or Eleanor Harrison? They've got money and power."

"No, I don't think that. I'm convinced that Eleanor is helping because she's honestly believes it's the right thing to do. On the other hand, she really isn't risking anything, and it's good copy."

Tony sipped his coffee, then wrapped both hands around the cup as he stared down into the dark liquid. "But McCall's another matter. I don't know what's driving him. I don't understand why he's risking his appointment as ambassador by bucking the President over dad's medal. From some things I've heard, what he's doing for dad may even be complicating life for him with his company."

Valerie reached across the table to raise Tony's head so she could look into his eyes. "While you're considering all of that, don't overlook the possibility that McCall may be just as angry and frustrated as you are over what's happened to your father. It could be as simple as that."

Tony reached for Valerie's hand. "Hell, honey, I'm not sure what's going on. Maybe I am kicking over all these rocks and there won't be anything hiding under them. It's just that we're shaking some big trees in Washington and anything can happen."

"Do you suppose your job is at stake?"

"I don't know for certain, but I think they're getting nervous because the district's first black assistant U.S. attorney is raising such a fuss about his old man."

"I guess if you speak out about dad deserving a medal, you can't do it without being critical of the Secretary of the Army."

Tony added. "And when you're critical of the Secretary of the Army you're also criticizing the President. Then when the bust went sour, there are people in Washington and South Bend who had to cover their asses. And who better to blame than the black attorney who looked like he was trying to avenge the murder of a black agent?"

"Did you know that black agent?" Valerie asked.

"I knew he was assigned to the Arnold investigation, but I never met him."

Valerie squeezed Tony's hand. "What are you going to do about your dad?"

"If you're asking whether I'm going to push for dad's medal, I admit that I've given that a lot of thought. It's going to cost us, however it turns out."

Tony looked into Valerie's eyes. "But I can't make that decision without you, honey. We've got to make it together."

"Let's don't play games, Tony. You know damn well you've made the decision, and you know damn well that I agree with it. Everything you've become, everything we have, we owe to your dad. So we both know we're going to do the right thing – whatever the cost."

Valerie smiled. "But I wasn't asking *if* you're going to do anything for your dad, smart guy. I wanted to know what's going to happen *next*."

Tony chuckled as he brought Valerie's hand to his lips. "Sweetheart, I'm sure as hell glad I don't have to face you in court. Well, I suppose the next thing has to do with the call I got from Spenser McCall. He called me at the office today and said the Chicago *Times* is going to run the story on Sunday about dad. The paper wants to interview dad and me tomorrow afternoon. They even want pictures of me in the office."

Valerie nervously ran her index finger around the rim of her coffee cup. "Oh, Tony, is that a good idea? I mean, pictures in the office?"

"Yeah, I know, but Spenser and Eleanor Harrison want me to do it. They say it'll help the story. I guess I've got to believe they know what they're doing."

Valerie got up from the table and put their coffee cups into the dishwasher. "Tony, doing the interview could be risky."

Tony sighed. "I know. But Eleanor has one of the best police reporters in the country on the Arnold case, and she's been giving me whatever he finds. He helped locate the girl and he traced Arnold to Gary, Indiana. I guess what I'm saying is that I've got to trust her judgment."

Tony, anxious to change the subject, asked, "How did dad do today?"

"He ate a good lunch. He spent most of the day in his room reading and napping. I'm happy that he seems so comfortable here, considering this is only his second day."

"Is he sleeping now?"

"No, I took him some coffee just before you came home and he was watching television in his room."

"Well, I'd better go talk to him and decide how we're going to handle the interviews tomorrow. He's not going to like talking about what happened during the war."

"Tony, I hope the reporter doesn't push him too hard during the interview. You know how they are."

Tony nodded. "We've got to have faith that Eleanor is going to do the right thing by us. I suppose we'll see."

June 2, 1967
Georgetown, Maryland
11:20 p.m.

It was the look in her eyes when he'd told her. It wasn't so much a look of disappointment, although she clearly was disappointed. Certainly it wasn't anger or recrimination. She wasn't that kind of person. Crawford had talked for almost an hour. Julie had listened quietly. They both had cried as they sat in the study. She held him closely. For long minutes they stood clutching each other. Finally she asked, "Ollie, what are we going to do?"

"I don't know. Those people are trying to destroy us," he almost sobbed.

Julie dabbed at her eyes with a crumpled tissue. "Whatever it requires, we'll do the right thing." Julie kissed him lightly on the cheek. "Whatever happens, I want you to know that I love you." Then she went up to bed.

Long after Julie had left the study, Crawford rose from the easy chair and opened the liquor cabinet and poured a drink. He looked at the tumbler he held in his hand. What he'd seen in her eyes was hurt. He recalled that she's asked, *Ollie, what are we going to do?* Crawford shook his head in amazement. She hadn't even realized that she'd said *we* instead of *you*. In all of their twenty-two years of marriage, he had never loved her more than he did at this moment.

Crawford drained the glass and poured another. *Whatever it requires, we'll do the right thing,* she had said. *...the right thing.*

Crawford carried his glass to his desk. He unlocked the bottom drawer, withdrew the presentation case, and placed it on the desk. He looked at the case, but didn't reach to open it. Then, slowly, tentatively, he reached into the drawer again and withdrew the pistol, the Model 1911A1 Army Colt .45-caliber that had been custom-made for his father. His father's name, inlaid with gold, had been engraved on the right side of the slide shrouding the barrel. His father had carried it in two wars, and had presented it to his son when he'd received his first command.

Crawford pressed the button on the left side of the grip that released the magazine. It was charged with seven rounds of copper-nosed military ball ammunition. He re-inserted the magazine. He then pulled the slide back, allowing it to snap forward to load a round into the chamber. Then, very carefully, he lowered the hammer and laid the pistol on the leather desk pad.

Crawford went to the liquor cabinet and refilled the tumbler. From a distance of ten feet, he looked at the pistol. "Yes, Julie," he said aloud, "I'll do the right thing."

He drained the glass and placed it on the cabinet. Then he sat at his desk. His mind was a whirlwind. He reached for the pistol and raised it until the barrel touched his head an inch above his right ear. His right thumb cocked the hammer.

Crawford closed his eyes, his finger lightly touching the trigger. The only image in Crawford's brain was Julie's eyes. The hand holding the pistol began to tremble. Why hadn't there been anger in those eyes? Why not disdain? His finger wavered on the trigger. What would his death do to those eyes? What would his father say? Crawford knew what his father would say. His father would say that, whatever the judgment, this is the ultimate act of cowardice.

Crawford slowly sat up. I am not a coward, he said softly. God knows I'm not a coward, but how will they all understand what really happened that day. He stared at the pistol, shuddering as he sighed deeply. Then he carefully lowered the hammer to the safe position.

Tomorrow the reporter will come. The right thing to do is to fight them, he thought. Whatever else happened on that day, my plan and my leadership are what held that road. The evidence is on my side.

Crawford ejected the live round from the chamber and pressed the squat bullet back into the magazine. Then he put the pistol back into the drawer. He held the presentation case for a moment, then put it away.

Yes, he thought, I'll fight and I'll win.

June 3, 1967
The Times Tower
Chicago
9:45 a.m.

"Talk to me, Strobe, before I read all this," Eleanor said. "What is it all going to tell me?" Eleanor sat at the conference table scanning the pages of copy in front of her. Around the table sat Russell Crowley, Harold "Strobe" Strobinski, and John Wilkinson.

Strobe Strobinski, who earned his nickname because of the intensity with which he ran the most important desk in any newsroom, puffed out his cheeks, then placed his hands palm-down on the table. "Ellie, you've got a story. Wilk and the rest of the team did a helluva job -- onc helluva job."

Eleanor could see that the city editor was tired. There were bags under his eyes and he needed a shave.

Wilkinson, the paper's chief investigative reporter, was slouched down, resting his head on the back of his chair. Although the reporter's eyes were closed, she knew he wasn't asleep. No other reporter on the staff would even consider being so casual while sitting in a meeting with the city editor, the managing editor, and the publisher. But Wilkinson was good at his work, so good that he not only got away with a casualness that bordered on insubordination, he even ignored the dress code. He never wore a tie, or even a white shirt. No one had ever seen him in anything other than a shirt or sweater and jeans.

"I know that, Strobe," Eleanor said patiently. "But first, I want the answer to one question: did Crawford lie to get the Medal of Honor?"

"He sure as hell did," Wilkinson said without opening his eyes. "At least he didn't tell the whole story. But..." Wilkinson opened his eyes and slowly sat up. "...but we can't make the statement in any of the copy or the headline."

No one asked why the statement couldn't be made. They knew that Wilkinson had graduated with honors from Notre Dame law school, and they knew that he'd already discussed the story with the attorneys representing the paper.

"Then how can you be so certain that he lied?" Eleanor asked.

Wilkinson gestured toward the city editor. "First of all, because Strobe pulled together the best people we've got, we were able to cover a helluva lot of ground in less than four days. And, frankly, we lucked-out."

Wilkinson's energy level began to increase as he talked.

"The statements from Bobby Geary and Cordell Jackson were important, of course, and we cover that in the main story. Strobe and I decided to combine the profiles of Cordell Jackson and Geary into one piece, and the other sidebar is about the medal. We're also doing a piece on the significance of the Battle of the Bulge, and a piece that contrasts the role of black soldiers in World War Two, Korea, and Vietnam."

Wilkinson shook his head. "The Crawford interview doesn't give us any surprises. He's got three key arguments: he says the record shows he was assigned command of the squad and planned the defense; Bobby Geary's recanting of his earlier testimony, he says, is obviously due to Geary's deteriorating physical and mental state; and Cordell Jackson's nineteen forty-six version of what happened came during a time when Jackson needed psychiatric care."

Eleanor held up her hand to stop Wilkinson. "I'll ask the question one more time: did Crawford lie to get the medal?"

Wilkinson nodded quickly. "Sally Ehrlich in our Washington bureau dug up the name of the officer who recommended Crawford for the Medal of Honor. She got a lot of help from Jim Austin, who works for Mr. McCall, and a Warrant Officer Parker. In nineteen forty-four, this officer was a captain, commander of George Company. He retired a few years ago as a full-bird colonel. He lives in Lexington, Virginia. His name is Albert Schumann."

"Why is he important?" Eleanor asked.

"On the morning after the action at the roadblock, Schumann said that General Crawford visited the scene of the fighting. Schumann said that the general *suggested* that he -- Schumann -- recommend his son for the Medal of Honor. Schumann explained to Sally that suggestions offered by generals, especially one as famous as General "Iron Ollie" Crawford, were thinly disguised orders."

"Well, aside from blatant nepotism, what does that prove?" Eleanor asked. "Did Schumann say that Crawford didn't deserve the medal?"

"No, he didn't say that," Wilkinson said. "Schumann said that, based on the evidence available at the time, Crawford appeared to be a regular Audie Murphy. But, Schumann said there were two things about the incident that bother him to this day. You see, he led the relief column that got to the roadblock just before dark. He said he found Crawford sitting in the middle of the road, among the dead, although there wasn't a scratch on him. He said Crawford was incoherent and sobbing. Schumann said he chalked it up to the shock of what he'd been through. When Crawford was told a couple of days later that he was a candidate for the medal, Crawford told Schumann he didn't deserve it and didn't want it."

"Did Schumann say why Crawford didn't want it?" Eleanor asked.

"Schumann said he asked him, but that Crawford just shook his head and walked away. Later, maybe a few days later, General Crawford talked to Schumann and said that it was clear to him that his son deserved the medal and that, although he wanted all procedures followed, he also wanted the review process expedited."

Strobe said, "That's probably why the review committee didn't spend a lot of time with Geary. They were afraid that Geary and the other witness, Wilcox, would die before they pulled their report together."

"Right," Wilkinson said. "But the most important thing Schumann told me -- and this is a key part of our story -- is that when he got to the roadblock, he found a black soldier lying near a machine gun without a tripod. He said there was a pile of brass -- expended shells -- around the gun. The black soldier's leg was missing and it appeared that he'd been shot in the head. In fact, Schumann said he thought the man was dead. He said he also noticed that most of the dead Germans were lying in front of that gun."

Eleanor, obviously excited about what she'd just heard, asked, "Well, didn't he tell anyone about that?"

Wilkinson nodded, "Yes, he said he mentioned it to General Crawford and to the investigators. At that point, they already had the testimony of the two witnesses -- Geary and Wilcox. Wilcox died of his wounds a short time later.

"But then, according to Schumann, General Crawford did something he thought was a little strange. He kept asking him about Cordell Jackson. By then they knew that Jackson was alive, but so badly hurt that he wasn't even conscious, so they couldn't interview him."

Eleanor asked, "What kind of questions was the general asking?"

"Things like what kind of soldier Jackson was. The general seemed particularly interested in Jackson's head wound. He found out that Jackson had been shot with a pistol. A few feet away from where they found Jackson there was the body of a German major. Schumann said that General Crawford was amazed that the German officer could get close enough to use his pistol. Schumann asked the question the general didn't ask -- but the question was hanging there and didn't have to be asked: where was Lieutenant Crawford when the German officer shot Cordell."

"Did Schumann and General Crawford discuss the fact that Cordell had been shot with a pistol?" Eleanor asked.

"Yes," Wilkinson said. "Schumann told the general that he had the Luger he'd found next to the German officer's body. General Crawford told Schumann he would discuss Cordell's wound with his son. There is no evidence that the review committee ever considered the question, but Schumann said the general seemed very concerned about how Cordell got the head wound.

"Schumann also said he thought it was highly unusual that Lieutenant Crawford didn't suffer a scratch, considering that every man in his squad was either killed or seriously wounded. Schumann said he had the feeling that the general was wondering the same thing."

Eleanor touched the stack of copy in front of her. "Obviously, if Crawford had run into the woods, he wouldn't have been exposed to the risk of death or injury during those terrible, closing moments of the fighting."

"What's confusing to me," Strobe said, "is that the evidence is clear that the relief column found Crawford on the road. Now, if he ran into the woods to hide, or whatever, he had to come back. But there's something more important that's been bothering me. In his statements after the war, Cordell describes how he was shot by the German officer. According to the psychiatrist's notes, however, Cordell's memory stops when that shot was fired. Now, if that dead major is the officer who shot Cordell and if -- according to Cordell's story -- he and Geary were the last two men alive, who killed the German officer?"

"Yeah, that bothers me, too," Wilkinson said, "assuming the dead officer and the officer who shot Cordell are the same man."

Crowley, the managing editor, said, "There could be a couple of explanations for that. Cordell might not have noticed that the officer who shot him was wounded and the guy died moments later. Or the dead officer was not the man who shot Cordell."

"There's something else," Wilkinson said as he turned several pages in his notebook. "Schumann said that in the several meetings he'd had with General Crawford after the war, Crawford never once mentioned his son or the medal. In fact, Schumann had the feeling that the old man and his son didn't have much to do with each other."

Eleanor asked, "Is Schumann suggesting that the general had second thoughts about whether his son deserved the medal?"

Wilkinson shrugged. "Maybe."

"Okay," Eleanor said. "We'll have to keep digging for that. Now, tell me about Oliver Crawford the man."

Wilkinson pursed his lips and nodded, again referring to his notebook. "Crawford was an above-average student -- nothing outstanding, but he worked hard for his grades. He was active in sports -- football, mainly. He was considered a team-player but, again, nothing outstanding. At West Point, he graduated in the upper quarter of his class. There is no indication that he ever cheated on an exam or got into trouble of any kind, not even a traffic ticket."

"He sounds too good to be true," Eleanor said.

"He was," Wilkinson said. "But it seems that he didn't have a lot of choice. His father, the infamous Major General Crawford, was a royal son-of-a-bitch. Apparently, the old man didn't see himself as a father; he saw himself as a drill instructor. He was on the kid's ass constantly. There's evidence that the general never felt that his son measured up to his standards."

"Wilk, how much of that do you have in the story?" Eleanor asked.

"Not much -- but enough of it to show that Crawford spent most of his life busting his buns to measure up to his father's standards. He was always pushing. And there were times -- like maybe right now and maybe on that roadblock in Belgium -- when he got in over his head trying to please his father."

Crowley held his hand up to stop Wilkinson. "Just a second; let's look at this whole matter from another perspective. Is it possible that Crawford -- even if Jackson was firing the gun -- was in command of the situation, and that he was fighting on the roadblock some place where Cordell couldn't see him?"

"But that isn't what Geary and Jackson say," Eleanor said. "If Crawford had been there, you'd think that either Geary or Jackson would have mentioned it." Eleanor leaned back in her chair. "I suppose that Russell's point touches on the greatest weakness in our story. Geary says that he saw Crawford running into the woods. Jackson says that after the first machinegun crew was killed, he didn't see Crawford anymore. On the other hand, Crawford and the army say that Crawford was in command until the very end."

Crowley turned to Wilkinson. "I'm curious about something. Why is Schumann willing to speak for the record? My experience in the army is that career officers -- even retired ones -- rarely are critical of the top brass, let alone the Secretary of the Army? And why is he willing to speak now, after all these years?"

Wilkinson shrugged. "I asked him if he felt that he was putting himself at risk in any way. Schumann said he wanted to talk because he was never certain in his own mind that Crawford should have gotten the medal. I also asked him why he waited so long to speak out." Wilkinson looked around the table and smiled. "His response was that no one had ever asked him. Like I said, Schumann said Crawford acted very strangely, both immediately afterward and when he was questioned by the review committee."

"What do you mean?" Crowley asked.

"Well, either Crawford was playing the role of the reluctant hero, or he really felt he didn't deserve the medal. Schumann said he noticed Crawford was very uncomfortable around his father when the roadblock thing was discussed."

"Sounds to me," Strobe said, "that if his old man hadn't pushed so hard, Crawford might not have received the medal -- maybe wouldn't even have accepted it."

Wilkinson nodded agreement. "Schumann also said that he can still see the image of Jackson lying with his hand near that gun, left for dead on that road. He said he has asked himself countless times whether Jackson was ignored because he was black. He said a black corporal who was a cook just didn't stand a chance against a general's kid who was an officer."

Eleanor said softly, as if she were thinking aloud, "You know, there is one man who can clear all of this up...a man who can substantiate what Geary and Jackson have said."

Wilkinson, an expression of doubt on his face, turned in his chair to look at Eleanor. "Who?"

"If he's still alive, and if he can be found, the Nazi SS officer who shot Jackson," Eleanor said.

Wilkinson shook his head quickly. "We just discussed the strong possibility that the man who shot Cordell was the dead major."

"Yes," Eleanor said more confidently, "but if Crawford wasn't there -- if he'd already abandoned his post -- then he wouldn't know whether the man who shot Cordell is alive or dead."

The room was quiet. Strobe smiled. "Jesus Christ, yes. But let's presume he's alive. How do we find him? Hell, how do we know he'll even admit being there. After all, he obviously intended to execute a wounded GI."

Eleanor nodded. "Spenser McCall asked one of his people, Jim Austin, to go to West Germany to see if he can find out. He's leaving this afternoon." She pointed to Crowley. "Strobe, assign one of our people to be on the plane with Austin."

Eleanor paused as she looked around the table. "It would be great if we can find this German officer," she said. "But, frankly, I think the odds are against us. However, it doesn't make much difference whether we do find him."

Strobe, puzzled, asked, "I thought we just agreed that the Nazi could clear this all up?"

"Yes, he could do that," Eleanor said, "but in this first story I want us to say that the German officer is one of the keys to settling this, and that we've got an investigative team in Germany trying to find him or any other German soldier who was there that day. Hell, if we have to we'll even buy ads in the major German dailies asking him to contact us. That alone should keep the story alive."

Strobe smiled. "What you're saying is that, at this point, the fact that we're looking, and that we *might* find him, is what's going to rattle Crawford's cage."

"Exactly," Eleanor said. "Wilk, play that up high in the main story.

"Finally," Eleanor said, "I want to know how Spenser McCall's involvement in this story is being handled."

The room was silent, then Strobe asked, "Ellie, why don't you tell us how you'd like it handled?"

Eleanor's face flushed. "Look, gentleman, I'm not going to tell you how to do it. I want to know how *you* intend to handle it, then I'll tell you whether I agree with you."

"Well," Strobe began uncertainly, "Mr. McCall is the person who got the ball rolling on this thing. He found Geary and got his statements. Frankly, Ellie, Mr. McCall's involvement gives the piece a nice human interest dimension. He's the big corporate guy who's willing to take on Washington -- take on a President who everyone knows he's tight with -- to make sure that the guy who shines his shoes gets the honor he deserves."

Eleanor smiled. "I like it," she said. "Run with it, but at this point I don't want anything said about the meeting we had with the President, or that Spenser had with Crawford. Maybe we'll use it later."

"Okay." She looked around the table. "Anything else?" No one responded. "All right, then. Let's get it all together. I want to read all the final copy in three hours. We'll have another planning meeting late tomorrow afternoon -- Sunday -- after we're on the street. I want to see the network reaction."

Eleanor rose and stood at the table. "All of this was very good work, people. Thank you."

The Hotel Metropolitan
Tel Aviv, Israel
June 4, 1967
11:35 p.m.

McCall knew who was at the door when he heard the knock. Oliver Crawford smiled when the door opened. "Hi, Spense. Did you have trouble crossing the border?"

"Hello, Ollie." McCall looked into Crawford's eyes as they shook hands, and he knew that tonight would at the very least be awkward. McCall waved Crawford toward the couch. "Yes, it got a little hairy. Troops on both sides of the border are very jumpy." McCall walked over to an ice bucket. "They just brought up a couple of bottles of cold beer. You ready for one?"

"Sounds good."

When McCall was seated, Crawford asked, "How did you get across?"

"The king's helicopter took me from Hummar to Amman airport. He provided one of his cars, a Chrysler, that was driven by his chief of palace security, a light colonel. Two people from our embassy came along. One of them drove me here when the colonel left us at the border. I suspect one of those damn embassy guys was CIA."

"He probably was." Crawford sipped from his beer bottle. "I talked to the President about an hour ago, Spense. He told me about your meeting with Hussein. I told the President that it's probably too late. I didn't get it officially, but it looks like the Israelis are going tomorrow."

"They're going to attack?"

Crawford nodded. "It'll begin with an air assault. They're going to hit every Arab air field that poses a threat."

"What about Jordan?"

"The Israelis are hoping that Hussein will stay out of it. If he does, I don't think they'll attack Jordan."

McCall recalled Hussein's dilemma, and their discussion of bravery. McCall said softly, as if he were alone, "I don't think it'll make any difference if Israel attacks Jordan. Hussein has convinced himself that he's got to fight."

"Then he's facing a lost cause," Crawford said. "Hussein won't be able to hold Palestine. The Israelis are strong and they're motivated. Their tanks will roll right over him."

McCall nodded slowly. He looked at Crawford. The Secretary of the Army was in his mid-forties, tall, and blue-eyed. His full head of sandy hair was graying at the temples. McCall once overheard a woman say that Oliver Wentworth Crawford was the most incredibly handsome man she had ever seen -- too handsome, she had said, to be real. McCall's better judgment told him that perhaps now wasn't the time. He was too tired, and he was concerned about Abby. He remembered the look in his friend's eyes when McCall boarded the helicopter at the villa. Then he remembered the scene in Cordell's hospital room -- Tony kneeling in front of the old man's wheelchair, his head bowed, covering his father's clenched hands with his own. Yes, McCall thought, it must start now.

"I suppose you're right, Ollie," McCall said evenly. "Maybe it is a lost cause. But, then, maybe it isn't. After all, those German tanks on that road in Belgium should have rolled right over you. But you held that road, and you got the Medal of Honor for it. Isn't that the way it happened?"

Crawford was closely examining the label on his beer bottle. Then he looked at McCall. "The President showed me the letter you gave him. That was a cheap shot, Spense. That's not your style. Why didn't you come directly to me? I'd have given you all the evidence you need."

"Ollie, the evidence I do have raises some serious questions about whether you deserved that medal."

"C'mon, Spense, all you've got is an old Negro who shines shoes for a living who says he should have gotten the medal."

"No," McCall said sharply. "Cordell has never said that. I and a few others who've seen the evidence are saying it."

"You mean Eleanor Harrison and Bobby Geary?"

McCall nodded. "Among others." McCall paused and looked closely into Crawford's eyes. "Ollie, you were seen running into the woods. Bobby Geary saw it."

Crawford slowly put his beer bottle on an end table. His reaction was as if McCall had struck him. His mouth was open, his lips moving, but the words seemed to be stuck in this throat. Finally, in a voice quavering with emotion, he said, "Spenser, that's a damned *lie!*"

McCall quickly shook his head. "No, I don't think so. Jackson had no reason to lie when he talked to that psychiatrist. He never took credit for organizing the defense. He still doesn't. As he and Geary described it, they were the only two men fighting at that roadblock. If you were there, one of them would have mentioned it. They had no reason not to."

Crawford leaned forward in his chair. McCall could see that he was fighting to control his temper. Then Crawford held out his hands as if to stop McCall from saying anything more. "Look, don't you realize what you're saying? You're accusing me of having lied. Don't you realize that the awarding of the medal is based on careful documentation? That witnesses were interviewed? That the scene of the fighting was carefully examined by investigators?"

"Ollie, we have evidence from--"

"Your evidence is based on what a pathetically ill man and a senile old Negro -- a man who's practically a vagrant -- say they remember after nearly twenty five goddamn years! Who the hell is going to believe them?"

McCall said very quietly, "I believe them...I believe them because they don't want anything out of all this. Cordell doesn't even know I'm pursuing it. It's important for you to know that Cordell's description of the fighting was recorded in nineteen forty-six during the interviews with the psychiatrist. And Bobby Geary's recollections of what happened closely parallel what Cordell said then, and neither man knew that the other had survived."

"Why are you pursuing it?" Crawford asked. "Don't you realize what you're doing to me? If you persist in this lunacy, I'll be ruined. Never in the one-hundred-year history of the Medal of Honor has anyone charged that a recipient lied to get it. It's just not possible for that to happen."

McCall didn't respond. The room was silent for a long moment. McCall could dearly see the panic in Crawford's eyes.

"McCall," Crawford said, "you've got to stop that newspaper story. The President wants it stopped. We know you can get that done because of your relationship with Eleanor."

"If you think that," McCall said, "then you don't really understand our relationship."

Crawford slowly nodded, as if he finally realized that the story would become public. Just ask yourself this question, Spense: what if I'm right, and you drag me and my family name through the mud? The investigation alone will ruin me." Crawford rose and started slowly for the door.

"Ollie." Crawford paused and turned to face McCall. "There's something I've been wondering about since this all came up. Think back twenty years or so, when you asked me to give Cordell a job. Why? Why did you care what happened to him?"

Crawford shrugged. "He'd been in my first command. As I recall, he'd been a good soldier. And he needed help. Simple as that."

"Okay, Ollie. I'll give you this: I'm still not absolutely convinced that you lied. Perhaps there's more to the story than I know at the moment, but what I'm convinced of is that something happened that day in Belgium that you're hiding. I'm going to dig out the truth."

McCall followed Crawford to the door. Crawford attempted a smile.

"I guess the President's hope that this meeting would resolve the matter wasn't very realistic."

"About as realistic as his hoping that I could convince Hussein not to fight." The two men stood quietly for a moment. "Ollie, I really didn't know what I expected to come of this meeting," McCall said without anger or emotion. "Maybe I hoped that I'd see or hear something that would convince me that you really do deserve the medal. As you say, it's been almost twenty five years."

"And I presume you're still not convinced."

"No, Ollie, I'm not."

"Well, Spense, I've always respected you -- as a man and for what you've done with your company. In two decades, you've made Horizon an international power. The President told me he respects you more than any other businessman he's ever met. He said you have a low-key way of getting things done. He said you're rightly focused and determined." Crawford smiled. "Which, I've got say, I've seen first-hand tonight." Then the smile faded. "But you've got to know, Spense, that I'm going to fight you on this."

"I understand," McCall said.

"I guess none of this means that we can't have breakfast together," Crawford said. McCall could tell that Crawford was attempting to temper the emotion generated by the meeting, and McCall was grateful for the effort. "Say, eight o'clock? Then we'll have to meet with our embassy people here in Tel Aviv. They probably will have more questions for you, and we should be there if the Israelis kick off tomorrow."

"Eight is fine. Good night, Ollie."

June 5, 1967
Jerusalem
11:50 a.m.

The black Cadillac sedan was northbound on St. George's Road in New Jerusalem when McCall heard the freight-train rumble of artillery rounds passing high overhead. "Those sound a lot heavier than the other stuff," McCall said. The sound reminded him of the V1s the Nazis used to pound London.

Crawford nodded. "Long Toms -- one hundred fifty five millimeter. We supplied them to Hussein." He pointed to the east, toward the hills surrounding Jordan's half of the city. "They're probably back there. They've got the range to reach Tel Aviv on the coast, and the airport at Lod."

Artillery had been falling in New Jerusalem since mid-morning, well to the west of the road, which paralleled the tangled and rusty coils of concertina wire that marked the no-man's land separating the Jordanian and Israeli parts of the city.

Despite the shelling, the traffic was heavy in both directions. There were a few civilian cars on the road, but most of the traffic was a mixture of military vehicles, buses, and cabs, all loaded with Israeli soldiers.

Earlier, when the CIA couldn't convince Crawford to leave Jerusalem, he was assigned a guide to help the driver. Both men were Israelis. The driver, who introduced himself as Gershon Stern, was in his forties. McCall thought the man, whose only comments were curt responses to questions, looked like an office worker.

The guide, David Ben-Dor, looked to be in his late twenties, his skin bronzed by the desert sun. Although both men were dressed in civilian clothes, McCall suspected they were either soldiers or agents of the Mossad, the Israeli intelligence organization. When they left the King David Hotel, Ben-Dor explained that they would drive toward the Mandelbaum Gate, which had been the only link through the no-man's land separating the Israeli and Jordanian halves of the city. McCall had passed through the gate the day before.

The traffic began to thin as the Cadillac neared the gate, which was north of Old Jerusalem. Just as Ben-Dor turned to talk to McCall and Crawford, they heard the reverberating thunder of jet engines. Several miles to the east, they could see a jet fighter diving toward the hills. Green tracers were arching up toward the fighter, which released its bombs and pulled up abruptly and banked hard to the right. McCall could see the explosion before he heard and felt it.

"Israeli Mirages," Ben-Dor said.

Three more fighters, one following the other, made bombing runs. The ground fire became more intense. Black, angry puffs of heavy caliber anti-aircraft fire punctuated the streams of green tracers reaching for the fighters. It did not appear that any of the Mirages had been hit.

McCall hadn't noticed the portable transceiver that Ben-Dor was using now, speaking in Hebrew. When the conversation ended, Ben-Dor turned to look at Crawford. "I've been ordered to turn west when we reach the Mandelbaum Gate, which will be in about five minutes, Mr. Crawford. We cannot stop. A helicopter is being sent to take you direct to the prime minister's office in Tel Aviv. It sounds like someone in Washington called him to order you both out of Israel as soon as possible. A special plane will be waiting for you at Lod."

McCall smiled. *Someone in Washington* could only be LBJ. McCall asked, "Then you men are soldiers?"

Ben-Dor looked back and smiled. Then he reached under his seat and held up a sub-machine gun. "Gershon is a sergeant; I'm a captain. We're paratroopers." Ben-Dor patted the driver's shoulder. "Gershon fought in the forty-eight and fifty-six wars -- through these same streets. He was--"

McCall didn't immediately realize what had struck the car. He heard a heavy thumping sound, then the windshield turned milky an instant before it was blown out. Just as he ducked to avoid the flying glass, he saw the top of the driver's head explode in a shower of blood and gore that sprayed over the other three men.

"Machine gun!" Ben-Dor shouted, "*Get down!*"

McCall looked up to see the driver slumped over the wheel. Ben-Dor reached across to grab the wheel to steer the car into the shallow ditch on the west side of the road. The riddled Cadillac plowed into the west wall of the ditch. McCall was thrown violently against the back of the front seat. He was dazed, lying on the floor of the car when he heard Ben-Dor shouting, "Stay low and crawl into the ditch. Get away from the car."

McCall pushed open the left door and he and Crawford crawled into the ditch. Ben-Dor -- carrying his radio, weapon, and a canvas shoulder bag -- went over the back of the front seat and dove through the back door. He pointed with his weapon to the south. "Crawl that way about fifty yards and wait for me."

Another long burst of fire slammed into the car and ricocheted off the road. McCall started to follow Crawford, then paused to look back. Ben-Dor had opened the driver's door, apparently to remove the driver's body, but he couldn't open it wide enough because of the crumpled left fender. The car was at a steep nose-down angle, its rear wheels on the edge of the ditch.

McCall turned back and crawled to within a few feet of the car. "Leave him!" McCall shouted. "We have to get away from the car."

"No, they want to see it burn." Ben-Dor's words were distorted by his struggle to remove the driver's body. "They'll keep shooting until the tank goes up."

McCall started to move forward to help the captain when a long stuttering burst of machine gun fire ripped the metal of the car and struck jackhammer blows on the road and along the edges of ditch. The fusillade created a furious whirlwind of sand and car fragments. Although he was lying in the bottom of the ditch, McCall felt an almost overpowering urge to dig even deeper into the dry sand. He'd never known such terror. He wanted to move, to help Ben-Dor, but it was as if his legs and arms were paralyzed. Then he felt someone crawling over him. It was Crawford.

"C'mon, Spense."

McCall was amazed that Crawford's voice was so low and steady.

Crawford patted McCall's shoulder. "Let's help this guy or we're never going to get out of this damned ditch." Crawford, disregarding the bursts of gunfire that continued to sweep the ditch, rose to his knees and reached over Ben-Dor to grab the driver's belt. "Pull!" Crawford shouted. The two men pulled the body through the partially opened door and into the ditch. Crawford seemed unaware of the blood that had smeared the front of his shirt.

Ben-Dor reached under the front seat for the driver's weapon. He held it out to McCall.

"Give us some covering fire while we pull Gershon clear."

McCall shook his head. "I've never fired an Uzi, and I don't know where the fire's coming from." McCall suspected that Ben-Dor had given him the gun to keep him busy, out of the way. *He thinks I'm too old -- and too scared -- to be of any real help.*

Ben-Dor quickly showed McCall how to cock the weapon, how the safety lever operated, and how to insert a fresh magazine. Then he gestured for McCall to move to the side of the ditch facing the Arab gun.

"When we raise our heads to look, I'll show you where the gun is. We have to be quick. It's a two-flat house, about three hundred meters straight back. There is a single-flat house in front of it that has a red tile roof."

McCall was impressed that the young captain had managed to spot the gun's location. "There are three or four windows on the second floor," Ben-Dor said. "The gun is in the second window from the right. We're going to look for three seconds, then get our heads back down." Ben-Dor pulled McCall closer to him, keeping a hand on his shoulder. "Ready?" the captain asked.

McCall nodded.

"Okay. *Do it now!*"

When McCall raised his head over the edge the ditch, he remembered the sight of the driver's head exploding. He felt a rising panic when he couldn't find the building Ben-Dor had described. Then he saw a white light flashing from a two-story building. It was the gun.

Both men ducked as bullets sprayed across the road. "Did you see it?" Ben-Dor shouted.

"Yes, I saw the muzzle flash."

"Okay, I want you to move to the north side of the car. They haven't seen any movement there. Fire bursts of only three or four rounds, then move twenty yards farther down the ditch. Don't fire more than once from the same position. Do you understand?"

"What if there are civilians in the house?" McCall asked.

"Everyone on that side of the wire is an enemy soldier," Ben-Dor said sharply, as if he resented McCall's concern about Jordanian civilians. Then McCall saw the captain's expression soften. "Don't worry, Mr. McCall, those houses have been vacant for months."

"How long do I keep up the firing?"

"All I need is three or four minutes. Then stay down. You've got three magazines. Save one in case they decide to come after us."

"You mean the Jordanians might attack us?" McCall hadn't considered that the Arabs would try to cross the wire.

"That's the Arab Legion over there. They're tough, and they're very good."

McCall remembered the Arab Legion colonel who commanded Hussein's guards. If they were all that impressive, he thought, the three of them wouldn't stand much of a chance.

Ben-Dor said, "We have a couple of tanks and APCs that are just down the road. I'll call them up. When the tanks knock out the gun, we'll pick you up in an APC and take you to the helicopter. Are you certain that you understand everything I've said?"

"Yes," McCall nodded quickly. He looked at Crawford, who smiled and held his thumb up. McCall felt a surge of anger, certain that Crawford knew he was afraid, that he didn't want to be alone on the north end of the ditch, that he didn't want to stick his head up to fire the damn gun. McCall felt that Crawford knew all of that, and was enjoying it.

Ben-Dor reached into his canvas bag. "Here," he said, handing McCall a large bandage, "you'll need this."

McCall, confused, looked at the bandage.

"You're head, Mr. McCall. It's bleeding." Ben-Dor pointed to the right side of McCall's head. "It doesn't look serious."

McCall gingerly felt for the wound until his fingers touched a gash above his right ear. He had been unaware of the blood that had flowed down the side of his face, soaking his collar.

Ben-Dor patted McCall's shoulder. "You should move now, Mr. McCall. And be careful."

McCall twisted around in the ditch and crawled on his hands and knees. He paused when he reached the car. It blocked the ditch. He'd have to climb over the hood, giving the Arabs a target for a second or two.

"Wait!" McCall turned when he heard Ben-Dor shout. "Go over the instant after the next burst."

McCall nodded, then crouched, ready to spring. The Arab gun fired a short burst, then McCall scampered over the hood and kept moving for another thirty yards beyond. When he stopped and looked back down the ditch, he realized the car prevented him from seeing Crawford or Ben-Dor.

There was a long burst of gun fire. McCall watched as the Cadillac trembled under the impact of the heavy bullets, then he felt a flash of heat as a mushroom cloud of fire erupted over the car. In moments the car was engulfed with flames that formed a thick, greasy pillar of black smoke.

McCall got onto his knees, raised his head until he spotted the house, then ducked down, pressing his back against the side of the ditch. He examined the Uzi and tried to recall what he knew about it, which was damned little. It's only a nine millimeter, he thought, and with this short barrel I'll be lucky to even hit the damn house at three hundred meters. He took a deep breath, rose to his knees, braced the weapon on the edge of the ditch, and fired several rounds. He couldn't see any of his bullets hit the house.

I've got to settle down, he said after he'd ducked back into the ditch. He knew he was a good shot, at least with a hunting rifle. He remembered the shooting match at the LBJ ranch, with the President and few of LBJ's cronies. Each of the five shooters put a thousand dollars into a hat. The tightest bullet group in a paper target at two hundred yards would take the prize. McCall won. LBJ, who had the second-best score, clearly didn't like being second-best at anything.

McCall moved a few yards down the ditch and fired again. This time he could see a few wisps of cement dust as his bullets struck far to the left of the window he'd aimed at.

Then he heard the rattle of a sub-machine gun to his right. Ben-Dor must be firing, he thought. Or maybe Crawford talked the captain into letting him fire the thing.

McCall moved and fired, this time the burst registered hits around the window through which the Arabs were firing. Instead of moving, he fired again, this time a long burst that emptied the magazine. He watched with satisfaction as the bullets chipped cement all around the window.

Then he saw the flashing light. Although he ducked immediately, he yelped when something struck his left forearm. He saw that a bullet had gone through the sleeve of his jacket. He quickly pulled up the sleeve. A bullet had grazed his arm. There was only a little blood. He was relieved, then chided himself for ignoring the young captain's order to move each time he fired.

McCall moved twenty yards down the ditch. He inserted a fresh magazine, then paused to catch his breath. He looked at his clothes, stained with dirt, sweat, and the driver's blood and brain tissue. He thought about his inability to help the young captain pull the driver's body from the car. He marveled at the captain's courage. The young man seemed oblivious to the bullets that struck all around him. How could any man have that kind of courage?

Then he remembered Crawford crawling over him to help Ben-Dor. If Crawford knew fear at that moment, he had control over it. *At least a lot more control than I had.*

McCall rose, aimed carefully, and fired. He ducked immediately, confident now that his bullets would be on target.

Perhaps Jerome Geary had been wrong. Perhaps he and Cordell couldn't see everything that was happening on that road. Perhaps Crawford deserved the medal. Perhaps. Machine gun bullets slapped and whined across the road, and McCall could see green tracers passing low over his head.

McCall heard the heavy engine of a tank approaching. He raised his head slightly and saw a tank followed by other vehicles coming toward them. He hunkered back down, resting the Uzi in his lap as he tore open the bandage. It was a large compress, the type he could tie around his head, but he decided that would look silly. He dabbed at the wound and saw that the bleeding had slowed.

McCall looked at the car. The fire had nearly burned itself out. There had been a jug of water in a cooler in the back seat. He was very thirsty, and badly needed a cigarette.

The tank was closer now. It had stopped by the Cadillac. McCall could hear of the hum of the turret as it turned ninety degrees. The Arab machine gun opened fire and McCall could see the flash of the bullets striking the armor.

The tank's main gun moved in small increments, up and down, left and right, as if the tank were a long-snouted animal sniffing out its prey. Then there was a sharp crack as the gun fired. McCall saw the right corner of the house disintegrate in a shower of cement and brick dust. The tube moved slightly left and fired again, then three more high explosive rounds. In less than a minute, the tank fire had nearly removed the top half of the house, apparently without hitting any of the adjoining buildings.

As the tank moved forward, McCall could see two armored personnel carriers and another tank following. The tank's turret hatch opened and the tank commander stood up to look into the ditch. When he saw McCall, he began to speak into the microphone attached to his helmet. The tank commander motioned for McCall to remain in the ditch as he stopped the tank on the far side of the road, apparently to shield the APC that was moving forward. Captain Ben-Dor, carrying his weapon and radio, trotted alongside the APC.

"Where's Crawford?" McCall asked when he'd climbed onto the road.

Ben-Dor pointed at the following APC. "He's okay. You get in this one. I don't want you both in the same APC."

McCall looked into the young man's eyes. "I'm sorry about your sergeant."

Ben-Dor looked across into no-man's land. "He was more than my sergeant, Mr. McCall. When I was in school he was my mathematics teacher. It was because of him that I became an officer in the regular army."

McCall looked at the Uzi that had belonged to the sergeant, then handed it to Ben-Dor."

"Do you know what a Sabra is?" Ben-Dor asked.

"It's what a native-born Israeli is called."

Ben-Dor nodded. "It's also a cactus that grows in the Negev. It's tough and prickly on the outside, and sweet on the inside." The young man's voice was shaded by emotion. "Gershon Stern was a Sabra."

McCall didn't know what more to say, and he started to walk toward the APC's rear hatch.

"Mr. McCall."

"Yes?"

"It's very difficult to be alone as you were in the ditch. You did well."

McCall looked at Ben-Dor for a long moment. "Captain, I was scared shitless. You saw that I couldn't help when you needed it. I froze. I was--"

McCall was interrupted by the tank commander who shouted from his turret to Ben-Dor, "David, we shouldn't stand here too long."

The captain motioned with his hand for the tanker to be patient. "It's okay, Dan. If there was another gun it would have opened up by now."

Ben-Dor turned back to McCall. "Gershon Stern believed that a man who knows great fear, and can overcome it, is the man who can be trusted to do what must be done. I knew you would do what was asked of you without taking unnecessary chances." Ben-Dor smiled. "That's why I sent you down the ditch, instead of Mr. Crawford."

"You mean you don't trust Crawford?"

Ben-Dor shrugged. "Why would such a man make a trip such as this one?"

"Do you know who Crawford is?"

"Mr. McCall, we know all about both of you."

McCall laughed. "Why am I not surprised." He shook hands with the young man. "Good luck, Captain."

Ben-Dor opened the rear hatch, and McCall saw that a half-dozen tough-looking troopers had been waiting in the sweltering APC. Just before he closed the hatch, Captain Ben-Dor said, "By the way, Mr. McCall, that was good shooting. Very good." Ben-Dor handed McCall the Uzi. "I'm certain Sergeant Stern would have wanted you to keep that."

As the APC lurched into motion, McCall saw the troopers exchange glances. They must be wondering what an old goat, splattered with dirt and blood, obviously an American, would be doing in the middle of their war. One of the troopers leaned forward and asked, "CIA?"

McCall knew it was rude, but he couldn't help it. He began to laugh, from deep within himself, his head back against the padded metal bulkhead.

"No," he said, "I sit behind a desk; I'm a businessman. Does anyone have any water?"

One of them quickly handed McCall a canteen. The water was warm, but it soothed his parched throat. He looked at each of the troopers and chuckled. "Now you guys are absolutely convinced that I'm a spook. Right?"

McCall leaned back and took another drink. He became aware of conflicting emotions. He had been under fire and he knew he had done well, despite the shaky beginning. He was pleased that these troopers had heard the young captain's compliments, and the way they looked at his blood-stained shirt. McCall wondered why he felt good about such things? Did he think he was a damned *warrior?* He touched the warm metal of the sub-machine gun in his lap. Perhaps, he admitted after a moment's reflection, that may be part of it. He had faced death, and he had functioned as he'd been ordered to. Then he remembered his fear and the horror of the driver's death.

McCall rubbed his burning eyes, straining to objectively analyze the emotions that surged and sputtered like a shorted electrical circuit. Then he thought of Cordell and Bobby—and, yes, Crawford—on the road in Belgium, and in the ditch. They had *seen* the men who were trying to kill them. They were close enough to hear the Germans scream when they died.

And Cordell. My God, *Cordell.* His leg blown away and metal shards in his body, the dead and dying all around him, and still he continued to fight. Cordell had looked into the eyes of the man who believed he was killing him.

McCall was glad he hadn't tied the bandage around his head. He now could better understand the depth of feeling shared by Cordell and Bobby. McCall wondered whether he shared some special camaraderie with Ben-Dor. Perhaps. Or, perhaps, the young Israeli captain was just being kind to an old man who was afraid.

That driver who taught young men mathematics -- Crawford and I were responsible for his death, McCall decided. I could have prevented it if I'd been more forceful with Crawford this morning.

Later, when this is all over, I'll have Jim Austin find that young captain, David Ben-Dor. The least I can do is to see if something can be done to help the sergeant's family; perhaps I'll establish a mathematics scholarship in his name. The young captain might like that.

McCall handed back the canteen and nodded his thanks. He looked at the young men seated around him and decided that wars should be fought only by old men in their sixties. They would be so paralyzed with fear that no one would be hurt. War would become a non-event.

No, McCall thought, I won't have Jim Austin find the captain. I'm going to call Eleanor the first chance I get, and we're going to deal with Crawford. Then I'll come back here and handle the business about the sergeant myself.

CHAPTER 15

June 8, 1967
Horizon Corporation
General Office
3:10 p.m.

McCall couldn't ever remember sitting slouched in his high-back chair, his feet on the desk. When the intercom buzzed, he reached awkwardly for it.

"Mr. McCall, Mr. Jackson is here and would like to know if he can see you for a few minutes."

McCall sat up. "Yes, have him come in."

When Tony entered the office, he noticed that there wasn't a single sheet of paper on McCall's desk. Tony also noticed, as he sat in one of the three stuffed chairs in front of the desk, that McCall's credenza was cleared of books and the personal items he'd seen there previously.

"Well, Spense, we've got to hand it to the sonofabitch. He's doing a helluva job."

McCall grunted, seemingly intent on examining a gold-plated pen from every angle as he turned it in his hand. "Yep, he's doing such a good job that my board decided that it would be a good idea for me to leave this office earlier than scheduled. Seems that some of them are a little concerned that I've made the wrong people in Washington very angry."

"How much earlier?" Tony asked softly.

"As of tomorrow morning, my young friend, I am, for all practical purposes, among the unemployed." There was no humor in McCall's smile. "That's probably the last thing I ever expected -- after all of these years -- to be thrown out of this place on my ear." McCall shook his head as if he still didn't believe it. "Oh, they'll handle it quietly. I'm supposed to be invisible for a few months, go some place where the media can't reach me. And my successor will quietly take over. No fuss; no muss."

Tony shook his head. "Damn, Spense. I don't know what to say. Who would have imagined that the bastard would have zeroed in on you? He knew better than to try to discredit a poor old black man, so he shoots at the big oil guy who's supposed to be pissed because he lost some government contracts."

"Get the story right, Tony. He didn't say big oil guy; he said fat-cat oil baron." McCall still seemed almost mesmerized by the gold pen. "Same thing, I guess, but his tune plays better." McCall put the pen on his desk. "The contracts were for lubes and fuel that we lost the bid on. Frankly, we only submitted the damn bid because the government asked us to. The loss was really our gain because we've never made any money on the damn stuff...hell, sometimes we've lucky to break even."

Tony grimaced. "It's those television bastards who are killing us, Spense. They show old footage of Crawford getting his medal from Truman, scenes from the Bulge fighting, then they show my father and his shoe-shine cart. People just can't believe that a white Anglo-Saxon Protestant -- some dude who looks like the all-American boy -- could be anything other than a goddamned war hero."

Neither man said anything for a long moment.

"Tony, I've had calls today from all three networks. They want interviews. What's your opinion, counselor?"

"Hey, man. My opinion doesn't count here. You've got too much at stake."

McCall laughed cynically. "What, my job?"

"You know what I'm talking about. If you screw up on national television -- supporting a cause that looks like it's dead on its ass -- LBJ might let you shovel cow turds on his ranch."

McCall picked up the gold pen, held it for a moment, then put it into his inside jacket pocket. "I would be very surprised, my young friend, if the President still wants me." He reached under his desk for his private phone and tapped numbers into the key pad.

"Ellie, Tony and I would like to come over. I'm going to need some advice on how to handle network television interviews. We'll talk about it when we're together. Okay. Fifteen minutes."

McCall looked around the room. He opened the center drawer of his desk, even though he knew it was empty, then slowly closed it. He put his hands on his desk as if to rise from his chair. "You know? I can't really blame them," McCall said, his smile genuine. "If the roles were reversed, I would have fired me."

Tony laughed. "That's because you're a hard-ass, McCall -- probably harder on yourself than anyone who's ever worked for you. Let's go have Ellie run you through charm school."

When Spenser McCall rode the elevator to the lobby, walked past the security desk and through the revolving door, he realized that he never again would set foot inside the Horizon Building.

June 9, 1967
The White House
The Oval Office
6:13 p.m.

Lyndon Johnson's secretary knew that no one was permitted to interrupt the President when he was watching Walter Cronkite report the CBS Evening News. The President was alone, sitting on the couch in the Oval Office, holding a glass of bourbon. He sipped from the glass as the image of his Secretary of Army appeared on the video screen.

Then the report shifted to the CBS owned and operated station in Chicago, where a reporter interviewed Spenser McCall. While McCall was speaking, the screen showed film of Cordell Jackson and of Bobby Geary in his hospital bed.

Finally, there was an unusually long interview with an Albert Schumann, a retired army colonel. The President sat forward on the couch and mumbled an obscenity. The President knew about Schumann. The goddamned Chicago *Times* had found him first, and CBS had picked up on it. Now the herd instinct was setting in and the other networks and the wire services and the major dailies would run with Schumann's story.

The President had Schumann checked out when his named first appeared in *The Times*. The report made him uneasy. Schumann was a "mustang," an enlisted man who'd earned his way into the officer ranks. Schumann earned his commission on the battlefield. There weren't that many decorations or awards in the file, but everything that Schumann did in his thirty years of service, he apparently did extremely well. Schumann's file didn't say it in so many words, but the President knew enough about the military that he could see plainly that Schumann was apolitical -- the kind of man who did a superior job and did it without kissing anyone's ass. That's probably why Schumann never got his first star. As the consummate politician, the President could admire an officer like Schumann, even though he couldn't completely trust any man who thought he was above kissing a little ass now and again.

As he had in *The Times* account, Schumann recounted how he'd found Cordell Jackson by the machine gun, how strange Crawford had acted, how uncertain he was that Crawford deserved the medal. He also described how hard Major General Crawford had pushed for the medal recommendation.

The President pointed the remote control like a gun and clicked off the television set. He stared at the black screen for a long moment. He walked to his desk and jabbed his finger at the intercom button. "Honey, call Ollie Crawford for me. He's either at the Pentagon or at home. Wherever the hell he is, I want you to tell him to get his ass down here in the next thirty minutes."

June 9, 1967
Waycross, Georgia
1:25 p.m.

Merlin County District Court Judge Claude Singletary endorsed the check, then handed it to the woman behind the admissions desk. "As I understand it," the judge said, "this check should provide for all of Mr. Geary's costs for the next three months. Correct?"

"Yes, sir," the woman said. She then gave the judge three forms. "Please sign each form where indicated."

Even Judge Singletary thought it had been remarkable. When Bobby Jerome Geary's story had appeared on national television, the

Waycross *Journal* discovered that the judge was involved. When he was interviewed by the paper, he said that Spenser McCall, chairman of Horizon Corporation, had given him a personal check for five thousand dollars. The judge said that McCall wanted the money to be used to make Bobby Geary's final days more comfortable.

Veterans' organizations, community groups, and ordinary citizens decided they would help. The judge established a fund for Geary at the First Georgian National Bank in Waycross. In three days more than twenty-two thousand dollars had gone into the account.

Judge Singletary had ridden with the ambulance to the nursing home to get Bobby. The judge had noted that John Mobley had reacted to the media interest in Bobby. The grounds of the old nursing home had been cleaned. When Mobley met him at the door, the caretaker was wearing a brown suit. The cuffs of the jacket were frayed and the pants were shiny, but the suit was a significant improvement over the tattered, bright green sweater.

When the judge had signed the papers, he walked down the corridor to Bobby's new room. It was more like a living room than a hospital room. It was carpeted and draped. There was a large-screen television set, a small refrigerator, and easy chairs and a couch for guests. The Haskins Med-Inn, a full-care medical center, was patronized by the very wealthy. There was no way to be certain that Bobby Jerome Geary was fully aware of new surroundings, but at least Bobby looked much better. His body had been scrubbed and his hair trimmed. He was breathing now with the aid of an oxygen mask. The doctors said his lung congestion was becoming chronic.

Occasionally, the bright blue eyes would open and the oxygen mask could be removed. Judge Claude Singletary looked forward to those moments when he could see those young eyes in the withered and maimed body, when he could talk to Bobby.

Today, Bobby was resting comfortably, so the judge pulled one of the easy chairs close to the bed. He reached into his brief case for his latest copy of the law revue. Later this evening he would have dinner with his granddaughter, Melinda. Then he would return to visit Bobby tomorrow, and the next day, and the day after that.

Judge Singletary had decided that however many days or weeks Bobby Jerome Geary had left, they would be spent in comfort. The judge knew it was his way to cope. He didn't know what else to do.

Two days before, the judge had received the telegram from the International Red Cross in Geneva, Switzerland. The Red Cross said it had been contacted by the Democratic Peoples Republic of North Vietnam.

The report said that Commander Robert Bentley Singletary, U.S. Navy, a prisoner in the Hao Lo prison camp -- the infamous "Hanoi Hilton" -- had died of dysentery on December 26, 1966.

June 10, 1967
The Times Tower
Chicago
10:25 a.m.

They all were intrigued by the phone call McCall had received the night before. Eleanor, McCall, and Tony sat in Eleanor's office discussing it.

"Why would Johnson want to meet tonight with the three of us and my father?" Tony asked.

McCall shrugged. "He didn't say, but since he wants all of us there -- including Cordell, he's probably got some new strategy for resolving his problem with Crawford."

"Did he say why he wanted my dad there," Tony said, concerned.

"No, but I don't think you have to worry about Johnson giving him a bad time," McCall said. "It may be that he's just curious to meet the man who he's heard so much about lately."

"What's Johnson doing in Chicago?" Tony asked.

"Apparently you don't read one of the best papers in the country," Eleanor said. "He's scheduled to speak at eight o'clock at the Hilton Hotel to a national convention of educators."

"He asked that we meet with him two hours after his speech," McCall said.

"It's my guess," Eleanor said, "that he's reacting to how the media have turned around. I know you didn't tell them, Spense, but when word got out that you...well, that you may have lost your job over this thing, your credibility went sky-high."

Tony smiled ruefully, "I guess the common folk have to see oil barons bleed a little before they believe them. Spense, you're the guy who helped the most, and you're the guy who is getting hurt the most."

"No, it wasn't really this business with the medal that's at the root of my problem." McCall said. "Although I have to admit that it got the board's attention. No, I think the media turned in our favor because of Bobby Geary. He not only helped Cordell's case, but he helped us all see how some disabled veterans are forced to live."

"Yes," Eleanor said, "but let's not forget about the piece CBS did last night about Bobby being moved into that new medical center. Everyone knows that if Cronkite said Washington was sinking into the Potomac, Johnson would start building an ark."

"And Singletary -- that judge in Waycross," Tony said. "He's doing a helluva job, despite how he must have been affected by the news about his son."

"Well," McCall said, "we can thank Jim Austin for finding him."

"Is Jim going to be okay?" Eleanor asked.

McCall smiled. "He called me last night. He said he'd submitted his resignation."

"Did they ask him to?" Eleanor asked.

"No, I don't think so. He said that he didn't think he could operate any longer in the corporate environment -- for Horizon or any other corporation. He said he can live on his military retirement, so whatever I end up doing, he said he'd like to be my dog-robber."

"Your what?" Eleanor and Tony asked almost simultaneously.

"I guess it's a term unique to the military. A dog-robber is a top aide to a general or admiral. He makes sure that things get done and that the right resources are found when they're needed, and used however they're needed. There are those who say -- and I agree with them -- that it's the dog-robbers who really win wars."

Tony chuckled. "Well, Austin's a dog robber, all right. He's a helluva guy. He just needs to learn how to lighten-up a little."

Eleanor nodded agreement. "What did you tell Jim?"

"I told him that when I find out what I'm going to do, I'd let him know if there's a spot for him. I like the man."

"Well, gentlemen," Eleanor rose from her chair. "I don't know how we can plan anything for this meeting tonight without knowing more about what we've got to plan for."

"I guess we'll have to play it by ear," McCall said. "And that always worries me -- especially with a man like Lyndon Johnson."

CHAPTER 16

June 9, 1967
Presidential Suite
Conrad Hilton Hotel
Chicago
10:08 p.m.

When Eleanor, McCall, Tony and Cordell were escorted into the suite by a Secret Service agent, McCall expected the President to be angry. He clearly was. He was slouched in a high-back easy chair, his jacket removed. Yet, despite his anger, he rose to shake hands with McCall, Tony, and he kissed Eleanor perfunctorily on the cheek.

"Mr. President, this is Cordell Jackson," McCall said.

At first Johnson didn't move or say a word. His expression was hard, and McCall was afraid he would ignore Cordell.

Then Johnson's expression softened. "I told your boy that I was looking forward to meeting his daddy some day, Mr. Jackson." The President extended his hand to Cordell. "I'm glad I've finally have the opportunity."

McCall could tell that Cordell was pleased.

The president waved one hand toward the couch and chairs. "Well, now, I figured that we ought to call a screeching halt to this shoot-out, and I want to know what it's going to take to do it?"

No one responded.

"Talk to me, Spenser," the President said. "What did you bring to the dance?"

"Mr. President, I don't have anything new to offer."

"Your board of directors apparently believes you've already too involved in this nonsense."

Eleanor couldn't help glancing at McCall. She knew that whatever emotion McCall felt, he wouldn't reveal it.

"With all due respect, Mr. President," McCall said. "That's a matter between the board and me...a matter that has been resolved."

Johnson rose and went to the bar to fix a drink. "Anyone else care for one?" he asked. When no one responded, he returned to his chair. He sipped his drink, looking at McCall. "Ah, hell, Spense. You know I never wanted to bump heads with you. I've got to say this about your board: you had some friends on it and I had some friends on it. Your problem was that they weren't the same people. You've got to believe that I didn't ask them to come down that hard on you, but you wouldn't cut them any slack, Spense, just like you won't cut me any slack. It was either run the company the way you wanted -- or scuttle Ollie Crawford the way you want -- or nothing." The President paused. "I don't suppose you're willing to help me find an alternative?"

"I'm sorry, but I don't see how I can compromise. I couldn't do it with the board, and I don't see how I can do it with you. Cordell Jackson deserves the medal that Crawford got." McCall shook his head. "No. I don't see how there can be an alternative."

Johnson grimaced. He looked at Eleanor. "And, Ellie, I suppose you're going to keep on bird-dogging the media parade on this thing?"

"I think Spenser just answered that question."

Johnson nodded slowly as he shifted his attention to Cordell. "How about you, Mr. Jackson? I suppose you believe you deserve the medal."

"I don't know if I *deserve* it, Mr. President. What I do know is that I don't want it -- at least for myself. If I do take it, it'll be for my boy." Cordell looked at Tony. "And for all the other boys on that road that didn't get to come home, including the boys I killed."

Cordell looked down at his hands clasped in his lab and said softly. "All this business has caused a lot of trouble for you and everyone else in this room. It happened so long ago, in another life." Then Cordell looked back up into the President' eyes. "I have to say that I don't understand everything that's going on today. But what I do understand -- what Mrs. Harrison, Mr. McCall, and my boy have explained to me -- is that there is some question about Mr. Crawford's honesty." Cordell looked at McCall and his son, then back to the President. "Sir, I don't think this trouble is just about some medal. It's really about whether an important man like Mr. Crawford told the truth."

"And what do you think, Mr. Jackson?" Johnson asked softly. "Do you think he told the truth?"

Cordell shook his head. "I'm not the man to judge him, Mr. President. All I can tell you for sure is that when the fighting got real bad, toward the end, me and Bobby were the only Americans fighting on that road. I don't know what happened to Lieutenant Crawford. He may have been fighting somewhere else. He may deserve the medal. All I know is that he wasn't there with Bobby and me."

Johnson, his voice still soft, said, "Every man wants something, Mr. Jackson. What do you want out of all this?"

Cordell looked at each person in the room before he answered. "I want two things, Mr. President. I don't want you to do anything bad to these people here for doing what they believe is right. And I want to see Bobby Geary before he dies."

Johnson nodded impatiently. "Fine, but my question was what do you want me to do for *you*?"

Cordell smiled. "Mr. President, what I just asked for is for me."

Johnson looked for a long moment into Cordell's eyes, then he leaned forward, his elbows resting on his knees. He was looking down into the glass of sour mash whiskey he held in both hands. Then he reached for the phone. He tapped four digits into the keypad. A moment later he said, "Come on in here." If there was a response at the other end of the line, the President hung up too quickly to hear it.

Less than a minute later, Oliver Crawford entered the room. He hesitated when he approached the couch, locking eyes for a moment with Cordell.

"Ollie, you know everyone here," the President said. He then gestured toward Cordell. "It's been a long time since you've seen Cordell Jackson." Each man nodded to the other, but neither offered to shake hands. Then the President pointed to a chair at his left. "Sit yourself over here, next to me."

Eleanor wondered how Crawford came into the city, and how he got into the hotel without a reporter finding out about it -- without one of her reporters finding out about it.

"All right," Johnson said. "I thought we'd have one more shot at this thing. Nobody wants to compromise; everyone wants to be a hard-ass.

So I figured we'd go head-to-head until something breaks loose, and if that takes all night, well..."

The President got up to refill his glass. "Ellie, sure I can't fix you something?"

"No, thank you."

"Any of the rest of you?"

Only Crawford accepted the offer. He rose to fix his own drink. The President noticed that Crawford's hand trembled slightly as he filled his glass with bourbon. The President also noticed that Crawford was working very hard at avoiding any more eye contact with Cordell Jackson.

When Johnson and Crawford resumed their seats, the President turned sideways to look at Crawford. "Son, until the last couple of days, things seemed to be going your way. Then Ellie and Spenser came up with that retired colonel -- Schumann -- and the national media picked up on his version. Ollie, you're hip-deep in alligators and they're snapping at your ass. We need to get to the bottom of this, and we need to do it now. Here. Tonight."

As soon as Crawford began to speak, it was clear that he'd already had several drinks. "Mr. President, I do not regard Colonel Schumann's statements as a different version. He did not contradict anything I have said previously, nor did he contradict the report by the review committee made twenty two years ago."

"Well, then, Mr. Secretary," Tony said, "how do you explain the fact that Colonel Schumann substantiates the fact that he saw a black man -- Cordell Jackson -- lying by a machine gun and that most of the German bodies were lying in front of that gun?"

Crawford nodded agreement. "I don't dispute that. I have never said that I had fired the gun. I was in command of that gun and the men who served it. Colonel Schumann did not say that I was absent at any time from the roadblock."

"No, but Bobby Geary did," Eleanor said. "He saw you run into the woods after the first machine gun position -- the one you were at -- was destroyed."

"I cannot speak to the man's motivations for saying that, so many years after the fact," Crawford said. "He made no such statement back in forty-five to the revue committee."

Johnson sat back, sipping his whiskey. The root of his political expertise was a fundamental understanding of people. He believed

Crawford, basically, but he felt that something had happened at that roadblock, something that Crawford was hiding. The President also knew that McCall and Eleanor did not take up causes lightly. They knew something -- or believed they knew something. The President felt certain that tonight he would be able to either clear his Secretary of the Army or ask for his resignation. Whichever, he wanted it resolved tonight. He couldn't afford the time this problem was demanding.

"Tell me, Ollie," McCall asked. "If you were there the entire time, did you see the German SS officer get down from the tank and shoot Cordell Jackson with a pistol?"

Crawford shook his head quickly -- too quickly, the President thought. "No, I do not recall that happening. But you must remember that there was chaos on the road. There were men screaming and dying and a great deal of firing."

"But isn't it logical," McCall persisted, "that if you were directing the fire of Cordell Jackson's gun -- or doing anything else on that road -- you would have been right there to see that tank drive up to the roadblock? How could there have been so much firing if that German officer -- as Cordell described it -- could casually walk up to him, take the time to cuss him out, then cock his pistol and aim with enough care to shoot him in the head?"

"No... no," Crawford said. "The flaw in your statements is that you are presuming that what Mr. Jackson is saying is the truth."

"Are you accusing my father of lying?" Tony asked softly, ominously.

"No, I'm only saying that...well, there was a great deal of confusion, and he may not be remembering the events as they occurred," Crawford said softly.

"Mr. Crawford." Everyone looked at Cordell when his deep voice silenced the room. "Will you accept a question from me?"

Crawford motioned with his hand for Cordell to continue.

"Mr. Crawford, you ordered us that day to stay on the road no matter what -- that we had to hold it or die trying. All of your men obeyed that order. Thirteen men died. You, Bobby, and me are the only ones alive, and we will carry that day with us to our graves. My question to you, sir, is did you obey your own order?"

"Yes," Crawford said. "Don't forget, when the rest of George Company showed up, they found me on that road."

The room was quiet while the President got up to refill his glass. While standing at the bar, he asked, "Ollie, let me ask you this: are you comfortable with the role your daddy played in this thing?"

"Mr. President," Crawford said indignantly, "I object to the fact that this discussion is becoming an inquisition. It's grossly unfair and my record speaks for itself -- as does my father's record."

Johnson returned to his seat, placed his drink on the coffee table, and leaned toward Crawford. "You're right, Ollie, it is unfair." Johnson's voice was almost conciliatory. "And I'm truly sorry about that. But you haven't answered the goddamned question."

"Whatever my father did or did not do has no bearing on what occurred on that road."

Eleanor shook her head. "But Mr. Crawford, his role does have a bearing on whether you would have received the medal. Everything we've found indicates that you might not have received it had it not been for how aggressively your father pushed for it. In fact, Colonel Schumann said that you initially did not believe that you deserved the medal."

"I think, Mrs. Harrison, that you will find that most Medal of Honor recipients feel the same way. Many of us feel uncomfortable about being singled out when so many others deserved recognition."

"But you obviously believe now that you deserve it?" McCall asked.

"Yes, I do."

"And you apparently believe," McCall said, "that Cordell Jackson and Bobby Geary deserve nothing for what they did?"

"I did not say that! There is no way I could have held that road alone."

Tony, his voice brittle, said. "That's damned generous of you."

The President drained his glass and put it on the table. Then he vigorously rubbed his face with both hands. "Well, ladies and gents, all this talk has been as empty as a bucket with a hole in it." He said to McCall, "Unless you've got something new, I've got to go with Ollie's version. I think your media blitz will keep the pot on the front burner for a little while more, but I think you're about to run out of gas."

McCall looked at Eleanor and Tony, then he got up and walked to the bar. When he'd fixed his drink, he leaned back against the bar and looked at the President.

"There is one thing more, perhaps the most important piece to this puzzle."

Johnson's eyes narrowed as he looked at McCall. He'd seen McCall and the other two exchange glances. "What've you got, Spense?"

"I'm sure that you are aware, Mr. President, that we carried ads in the major German dailies. The ads briefly told Cordell Jackson's story and asked any former German soldier who was at that roadblock to contact us."

"Well?" Johnson asked. "Am I going to have to drag this out of you one damned word at a time?"

"No, sir. We've been contacted by three men, all former SS Panzer officers. Two have said they will speak to us only if we can guarantee anonymity. The third said he will speak for the record. We have people interviewing them now, and we are authenticating their preliminary statements with German army archivists. All three say they were in the area of Hotton in Belgium during the Bulge fighting."

Johnson didn't like what he saw in Crawford's eyes. He asked McCall, "Are they going to talk?"

"One of the two requesting anonymity may be our man. If he checks out, he is willing to give his statement on the condition that the media not identify him."

"How much time will it take to check him out?" the President asked.

McCall looked at Eleanor. "Ellie, don't you agree that we'll need about two more days?"

Eleanor slowly nodded agreement.

Crawford moved to put his glass on the table, but he misjudged the distance and the glass fell to the carpet. "I cannot imagine," he said, shaking his head in disgust, "that you people would even consider the word of a damned Nazi!" He turned toward the President. Furthermore, I am disappointed that you would permit these people to carry on with this witch hunt...that you are just sitting there while they try to destroy me."

"They're not trying to destroy you, Ollie." The way the President said the words indicated that he really cared for Crawford. "It's just that I can't afford any more surprises. Son, I need to know what that German is going to tell these people. I need to know it now."

Crawford looked at the President, then at each of the others in the room. Crawford's eyes were red-rimmed, his face haggard. Slowly, he leaned forward and put his face into his hands. For perhaps a full minute no one moved.

Then McCall rose and stood beside Crawford's chair. He rested his hand lightly on the man's shoulder and said, "Something terrible must have happened on that road, Ollie...something other than the fear and the confusion that all men must experience in that kind of fighting. Whatever it was, I think you've been carrying it with you for all of these years."

Crawford raised his head to look at McCall, then he sat very straight in his chair.

"None of you can know what it is like to have a man like Major General Oliver Crawford for a father. That roadblock was my first combat command. I knew that, wherever he was, he would be watching me. His tolerance for mistakes, for bad decisions, was absolute zero. He could not understand even the concept of fear in combat."

Crawford looked closely at each of the others, as if he were seeing them for the first time. "I've heard stories from men who served with him in both world wars. They said his life was charmed, that he was disdainful of enemy fire. My father did fear one thing -- growing old. He told me that. He said a professional soldier should be killed in combat. Patton said something similar. His idea of a proper death for a soldier was to be killed by the last bullet fired in the last battle."

Crawford reached down to pick up his glass lying on the carpet. He held it in his hand, turning it slowly, watching the cut crystal catch the light.

"No, I didn't fear the enemy that day, and I wasn't afraid of dying, but I was so God-awful afraid of doing something dumb, of making a mistake. I told those men that we were going to hold that road or die trying." Crawford shook his head. "What bullshit. Nobody gave me that order. No, it was my order, the kind of order I thought my father would give, the kind of order that I knew he would hear about and that would make him proud."

"Mr. Crawford." Everyone looked at Cordell. McCall could see the shock on the old man's face. "Are you saying that the only reason you gave that order was to impress your father? My God, man, are you saying that I could have told Bobby and the others to pull back? Did all those men suffer and die on that awful road just so you'd look good to your father?"

Crawford didn't answer. He wiped his face with his hand.

The President was certain now that very soon they all would learn what they needed to know. He leaned toward Crawford. "Tell the story, son."

Crawford nodded. "When the fight began, I remember clearly that I was not in the least frightened at the thought of dying. Despite what is said about war, it can be exhilarating. The men were responding to my commands, and we were holding the Germans -- beating them back, in fact -- and I could hear and feel the snap and whine of the enemy fire all around me and I did not know fear. Like my father, I thought my life was charmed, that I couldn't die. For that very brief moment in my life, I felt that I had finally become the man that my father had always wanted me to be."

Crawford's head turned quickly to Cordell. "You did an outstanding job of knocking out those tanks, Mr. Jackson. I remember that I gave the bazooka to a very experienced noncom. It wasn't until I read your account that I learned that the sergeant had been killed so early in the fighting." Crawford nodded slowly. "Yes, you did a very remarkable job."

Crawford sighed deeply, shuddering as he emptied his lungs. "I clearly saw what you did. Everything was just as you said -- except that you made it sound much too easy. The Germans were concentrating nearly all of their fire on you and Geary...I don't know how either of you could have survived that. I was close enough that I could see when you lost his leg, and how you crawled into the woods to get the other machine gun, and how you came back and killed all of those men. I saw the German officer -- he was a major, SS -- walk up to you, say something I couldn't hear, then shoot you." Very quietly, Crawford said, "Yes, I saw all of that."

Crawford was looking at the empty crystal glass in his right hand.

Finally, Johnson asked gently, "When you saw all those things, Ollie, when you saw the German officer shoot Jackson, where were you?"

Crawford turned to look at the President, then attempted a smile that became a grimace of pain. "Why Mr. President, I was in the woods, just like Private Geary remembered." Crawford's eyes filled with tears and he reached for his handkerchief. He wiped his eyes and very carefully refolded his handkerchief exactly as it had been folded.

"At the time, I didn't know what had happened to me. It wasn't until the review committee went to work that I learned that the machine gun position I was at had been hit by an eighty-eight... ah...a tank shell. One moment I'm throwing grenades and shouting orders and the next moment I'm in a ditch, maybe twenty or thirty feet back down the road. I remember lying there for a few seconds trying to determine whether I'd been wounded. Then something heavy rolled into the ditch and landed on my stomach."

Crawford looked up from the glass and searched the eyes of the people around him. McCall could see that Crawford was gripping the glass so tightly that his knuckles were white.

"It was a man's head. It was still in the helmet. The strap was still hooked under the head's chin." Crawford seemed to be strangling on the words, the effort to force them out creating a sing-song quality to his voice.

He took a deep, shuddering breath and leaned back in the chair. "He was one of my men. His eyes were opened wide, and he must have been yelling when it happened because his mouth was open. When the head had rolled it picked up snow, like a snowball does. It was as if the head were framed in a white scarf, or a wreath. The face was unmarked. There wasn't a drop of blood on it. It was a young boy's face, only inches from mine. The face and the eyes and the mouth seemed to be shouting, *What have you done to me?*"

The room was quiet except for Crawford's rasping breath. Gradually, he brought his emotions under control.

"Earlier that day, when we were on our way to the roadblock, I stopped the column when I saw a wrecked Belgian home. One wall had been blown away and there was a young boy standing there looking into the house. I don't why, but I wanted to see what he was looking so intently at. It was a kitchen, and the whole family, apparently except for the boy, was sitting around the table as if they were about to have breakfast. They were all dead. I guess the concussion killed them. But there wasn't a mark on any of them -- except for the father. His head had been blown off. He was still seated there at the table, except that his head was gone. The others -- his wife, an old lady, and a teenaged girl, were sitting there with their heads bowed, as if they were afraid to look at what had been placed on the table. The man's back had been to the wall that was blown away. His head...his head was lying in the middle of the table."

Crawford shuddered. "That's what I remembered when that man's head rolled onto my chest. I pushed the head away and ran into the woods. I guess I kept running until I tripped over something and fell. I didn't even realize I was running until I fell. I knew I had to go back, but I think it took a long time for me to get to my feet. I followed my footprints in the snow until I got back to the road."

Crawford shook his head. His voice was very soft now. "But I knew there was no way I was going to crawl out to that roadblock. I just didn't have the courage to do that again. Everyone was dead, or nearly dead, except for Jackson and Geary, and I knew they would die soon. There were too many Germans; they had too much firepower. So, I just stood in the trees and watched. I watched it all, and I realized that I'd deluded myself into thinking that I was my father's son. I never had been and never would be."

Eleanor got up and filled a glass with tonic water. When she handed it to Crawford, he looked up and smiled.

He sipped from the glass before continuing. "When the shooting stopped and the Germans left, I went out onto the road. I pulled Jackson away from the logs. When I moved him I saw that a chunk of red ice was stuck to the stump of his leg."

McCall saw Tony look at this father. Cordell's eyes were riveted on Crawford.

"The ice apparently had stopped the bleeding," Crawford said. "I put a tourniquet on it anyway," Crawford said, as he looked at Cordell, "even though I was sure that the bullet wound to your head had killed you. I couldn't detect a pulse."

Johnson cleared his throat. "How long was it before the relief column came up?"

"I'm not sure, but there still was some daylight left. I was told that I was just sitting there, among the dead and wounded, when they arrived."

Crawford drained his glass. "You have to understand, Mr. President, that the whole business about the medal just got out of hand. I didn't want it. I felt I didn't deserve it, but the process got rolling and there was no way to stop it. There was no way in hell that I could have told my father that I ran -- although God knows I tried to tell him. But he seemed so excited about it and he kept patting me on the shoulder and shaking my hand. You have to understand...he'd never done anything like that to me before."

"But you could have rejected the medal or returned it," McCall said.

"Oh, I had thought of that many times, especially after my father died. I've never worn the medal, or even the lapel pin on civilian clothes. But, no, I couldn't return it. I feared the personal disgrace for me and my family. But most importantly, I would have disgraced the medal. The thought of dishonoring the medal and all that it means was just something I couldn't even think about."

Eleanor asked, "Do you suspect, Mr. Crawford, that your father knew...well, knew the real story?"

Crawford nodded slowly. "Yes. When we were on our way to the White House to receive the medal, my father asked me if I'd seen the German officer shoot the black soldier -- Cordell Jackson. When I said I hadn't, he asked how that was possible, if I'd been on the road. I said I just hadn't seen it, but I could see in his eyes that he didn't believe me. From that day until he died, I only saw my father at family gatherings. It was clear that he never again wanted to be alone with me."

"Something I don't understand, Ollie," the President said, "Why, after all these years, did you decide to tell the story tonight? Were you afraid that they'd found the German who'd shot Jackson?"

"No, sir. I wasn't the least bit concerned about that."

"But the German's statements could have cut you off at the knees, boy," the President said.

Crawford smiled, and looked at McCall and Eleanor. "I knew they didn't have the man who shot Jackson, Mr. President."

"How could you possibly know that?" the President asked, his head cocked with suspicion.

"Because I killed that SS officer."

Crawford could see the surprise register on the faces around him. "When I saw the German climb down from the tank, I thought he might take Jackson prisoner, but then I saw him pull out his Luger. I'd lost my carbine, but I still had my forty-five. I ran forward through the woods to get closer. I got to within twenty feet or so when the German fired. I was behind a tree and he didn't see me. He was taking aim to shoot Jackson again when I fired. One of the crewman got out of the tank to help his major. He was carrying a machine pistol and I killed him too. Then I ran around to the side of the tank and dropped a grenade through the open hatch."

Crawford looked at McCall. "So you see, the odds are that no German witnesses -- at least German officers -- survived. I've never told anyone about any of that, so I guess you'll just have to take my word that it happened that way."

McCall nodded. "In light of that, I suppose it's appropriate for me to admit that we have not received a single response to our stories and ads in the German dailies. But what I don't understand, Ollie, is why you didn't tell the review committee about killing the German officer and knocking out the tank? If you had, it's likely that none of this would have come up -- we wouldn't have had a case."

Crawford smiled. Then he laughed. "Because I was afraid they'd give me a medal or at least think I was some kind of hero." His smile faded. "Mr. McCall, I've lived most of my life as an honorable man. I felt I didn't deserve a medal or any other honors because I knew I ran -- I left my men and I ran into the woods. I couldn't admit *that*, for God's sake, but I knew I wouldn't accept a medal. What Jackson and Geary did, what they accomplished, was the only thing that gave some balance to the loss of all those American lives."

"Well, hell, now I am confused," McCall said, "because you did accept the medal."

"My father wanted that medal. He'd always admired the men who had it. He considered them to be the warrior elite. Once I saw that the only way I could avoid accepting it would be to admit that I was a coward, well...things got out of my control. I just couldn't stop my father."

The President got up and paced the room. "Well, Spense, where does that leave us?"

McCall sighed, shaking his head slowly. "I really don't know, Mr. President."

Crawford rose to his feet and faced the President. "If I may be excused, sir, I'd like to return to my room. I am very tired. I would like to call Julie...my wife." Crawford hesitated. "Mr. President, my resignation will be on your desk in the morning. I want you to know, sir, that I will cooperate fully with whatever investigation you authorize." Crawford slowly walked toward the door, then stopped. He turned and looked for a long moment at Cordell Jackson. McCall thought Crawford was going to say something, but then he turned and left the room.

June 10, 1967
Presidential Suite
Hilton Hotel
2:14 a.m.

The President yawned and stretched. "Well, we've talked this thing every way but loose. But I'm not going to make any decisions until I know what you people are going to do."

Tony, who did not seem the least bit tired, got up and walked to the window. Even at this hour, he noticed, Michigan Avenue traffic was heavy. Without turning, he said, "I feel differently about Crawford. Christ, after having a man's head roll into my lap, after what he saw in that house, I'd probably still be running. What I think is important is that he came back, and I believe he saved my father's life."

Tony closed the curtains and walked behind his father's chair, placing his hands on the old man's shoulders. "As far as I'm concerned, I'll always believe that my father deserved the medal for what he did. But the way I feel about it now, I'd hate to see Oliver Crawford destroyed. Speaking for myself, I believe everything he told us tonight."

Cordell cleared his throat. "This whole business involves feelings that are too raw, too complicated. I guess what I'm saying is that Mr. Crawford should keep the medal and we should drop the whole thing."

Johnson looked at Eleanor. "And what about you, Ellie?"

"Mr. President, no one in this room -- yourself included -- has ever heard me apologize for being aggressive. And don't anyone get his hopes up, because I'm not going to do it now."

Johnson chuckled.

"The story was legitimate," Eleanor continued. "There was some very good journalism involved here. I'm proud of the job we did. However..."

Eleanor looked around the room. "...if I would have known what we heard tonight, I honestly don't know how I would have handled the story. I want to drop the story, but sometimes these things have their own momentum. Besides, we have an obligation to our readers to tell them how it all was resolved. Frankly, I agree with Tony. I don't want to see Crawford destroyed."

McCall sighed. "At the risk of being the curmudgeon, I think we have to guard against over-reacting to what we heard tonight. I, too, have great sympathy for what Crawford has had to live with. I don't want to see the guy destroyed. And, I also would like to see the whole thing end." McCall looked at the others. "But what about Cordell Jackson? Do we just forget about what he did? And what about Bobby Geary. My God, what hell that man has lived through over the last twenty-two years."

Johnson pursed his lips in thought. Then he slapped his thighs with the palms of his hands and got to his feet and walked to the bar for one last drink.

"Here's what I propose," Johnson said when he resumed his seat. "I'll let Ollie keep his job. I'll tell the media tomorrow that an investigation of the matter supports Ollie's right to keep the medal. After all, he was in command, and the defense he set up was key to turning the Germans back. I can say that the investigation turned up additional evidence proving that Cordell Jackson and Bobby Geary also deserve recognition. I'll announce that I'm asking Congress for a special statute to reopen the case for Jackson and Geary and that a review committee be established. I will recommend to the committee that Cordell Jackson also be considered for the Medal of Honor and a Distinguished Service Cross for Geary. I'll also see if the Veterans Administration can't find a way to increase the level of Geary's care."

Johnson drained his glass. "That solution takes care of Crawford, and it gives you, Ellie -- and all of your colleagues -- a way to resolve the story for your readers and viewers. Your paper will certainly be the hero for leading the good fight for Jackson and Geary."

Johnson looked at McCall. "Spense?"

"I guess I have only two questions," McCall said. "Ellie, are you going to report any of what Crawford said tonight?"

Eleanor nodded. "Yes, Spense, it has to be told. How else can it be explained that Crawford can keep his medal and that Cordell also deserves one?"

"Okay," McCall said. "It has been my hope all along that Crawford would be the eyewitness Cordell needs for his medal. Together with Geary's testimony, we have the two witnesses for Cordell's medal."

McCall turned to the President. "What about Colonel Schumann? He has a lot of credibility with the media and will have considerable influence on the review committee."

Johnson nodded. "You're right. He'll have a helluva lot of influence because he commanded those troops. In fact, without his support, we're not going to get anywhere. I'll give him a call tomorrow."

McCall said, "Mr. President, you're not going to pressure him in any way."

Johnson smiled. "Only people who can't negotiate need muscle. Besides, he's the kind of man who'd tell me to go to hell if I turned on the heat. I just want him to know that there have been some developments that he should know about and that we'll make available to the committee."

Johnson leaned forward as if to rise from his chair. "Okay?" He looked at each person for a response. They all nodded. "Okay!" The President slapped his hands together. "We got us a done deal."

Johnson got up and walked to Cordell. With some difficulty, Cordell rose to his feet. The President took Cordell's hand and held it with both of his. "Mr. Jackson, I hope you will accept the apology of your President for the wrong that has been done to you."

"Mr. President, my country has been good to me." Then Cordell smiled. "But I would like to talk to you sometime soon about some black folks who are neighbors of mine who the country hasn't been so good to."

Johnson tilted his head as he looked into Cordell's eyes, as if he didn't quite believe what he had heard. Then he laughed aloud, and he began pumping Cordell's hand."

"Mr. Jackson," he said, "I have the feeling that you and I are going to be good friends. Yes, sir, damned good friends. When all of this is behind us, I'm going to call you to come visit me and we'll sit down and talk."

Then Johnson turned to the rest of the group. "We're going to get this thing wrapped up in a couple of weeks, because I'm going to build a fire under some people."

Everyone rose. "You folks keep your seats," Johnson, motioning them back with his hands. "I'm going to have someone send up some steak and eggs and we'll have breakfast together." He smiled at Eleanor. "I always like to have breakfast with a beautiful woman."

The President walked toward the hall door, then paused and turned back. "Before I do that, though, I'm going to wake up Ollie. I'm going to tell him to get his ass back to the Pentagon in the morning, because I don't want my Secretary of the Army cooling his heels in this damned bordello."

CHAPTER 17

June 17, 1967
Waycross, Ga.
9:04 a.m.

The chartered Learjet, its twin turbine engines sighing as they spooled down to an idle, braked to a halt in front of the airport terminal. The copilot opened the side door and McCall was the first out of the aircraft. He waited at the foot of the steps to help Eleanor. Then Tony followed and helped Cordell.

As the four walked to the terminal, McCall could see Judge Singletary standing with Jim Austin at the entrance.

"Judge Claude Singletary," McCall said, "let me introduce Eleanor Harrison." The judge removed his hat and took Eleanor's hand. McCall gestured toward Tony. "You've met Tony, and this is his father, Cordell Jackson."

The judge shook Tony's hand, then looked at Cordell and smiled warmly. "Bobby and I have talked about you. He was excited about seeing you again."

Then the judge lowered his head, shaking it slowly. "I am so sorry. It happened very quickly. They say he just stopped breathing. Thank the good Lord that He permitted me to be with Bobby." The judge looked at Cordell. "I thought you would want to know that I held his hand at the end. It seemed to comfort him."

The group stood quietly. The judge looked around the group and smiled. "Where are my manners? I have a limousine that your Mr.

Austin was kind enough to arrange for. Would you folks like to check into the hotel first?"

"I'd like to see Bobby," Cordell said.

McCall was surprised that the funeral home's parking lot was nearly full, even though the service wasn't scheduled to begin for another forty minutes. There were at least five television crews present.

When one of the parking attendants saw the limousine, he recognized the judge and directed the car to the front entrance of the chapel.

The funeral director, Morris Thompson, greeted the group. "Judge Singletary said you folks would like a few minutes of privacy with Mr. Geary. Please follow me."

When they entered the chapel, the group could hear organ music playing softly. At the far end of the aisle, they could see Bobby's open casket surrounded by flowers.

They stood quietly. Then Cordell began to limp slowly toward the casket. McCall and the others followed at a distance.

As Cordell lowered himself to the kneeler in front of the casket and bowed his head, McCall reflected on all that had happened since Cordell had been shot by the mugger that night that seemed so long ago. President Johnson, true to his word, had built a fire under those involved in determining whether Cordell would receive the Medal of Honor. In only twenty-seven days the recommendation had been approved. Aside from the President's support, one of the keys to the success of the recommendation was the endorsement by Secretary of the Army Oliver Wentworth Crawford.

Crawford had held a press conference to announce the findings of the review committee, revealing that it was based in part on his personal testimony of what had occurred on the roadblock. Without the prior knowledge of the President, Crawford also told the media everything he had revealed that night in the Hilton Hotel suite. He said he had offered his resignation, but that the President had asked him to remain at this post.

However, Crawford said he felt it would be in the best interests of the Army and the administration if he resigned, and that he would do so immediately.

The media locked onto the story and interviewed members of the review committee to find out whether Crawford deserved to keep his

Medal of Honor. The committee announced that it was its unanimous decision that Crawford's leadership during the fighting at the roadblock played a key role in its defense, despite the fact that he had "temporarily abandoned his post." The committee had accepted Crawford's statement that he had returned to the road, had killed the SS officer, and had destroyed the tank.

The committee said that it had developed fresh testimony from a retired army colonel, Albert Schumann, which supported Crawford's statement. Schumann said he remembered seeing the knocked-out tank and the corpse of an SS major lying near Cordell Jackson. Schumann said the German appeared to have been shot in the face and throat with a large-caliber weapon, probably a .45 pistol. The colonel said he found the German officer still holding a Luger in his right hand. Schumann said he confiscated the weapon, which he still owns.

In light of Cordell's statement about the position of the tank and that the last thing he remembered was being shot by the German, and since no other Americans were alive or capable of fighting, the committee accepted Crawford's statement.

The committee said that it lacked sufficient evidence to award Bobby Jerome Geary the Distinguished Service Cross. He did receive the Silver Star.

When he received the news, Cordell made one request. He asked that Bobby's name be engraved on the back of his medal instead of his own. Moved by the sentiment, President Johnson approved the request. Therefore, the name on the medal, and the name entered onto the Medal of Honor rolls, is Bobby Jerome Geary.

The President later said he regretfully would accept Crawford's resignation. However, the President said he had great admiration for the courage demonstrated by Crawford during the controversy, and that he would urge Crawford to take an important post in the Veterans Administration.

On May 14, shortly before noon, President Johnson presented the Medal of Honor to Cordell Jackson, nearly twenty three years after he had earned it. Cordell at times seemed confused, even frightened, by all of the attention. During a media interview in the Rose Garden afterward, Cordell was asked what he would do now that he'd earned the nation's highest military honor.

"All I want to do right now," Cordell said, "is to go see Bobby Geary." Judge Singletary had phoned McCall the night before to tell him that Bobby Jerome Geary had died.

When the ceremony was concluded, the President asked to speak privately with McCall in the Oval Office.

"Well, Spense, I jumped on this thing like a duck on a June bug, just like you wanted," the President said as he poured two glasses of sour mash whiskey. "What you did for Jackson...well, it was a damned fine thing."

"Cordell is a fine man."

"He's a helluva man. And I've got to say this -- you were right to push it. The Nigra leaders have been calling to thank me for doing right by him. Maybe now I have even more support there than I had before."

The President held out one of the glasses, looking intently into McCall's eyes. "Now, old friend, today's the day we fish or cut bait."

McCall took the glass, holding it with two hands as if it were a chalice. He pulled his eyes away from the President's and looked down into the amber liquid. "You know, the board was right in throwing me out," McCall said.

"That's bullshit, Spense, and you know it." The President moved to the couch. McCall took the easy chair facing him.

"No, I really believe that -- for two reasons. The first is that I'd been there two long. Ellie tried to tell me that. I guess I began to believe that I owned the company, and that I expected people to just follow along when I wanted to do something."

"And the second reason?" McCall could sense the President's impatience.

"I fell into the biggest trap any manager..." McCall leaned forward to emphasize his words. "...or leader, can fall into. I wanted to follow a course of action that I knew intuitively was right, and because I felt in my gut that it was right, then I knew it had to be right."

The President shook his head. "Spense, I don't have the foggiest idea of what the hell you're talking about."

"I'm talking about the fact that this nation is running out of oil, that we're getting hooked on foreign oil, and that the CO2 project was one way to help cut that dependency. You and I know that it's not a question of *if* the Arabs cut off our oil; the question is *when* it will happen. When it does, you and I are going to be among the people who are going to have to explain to the American public how such a thing could happen."

"Well, if you're so goddamned sure it's going to happen, then you're probably right, and what you wanted to do with CO2 was probably right."

"I know damned well I was right, but the point is I didn't do my homework; I didn't bother to do all I could to convince my board and the stockholders and the American people and the government that we had to look this thing in the eye and deal with it. I figured that if *I* believed it was a problem, then because I believed it everyone else should."

Johnson's eyes suddenly narrowed, and he began to nod his head slowly. "McCall, why am I beginning to suspect that I'm getting another goddamned picket-fence lecture on Vietnam?"

"Mr. President, I failed as a CEO because I didn't work to get the consensus I needed to get the job done. I guess I figured that because I was the boss, I had to be right."

"What are you saying, that I haven't tried to get Congress and the American people on my side? If you are, you're a brick short of a full load, son. There isn't anybody who wants that war over sooner than I do, but the sumbitches won't negotiate. What the hell do the pepper pots want me to do, just pull up stakes and get out of that sorry-ass country? Americans have never done a thing like that before. We've never just given up, and I won't be the first American President to cut and run."

Johnson rose and walked toward the window, then turned back quickly to face McCall. "God*dammit*, Spense, Americans can do anything we set our minds to. The Texas Rangers have a saying that you can't stop a man who keeps on a-coming. That's the way Americans are; that's the way I am."

Pacing the room, his arms waving, Johnson said, "Hell, at Valley Forge the American's were eating moss and leaves and their asses were hanging out and they didn't have bullets for all the rifles and still they sucked it up and whipped the most powerful king in the world. We not only got through the Great Depression, we whipped it about the head and ears and came out stronger than ever -- and that was after and before winning two world wars."

Johnson paused in front of McCall's chair. "Do you realize that in less than two years we're going to the moon? The *goddamn moon!* And *Americans* are going to be walking on it, Spense. Not the goddamned Russians. Not the goddamned Chinese. *Americans!* I know what I'm doing in Vietnam. I just need a little time to pound more sand up Ho Chi Minh's ass. Then he'll have to sit down and talk peace. Just wait and see if he doesn't."

Johnson came back to the couch and leaned forward, touching McCall's knee. "Spense, that's all I need -- a little time. I need a little slack. This goddamned war is a cancer eating at my domestic programs. For what it's worth, I think you're right about our oil problem. And you're right about how the people are going to react if our oil's cut off. But I've already got a full plate, and I don't want to have to deal with a goddamned oil shortage. That's why I want you to help me, to go over to the Middle East, to promise the Arabs candy and flowers if they'll keep their hands away from the oil spigot. I need you to help me keep that pot from boiling over."

McCall knew that Johnson wanted desperately to end the war, that he wanted to quickly move the nation to what he believed was its potential, toward what he believed was its destiny. But McCall knew that the President now would resist anything less than victory. Now his ego and pride were involved, and McCall knew that once LBJ took something personally, he was utterly controlled by his ego and pride. He'd put his monogram on Vietnam as he had his boots, shirts and cufflinks. The kind of pride and ego that had seen to it that Lady Bird Johnson -- not Claudia -- and Lynda Bird Johnson and Luci Baines Johnson had the magic initials LBJ. And when he was at the ranch, he flew his private LBJ flag.

McCall knew that he and Lyndon Johnson had failed because they hadn't heeded the warning signals, had misread the wants and desires of their respective publics. McCall had finally come to accept his mistakes; Lyndon Johnson, McCall felt, never would.

"Mr. President, I will work for your campaign, full time, in whatever capacity you feel I can best serve." McCall placed his whiskey glass on the low table. "But I can't be your ambassador to Iran. Although you said your plate is full, mine would be empty. I would have nothing to offer the Middle East oil producers that could deter any embargo they might choose to impose. We are in no position to bargain, partly because this nation doesn't have an energy policy, and partly because I and the other oil company CEOs, and the government, have not prepared the American people for the consequences of being hooked on cheap oil."

"That's bullshit, Spenser. You know more about the oil business than anyone I know. You're the kind of man who can fix this problem before it gets to be a problem."

"The problem won't be solved by someone who is knowledgeable about the oil business," McCall said. "It's not a business or technical or even an economic problem. It's a political problem, and I don't presume to have answers for political problems. I can't serve you as a politician or a diplomat. I'm just an oil man -- an unemployed oil man."

Johnson leaned back on the couch and puffed out his cheeks. "So that's your final word?"

"Yes," McCall said firmly.

LBJ was not a man who could hide his feelings, and McCall keenly felt the President's disappointment. The atmosphere in the room now was awkward, strained. They talked about the campaign for a few minutes, but the President's interest and enthusiasm had evaporated.

When McCall quietly closed the door as he left the Oval Office, both men believed they never again would see each other.

Cordell looked for long minutes at the man lying in the casket. Bobby's hair was white as snow. The face was pulled taut by the massive scars at the throat, which was as thin as a child's. Cordell struggled to remember the young face, the frightened face, on that frigid road so long ago. He remembered the blue eyes, bright with the hope of youth, looking back down the road, looking for the help that never came. He remembered how he'd held the boy in his arms to warm him, to reassure him, and to quiet the tremors. He remembered how Bobby Jerome Geary had trusted and respected him.

Slowly, Cordell reached to touch Bobby's hand. "Oh my...oh my," Cordell said, his voice soft and deep. "You are still so cold, Bobby. That road has made us both cold forever. If only I had known you were alive, I'd have come to take care of you, like I promised."

Cordell tightened his grip on Bobby's hand, and his voice was stronger. "Rest easy, son, I have you now. I'm finally going to pull us both from the awful river of blood."

McCall, Eleanor, Tony, and Austin stood in a semi-circle behind Cordell. Judge Singletary stood behind them. They watched as Cordell reached into his coat pocket and withdrew the presentation case containing his medal. He placed the case on the edge of the casket and opened it. He took the medal from the case, then, gently, he placed the Medal of Honor on Bobby's chest, very near his throat, smoothing the blue silk ribbon spangled with thirteen stars.

Cordell bowed his head in prayer, placing his hand on Bobby's.

Eleanor and McCall reached for each other's hand, each clutching tightly.

The President had ordered that Bobby be buried with full military honors. The flag that had draped Bobby's coffin was presented to Cordell, who embraced the colors tightly to his chest.

Later, the mood was somber in the dining room of the Georgian Hotel in Waycross. Few words were spoken during dinner. As coffee was served, Tony asked, "Spense, have you decided what you're going to do?"

McCall smiled. "Well, I'm certain that I won't be going to Iran..." He looked at Eleanor. "...and I don't know whether the President will be asking me to work for his campaign, but I did make the offer. I guess we'll have to wait and see." McCall shrugged. "Maybe I'll just take it easy for a while."

Tony turned to his father, placing his hand on the older man's arm. "Pop, what would you think about your son being a U.S. representative -- a member of congress?"

Cordell seemed confused, his mind still occupied with Bobby. "What are you saying? That you're going be a congressman?"

"Well, I've got to be elected first," Tony said. "It's too late for the sixty-eight election, but we can start getting ready for nineteen seventy. And I'm going to need your help, Dad."

Cordell shook his head. "Son, I don't know nothing about becoming a congressman."

"Oh, there a lots of things you can give me some advice on, dad -- things like veterans' benefits and care for the elderly and civil rights." Tony looked at McCall and Eleanor, both of whom were smiling broadly. "Besides that, it looks like you're going to have a direct pipeline to the President of the United States -- he said he'd be calling you."

For the first time in a long while, Cordell smiled. "Son, I'm not holding my breath waiting for *The Man* to call me on the telephone asking for my help. But if he does, I have the feeling that he'll listen to me."

"Well, besides some influence with the President, there is some very important help I know you can get," Tony said. "There's another man whose help I need who you also seem to have a lot of influence with, the kind of man who knows how to run a political campaign."

Cordell looked at McCall and chuckled. "Well, son, I think I can get that done for you." Cordell's eyes lingered on McCall. "He's a man who doesn't have any trouble doing the right thing." Cordell was warming to the discussion now. "But it appears to me -- mind you now, that I don't know nothing about getting to be a congressman -- that you also need some powerful newspaper folks helping you. I'll see what I can do about that, too."

Eleanor laughed and reached across the table to squeeze Cordell's hand.

McCall called the waiter over. "Another round of coffee, please. We're about to make a very important toast."

As the four lifted their cups, Cordell said, "To U.S. Congressman Tony Jackson." The old man looked around the table, smiled broadly, and cocked his head as if he were listening again to the words he'd just spoken. "You know? That sounds awfully good to these tired old ears."

# # #